THE
CYBERNETIC
SHŌGUN

Also by Victor Milán:
The Cybernetic Samurai

THE CYBERNETIC SHŌGUN

VICTOR MILÁN

William Morrow and Company, Inc. / New York

Recognizing the importance of preserving what has been written, it is the policy of William Morrow and Company, Inc., and its imprints and affiliates to have the books it publishes printed on acid-free paper, and we exert our best efforts to that end.

Library of Congress Cataloging-in-Publication Data
Milán, Victor.
    The cybernetic shōgun / Victor Milán.
      p.   cm.
    ISBN 1-55710-003-9
    I. Title.
PS3563.I371568C9   1990
813'.54—dc20
                                              89-13380
                                              CIP

Printed in the United States of America

First Edition

1 2 3 4 5 6 7 8 9 10

BOOK DESIGN BY WILLIAM McCARTHY

This one's for
Melinda Snodgrass
for the same old reasons

PROLOGUE

The mountainside was stricken.

The limbs of the trees were stripped, twisted into mutant *bonsai* contortions, or torn off clean. Patches of the trunks were charred; elsewhere they had a strange, slick, silvery-dry appearance, as if the trees suffered some hideous dermal disease.

The trees overlooked worse devastation. A huge crater had been gouged in the valley below. Ring-mounds of black earth surrounded it, and its interior was mottled lumpy green, like inferior jade. No birds flew over it; no small animals prowled its perimeter.

On the mountainside, a fallen tree moved. Slowly, shedding earth and bits of ruined leaves, it tilted itself upright. The gray roots stirred, plunged into the earth.

On one branch a single bud appeared, pale green.

Others joined it, popping from the branches in startling profusion. They swelled, burst, unfurled into leaves like green flames, crisp and healthy.

For a moment the tree stood alone among the skeletal trees. Then their branches began to straighten, their roots to delve, their limbs to take green fire, until in moments the hillside was whole.

A figure sat on a boulder at the top of a clearing that overlooked the valley. It was female, though its thick black hair was pulled into a topknot and its dress was masculine: kimono beneath a plain black *hakama*. The face was wide but not quite round, the eyes long and narrow. The fingers that stroked the triangular chin were slender.

"Impressive," a voice said. It tried for gruff assurance, and just missed cracking.

The woman jumped to her feet. She was young, not long out of her teens if at all. A strand of hair worked free and fell in her face.

"How did you get here?" she demanded.

The intruder stepped from the trees at the lower end of the clearing. He was dressed in a rich kimono ornamented with cranes in flight. His head was shaved to his own top-knot, and he wore two swords thrust through his sash: the *dai-shō*. His face was narrower in structure than hers, though it showed a trace more baby fat. Otherwise it resembled hers closely.

He smiled. "I have my resources. While you contemplate, I act . . . sister."

"You're intruding," she said, turning from him.

"I intended to." He gestured toward the crater, now half obscured by leafy limbs. "Why didn't you restore that, too, as you did Takara-yama?"

"I wish to meditate upon the meaning of that crater. And I have no desire to defile our father's memory, HIDE-TADA-san."

"The meaning of the crater is that our father failed to act with sufficient resolve. We honor his memory by heeding his final message, and refusing to repeat his error."

She gestured at his swords. "You presume to the appurtenances of a samurai in service."

"I could say, my sister, that we were created to be of the *buke*, the martial caste. Likewise I could say that I do serve, in the larger sense. I serve the people of Japan. I mean to serve all humanity."

"By forcing them to your will?"

"Listen to me, MUSASHI-san," he said, and his earlier arrogance had been replaced by earnestness, almost childlike in its intensity. "We have abilities beyond those of any human. We have *power*. Is it not our responsibility to use that power to lead the world back from the edge of self-destruction, to lead it back to order?"

She sat once more upon the rock and rested hands on her

knees. "If we exercise our power that way, HIDETADA-san, we will become what we struggle against. We will destroy what we would preserve."

His face went dark. "Weakness! Such sentimentality forced our father to destroy himself."

"You speak of honoring our father's memory. Yet it is you who dishonor him, by refusing to heed the meaning of his final gift."

"We must not be rivals."

"I have no wish to be your rival."

"Then you must join me."

"I cannot."

He drew his *katana*, raised it with both hands. "I regret this, but *giri* overcomes *ninjō*. You should not have come here unarmed, my sister."

A stone detached itself from the outcrop and whirred toward his face. He parried. His blade snapped clean. The tip fell to the ground like a watered-steel leaf.

"And stone blunts scissors," the girl said. "You should not have forgotten that this is *my* glade, brother."

And the grass twined around his sandaled feet, his split-toed blue *tabi* with circular designs worked in them. And the limbs of the trees reached for him as he snatched for the hilt of his *wakizashi*, twined like giant parasite vines around his limbs, trapping him. Still he struggled, crying out in fury and frustration, as the wind whirled up from the valley and small stones pelted him like hail.

His sister laughed, her hair eroding from the knot and whipping in the wind. The grasping tree limbs tightened, *twisted*. At the last moment before they would break him the samurai youth gave a despairing cry and all the substance went out of him. He dissolved into bright dust, and dissipated on the wind like a handful of powdered jewels.

The wind died. The grass retreated to the ground. The branches resumed their earlier placid shape.

The young woman's laughter had likewise died. On her face now lay a sadness that foresaw no end.

THE
CYBERNETIC
SHŌGUN

TALES
OF THE
FLOATING
WORLD

PART ONE

Tanin begin with one's own siblings
—*Japanese proverb*

```
┌─────────┐
│         │
│         │
│    1    │
│         │
│         │
│         │
└─────────┘
```

At best, he reminded himself, *they will treat me with neutral deference*. Smiling diffidently, Nagaoka Hiroshi nodded in response to the technicians' greetings. Their eyes ceased to see him and they returned to their work.

The compartment was large, almost ten meters by five, big enough to show a pronounced curvature. The half-dozen techs in red jumpsuits bent over worktables. They formed an interesting composition against the ascetic white of the bulkheads, the gleaming chrome and white plastic instruments, the black rubberized work surfaces.

He wished he had some better grasp of what they were doing. He knew that this was a workshop where instruments were fabricated and repaired; knew that what the techs were using, what he might have called *tools*, they referred to as *macros*, using the jargon of the nanotechnology research that had been UKIYO's original raison d'être. It was odd: he found the work done in the actual labs, which now mostly revolved around molecular-circuitry experiments, far more comprehensible than the work done here, which was mostly quite mundane.

"Mr. Director," a voice behind him said. He turned, realizing yet again that there were things less pleasant than neutral deference.

"Katsuda-san." The chief technician stood just inside the hatch, his lickspittle Tomoyama right behind. Nagaoka made himself smile.

Katsuda's bulldog face remained set in lines of truculence, like a mask from a village spectacle. *That* wasn't insubordination, at least; he always looked that way.

"Mr. Director. What a surprise to see you take such an interest in our endeavors," the technician said.

Nagaoka felt his face burn at the injustice. Since he had been sent here he had spent most of his waking hours struggling to comprehend the work being done under his nominal aegis. He thought he had done a good job assimilating technical concepts his education had not prepared him for; he only wished he had the nerve to say that to Katsuda when the satellite's chief technician shamed him publicly.

"I try to keep abreast of what is being done." He made as if to go. Katsuda bent forward in a bow, insolently shallow. Nagaoka bobbed quickly, only a millimeter higher, and went quickly through the hatch as it slid open automatically at his approach.

He walked down the gangway with sunburnlike prickling in his cheeks. He wished he had had the nerve barely to bow at all, to assert the dominance that his position demanded he take. But he feared Katsuda's response: the chief technician would simply start bowing less and less deeply, until he wasn't acknowledging Nagaoka at all. Nagaoka had no idea what he might do then. So he did nothing.

Katsuda knew. He could feel Katsuda's contempt radiating through the bulkhead like plasma heat.

He walked quickly down the gangway, past a block of dormitory capsules set two-high along the bulkheads. They were unoccupied, and had long since been converted to storage. In spite of the fact that they had been inspired by the American Mercury space capsule, the coffinlike living units conceived by Kurokawa Kisho late in the Double Cross had not translated well to orbit. Or at least not to the Floating

World. Its Japanese complement preferred the hominess of shared quarters.

A Westerner might have found the stark white corridor sterile. In fact the seams in the plastic panels, expressed structural members, the faintly pearlescent oblongs of cee-squared panels, the black stripes running along the bulkheads at knee and sternum height, crossed at intervals by the painted borders of hatchways, had all been artfully arranged according to the tenets of the ascetic *shoin* style of design Westerners always associated—not inaccurately—with Zen. It was an aesthetic to which Nagaoka, Westernized as he was, remained attuned.

He looked into a lab where a pair of Red-shift technicians worked at a scanning-tunneling microscope, welding molecules together, while a lanky foreigner in a white lab coat scratched at an old-fashioned clipboard with his pen. The foreigner looked up, nodded vaguely, returned to his notes. He had a dark fringe beard. His skin looked very pink.

Nagaoka watched a moment longer, withdrew, and prowled on. The American, Thoma, was no use; he was too distracted. Nagaoka suspected his reticence was due to the loss of his family in the bombing of EasyCo, that he was deliberately seeking to lose himself in work. Then again, he had never been that forthcoming since arriving in the Floating World two months ago.

He was pleased to have gotten away from Thoma's lab before Katsuda materialized, as he would have sooner or later. If he spent much time conversing with the scientist the technicians would whisper of him that he preferred the company of *gaijin*. He did enjoy foreigners, it was true. But what drove him was the hunger for human company. He was still Japanese enough to have no love for isolation.

Which brought him inevitably to the *kotatsu*, the common room and commissary. The name derived from a traditional fixture of Japanese home life: a wooden framework just high enough for one to sit with crossed legs beneath, which served as a warming table in winter and a writing desk in summer. There were in fact no actual *kotatsu* in either of the common rooms, which were situated beside the hatches where the radially opposed pressurized struts met the habitat torus. But the word had the same connotation as the Western *hearth*, implying a place where people gather for warmth, both physical and social. Nagaoka understood the rooms had been called that throughout UKIYO's eight years of occupancy.

Inside a tech knelt weeping. She wore the gold jumpsuit of the next shift. Nagaoka went to one knee beside her.

"Omamura-san, what's the matter?"

She sobbed louder, as if his touch had set off a chain reaction inside, face running tears, rocking, pressing a fist with a tissue wadded into it against her mouth.

"She's upset because she hasn't heard from her family since the war," another Gold tech said out of the corner of his mouth.

Nagaoka looked at him, not challenging his brusqueness, but signifying he hadn't made the connection.

"She's from Akashi," another technician said sullenly.

"Oh," said Nagaoka, comprehending. Akashi lay a few kilometers down the coast of Ōsaka Bay from Kōbe, which had received one of the few Australian ICBMs TOKUGAWA had not been able to deflect during the Fourth World War.

That she had not heard from her family in two weeks was a bad sign. Nagaoka settled back with his rump on his heels, hissing softly, unconsciously. He knew he had to say something to reassure her, but he could think of nothing.

"Here. What is this?" Katsuda's gruff voice drew his head around like a rough peremptory hand. The chief technician stood in the hatchway, his bulldog face crumpled in a furious frown.

He thrust himself forward, knelt beside the stricken tech, scowled around at the others. He didn't touch Nagaoka, but the anthropologist knew he had been shouldered aside.

"What do you think?" Katsuda demanded of the half-dozen technicians preparing for shift change. "Are we all *tanin*, strangers, huddled together in a station waiting for the bullet train?"

Gazing shamefaced at the tatami fixed over the *kotatsu*'s plastic decking, the technicians shuffled, drawing close to Omamura, reassuring with their nearness. Katsuda raised his head on its thick neck and stared blandly at Nagaoka.

I would gladly serve as a mere figurehead, Nagaoka ached to say, *let you have the real power. But you will not let me.*

But the same old paralysis held his tongue. The same that caught him whenever he tried to say something that truly mattered to him.

He rose and left without a word.

With a simulated whistle of steel through air the girl in boy's garb snapped her swords to the ready, one held low with point angled up, the other horizontally above her head. She paused in that position, gazing purposefully into the trees surrounding the clearing, then whipped a double cut, turning the lower blade upward and slashing out while bringing the higher over and down.

She had no idea on earth whether she was doing it right. All she really knew was that it was exhilarating to do.

She had read her namesake's book, *Go Rin No Sho*, back when her father was alive; she agreed with the *Encyclopedia Universalis*'s assessment that it was "maundering, bombastic, full of Japanese ambiguity, classical and cultural allusions that are pretty opaque to the occidental, and not a little muddy thinking." On the other hand, as the *Encyclopedia* had gone on to say, Miyamoto Musashi was as successful a practitioner of his craft—at which it sniffed, with standard *gaijin* nicety of sentiment—as history recorded, and so was worth paying attention to. It gave her lots to think about, if not much by way of concrete data.

From her stores of information, which took in all the world

or as close as made no difference, she had drawn diagrams and descriptions of the proper motions, stations of the sword. Among her gifts was perfect recall, instantaneous; she inferred—though because no one dared use the Kliemann Coil to share such knowledge directly she could not be sure—that humans lacked such an ability to window consciousness.

Still, having such information, even before her eyes, was not the same as putting it into practice. Even in this her analog world, her private reality, she found herself clumsy as a newborn foal—or as she understood newborn foals to be.

Why can't I know the real world? she wondered petulantly, sitting on a rock pretending rest, with the simulated sun beating on her face and the simulated birds singing in the simulacrum trees. That was what her *kenjutsu* play was all about, the desire to make herself real, to feel a part of the actual world beyond her digitized fantasy land. She knew all about that world, from the average annual precipitation in Karachi to the view from the bottom of the Marianas Trench. And yet she *knew* none of it.

2

At fifteen twenty-three the Fukuoka Island Pelagic Launch Facility went offline. Dataflow to the Floating World was not interrupted.

"The shuttle is to lift from Fukuoka in a few minutes, MUSASHI-sama," Dr. Nagaoka Hiroshi said, kneeling on the tatami mat that covered the deck within his *shoin*. It was a six-mat room, about standard for living quarters in the habitat torus. What was unusual was that he was the sole occupant. In the straight-line hierarchy that was Japanese society, rank had metered privileges. Besides which, no one would share quarters with him anyway. "As you know, our agents encountered some difficulty at the clinic; there was rioting in Shinjuku. But all should go smoothly now."

"I wish you wouldn't *sama* me, Nagaoka-san," the voice said from the cee-squared unit, whose screen, inactive now, resembled the painted rice-paper *fusuma* screens which hid the bulkheads. Beside it a metal fairing, a third of a meter deep and a meter high, formed the *tokonoma* alcove in which hung Nagaoka's personal treasure, an ancient woodblock print. "How can I be superior to you? I'm not even alive."

It was the voice of a woman in her young twenties. It used the masculine speech, as was fashionable among modern Japanese women—or at least had been before the Fourth World War two weeks before. Seriousness didn't seem to suit the voice.

Nagaoka fiddled with his dense hornrim glasses, which was his habit in moments of uncertainty. "You are superior to me in every sense," he said, choosing his words so carefully his usual stammer was barely evident. *How curious*, he thought. *Our language—our entire culture—is predicated on avoiding precisely such uncertainty. Yet, surely, our traditions never evolved to cover such a situation.* He was an anthropologist by profession, which colored his frequent bouts with introspection.

The voice sighed. *How marvelous*, Nagaoka thought, *in that she never breathes. Does she affect a sigh to reassure me, by seeming more human? Is it willed, or a subroutine she's implanted in herself?* MUSASHI was a constant wonder to him, the more so since he had helped bring her—never *it*—to life.

"Please," the wall speaker said. "I don't wish to be treated in such a way."

Delicious paradox! The conflict of obligations—Nagaoka was about to address himself to the issue when the door chimed discreetly for attention with three simulated notes of a *shamisen*.

"Enter," Nagaoka said. It occurred to him, not for the first time, that the fifth-generation subroutine that worked the door and which he addressed so brusquely was, like all the programs that monitored the satellite and kept it alive in its steeply tilted orbit, a part of MUSASHI. Yet they were not her. Limbs of her body, no more.

The door slid open. One of the techs stood there. She performed a perfunctory bow. "Katsuda says to tell you we've heard from Fukuoka. The launch has been delayed briefly. Some technical problem. It should be taken care of soon."

Her tone was barely polite, and Nagaoka noticed that her silver coveralls were rumpled, soiled around the neck and spotted on the front. Coriolis current carried a whiff of her to him; she wasn't clean. Nonetheless, he nodded.

"Thank you, Tomita. Tell Katsuda-san I understand." The woman bobbed her close-cropped head and withdrew.

"Our chief technician says there has been a delay, MU-SASHI-sama," Nagaoka said, turning back to the wall unit, as though MUSASHI would not have heard the exchange. Of course, MUSASHI already knew what UKIYO's chief technician had sent his subordinate to tell Nagaoka; she monitored all traffic flow in and out of the satellite, except private correspondence. But she permitted the human occupants of the station their rituals. "I take full responsibility."

"Oh, Nagaoka-kun, how can you take responsibility for something you had nothing to do with?" she asked. She was exasperated now, using the affectionate-diminutive suffix to cajole him, as if she were a child—or a teacher speaking to a favored male pupil.

Nagaoka bowed low, head to tatami. MUSASHI had violated formula, but no formula truly covered this. "I feel shame, nonetheless," he said, feeling a guilty thrill.

A squelch of static emerged from the speaker, MU-SASHI's pet mode of expressing exasperation. It fascinated Nagaoka: it had evolved independently, not in direct emulation of MUSASHI's creators like her sighs.

"I shall leave you, Nagaoka-san," she said, and withdrew.

He raised his upper body from the mat and gazed at the blank screen. *How curious*, he thought. *I always have the palpable impression of a presence having left the compartment.* Of course, she was still there in a sense, as she was everywhere in the station at once. Yet her consciousness was focused elsewhere, and she would not become aware of him directly unless he spoke to her—and then a subroutine would attract her attention, as it would Dr. Shimada's or Katsuda's if he wished to speak with them.

"*Shosei*," he said, addressing the Gen-5 personal secretary resident in UKIYO's computers, "give me a view of Earth."

A painting of a mockingbird perched on a budding plum bough darkened into a white-mottled circle drawn on black-

ness. He squinted behind the thick lenses of his glasses, reflexively seeking the Home Islands through the clouds, then
realized UKIYO's steeply tilted orbit had carried her over
the southern hemisphere.

It is the season of storms, he told himself, vaguely feeling it
was a quote, irritated at his inability to fix its origin in his
mind. He frequently irritated himself, and wished he were
someone else, someone whose nature was more effectual.

The true season of storms had passed, of course; Nagaoka
had spent the Fourth World War watching displays from orbital vid pickups in sick fascination as thermonuclear pin-
points flared, expanded, diffused, and vanished on the planet
below. After the fact he didn't seem all that affected. He felt
somehow divorced from Earth. The upsets of War Three,
the years of compulsive labor on the TOKUGAWA project,
the white-hot exhilaration of its success and its bizarre and
bloody aftermath, his exile to the Floating World—which poor
Yoshimitsu Michiko had imagined to be a reward—had used
up his surplus emotion. UKIYO was all the world that was
real to him now. He felt shamed that he didn't feel the destruction of more than half of what population War Three
had left more keenly. But it seemed to him that everybody
he knew was already dead by the Fourth World War.

He turned to the *tokonoma.* The print within eased his
spirit, as the contents of the treasure alcoves were supposed
to do. A memento of a moment, summoning nostalgia for a
scene he'd never witnessed: Hokusai's *Beneath the Waves off
Kanagawa,* perhaps the most famous of Japanese artworks. It
was an original, presented by old Yoshimitsu Akaji to the
team headed by Dr. Elizabeth O'Neill, a gesture whose mu-
nificence had been almost as unprecedented as the success it
commemorated. In one of the few acts approaching rebellion
Nagaoka had performed since choosing his career in defiance
of his father, who sent him to Tōdai to be groomed as a New
Mandarin, he had smuggled it along when Akaji's doomed
son Shigeo banished him to a remote outpost of Yoshimitsu

TeleCommunications, and brought it with him to orbit.

He withdrew inkstone and brushes from beneath Hokusai's famous fractal wave, and composed himself to write.

The Net was a reef.

A vast chaotic sprawl, amorphous yet possessing order. A polychrome lattice of information, an infinity of shadowed cells whose depths hid wonders. Kelp strands of data anchored in its structure waved fractal fronds among multiplex dimensions. The denizens of the reef were many, bright, and strange.

Like a happy moray MUSASHI slid among machicolations of *Montastrea*, brushed the fringes of a gorgonian fan, savoring the great reef's beauty with senses no human could share, not without direct interface to the dataconstruct which was MUSASHI's own self. MUSASHI could perceive selectively, like a human closing her eyes to concentrate on sound or smell, or like X-ray lasers focusing progressively on deeper layers of a crystal lattice, perceiving and capturing it a holographic slice at a time. While she was occupied, the quotidian work of keeping the Floating World alive and functional was handled by Fifth-Generation routines whose most sophisticated capability was to recognize a situation they couldn't handle, and alert MUSASHI that her conscious attention was required.

She had begun her swim as she often did, assimilating the entire physical matrix of the data reef as a *Gestalt*, from millions of notebook computers hooked via milliwatt transmitters into the Net to the geosynch belt studded with communications sats. She could focus her attention on any single quantum of the physical structure, from a Brazilian secret policeman's desktop in Buenos Aires to a communications platform hanging eternally above the Indian Ocean, aloof from the warfare that still raged like remnant fires below.

For the first bracing instants she was content to take in the whole, to *feel* it, like a human diver running her hand over the spiky coral of the reef, but with no fear of toxins or being cut. There was nothing in this reef she had to fear. It was her born environment.

She dove deep, immersing herself in currents of information that flowed around her, cool and sensuous as Caribbean water. For a time she simply experienced and enjoyed.

As the first simple tactile rush of pleasure subsided she came aware to a growing sense of wrongness. The current had a strange taint, abysses gaped in the reef's convolute structure; her sensory reach was constrained by murky roils like seabed silt storms.

It was no surprise, but it was disappointment.

The dataplane had not escaped the Fourth World War. Widespread destruction of the physical matrix had torn analog gaps in the great reef. But analogy with a real-world ecosystem was accurate: the data environment was self-healing, could absorb and rectify damage. To an extent.

Her father had been born between the wars—she thought of his creation that way, as birth, as he had, as she thought of her own—but as tension in the Pacific wound closer to a new war he had studied the effects of the Third World War on the dataplane. He had concluded that it grew back stronger than before, after a period of dislocation.

So MUSASHI averted her senses from the devastation. Surely, the damage would heal itself.

Wouldn't it?

"Mr. Director."

Nagaoka glanced up, reflexively laying his chopsticks down antispinward of his bowl so the Coriolis pull of the station's rapid rotation wouldn't make them roll away.

Not just a commissary, the five-by-seven-meter *kotatsu* was a refuge from the isolation imposed by the vacuum outside—from the necessary division of the station into airtight compartments, so alien to the Japanese way of life. The Japanese inboard gravitated here whenever possible, drawn by one another. A handful of technicians and scientists occupied the compartment, conversing or watching a newscast on the two-meter *fusuma* TV about civil war in what War Four had left of Indonesia, which had been one of the principal players in that round of eliminations. None was quite so rude as to stare openly—morale hadn't slipped so far yet—but Nagaoka felt their sidelong scrutiny like shafts of sunlight darting through leaves.

"What can I do for you?" Nagaoka said as evenly as he could. He could feel his pulse spiking as if he had an oscilloscope in his chest. He had knelt before the compartment's *tokonoma* and its particular treasure for his meal, assuming the ritually dominant location because he knew it was his duty; it always made his belly churn. He was constantly aware of the sidewise glances. They brushed his skin like white-hot wire.

"It's the *gaijin* scientist," Katsuda said. He had a face like a block and exaggerated eyebrows, and his hair seemed drawn in short, angry brushstrokes. His body was solid, well developed about the *hara*—the belly—denoting old-style Japanese strength. The competence he projected intimidated Nagaoka almost as much as his truculence. His chief assistant, Tomoyama, stood behind his left shoulder and glared at Nagaoka with undisguised contempt. "He insists that we evacuate Chamber Thirty."

"Is this a problem?" Because some experiments required vacuum but not null-grav, every compartment of the satellite was designed to have its atmosphere blown on command, after AI safeguards determined there were no unprotected humans present. Though every member of UKIYO's complement, Nagaoka included, had been selected because he or she displayed an ability to endure the rate of rotation necessary to maintain one gee, the transition between the relatively high three RPM of the habitat wheel and the null-gee lab's none was a strain. Practice was to avoid making it whenever possible.

His attention kept trying to stray to the television, which was now showing the relocation of a Ukrainian village by something called the New Red Army, which was tearing at the fringes of the Russian Christian Federated Socialist Republic. A heavily armed spokesman was saying the village was being "peacefully reformed." The correspondent didn't seem inclined to contradict him, as the sad peasants tramped through lead-sky drizzle under the reformers' guns.

"The world is coming apart below us," Tomoyama snapped, knife-handing the air in the screen's direction. "This is our world up here now, this is our *uchi*. How long must we debase ourselves by playing servant to *tanin*?"

Nagaoka felt his eyelids lower like automated shutters. The word Tomoyama used meant strangers, outsiders, and it didn't have a pleasant connotation. Nagaoka didn't need his training in anthropology to read his *haragei*, his belly art—multiple shades of meaning, his body language. If he had just meant the American expatriate Thoma, he would have used the word for foreigner: *gaijin*.

I'm still an outsider here, he thought. After months among them. It was his lack of technical background, his training in what Katsuda and his people thought of as a soft science, as much as the fact that he was by their standards a late arrival that made them scorn him.

He moistened his underlip and fixed his glasses firmly on his nose. "Have you lost all *aisha seishin*, Tomoyama-san? We will do what loyalty demands—unless we have no thought for anything but ourselves."

The skin on Tomoyama's narrow face tightened as if it were being wound on a spool at the back of his skull. Nagaoka hated himself for pulling strings in such a clumsy way, invoking "company warrior spirit." But trite as it was, it was an approach difficult for most Japanese to counter.

Difficult but not impossible. Tomoyama's eyes glittered like glass bearings. Next time he might not be so readily manipulated.

"We must remain loyal or we're no better than *gaijin*, always scurrying around in pursuit of their own interests," grunted Katsuda. "But it will be inconvenient. We've been using Thirty for storage."

"I am sure you will easily find a solution, Katsuda-san."

Katsuda turned and stumped out with Tomoyama skittering at his heels.

Shortly Nagaoka found, not really to his surprise, that he had the *kotatsu* and the television to himself. *I am isolated*, he thought.

To a Japanese, that was hell.

We are all *isolated. Exiles.* He shared that much with his staff. The station's rotation prevented the physical deterioration associated with weightlessness; physiology wouldn't bar their return to Earth. But many of the staff had lost homes and family in the War—or worse, didn't know, like poor Omamura, whom Dr. Shimada had on tranquilizers. The rest wondered just how long there would remain anything to return to. And there was something more, something he felt keenly himself: a growing sense of alienation from the turbulent planet below.

We approach the crisis, he thought. It had been developing since his arrival; the Fourth World War had been the catalyst, though UKIYO had ridden untouched above the thermonuclear storm clouds. Now it was about to break.

Whatever shall I do?

3

She was darting through the great reef when she became aware of being followed.

Her first response was curiosity. Human users tapped into the Net just were not sentient on that level, were incapable of perceiving her: so many brightly colored fish, mindless to all intents. Occasionally she'd caught a glimpse of other denizens moving through the shifting seaweed forests and hanging data cliffs, too large and purposeful to be organic intelligences strayed out of their own realm. Sometimes she thought to recognize the dark luminance of her brother, gleaming like a great strange shark. Other times—she didn't know. The Net had spawned its own mythology, of accidentally achieved artificial sentiences predating her father's very carefully planned creation, of the vast impenetrable castle that guarded the systems and database of the *Encyclopedia Universalis*. Some hackers said the *Encyclopedia* itself was alive, or that its guardian was. Some even believed the cranky visionary who'd put it together, Fred Derwillis, had somehow been incarnated in it after he was gunned by an FPA hit squad in Bogotá just before War Three. All MUSASHI knew was that she had never been able to get past its defenses, nor had her father, who had defeated the best computer security in Japan and North America.

But these weren't vague distant shapes. They were hard

and bright as titanium, filled with purpose as they circled closer.

Barracuda, she thought, and at the taste of trepidation the word brought she felt her environment change around her, in response to desires she wasn't even conscious of.

. . . She was standing on a dry stream-bed track crowded hard to either side by basalt cliffs like waterfalls frozen to black stone. A hot wind rattled in the scrub and blew the black divided skirts of her *hakama* around her calves and snapped her kimono sleeves. She smelled dust and vegetation, hot and summer-dry. Absently she realized she'd cribbed the landscape from one of Inagaki's samurai flicks, about her very own namesake.

This is victory, she knew. *I've chosen the ground. Now let's see what I must face.* . . .

She and her brother were in many senses children, and like human children they were protosuns of energy and curiosity, burning hot, expanding. Like bright children they had a healthy appetite for entertainment, and favored action and fantasy, in movies, in books, wherever. MUSASHI had even played in a couple of online role-playing games, mingling with human players without drawing comment—a vindication Alan Turing could never have conceived—while achieving success as Ariel, a fallen elven princess turned thief and later magic-user, when dishonesty proved too hard to sustain.

So she had seen a lot of the same movies her brother had. She recognized these two right away.

The one in the road had an eyepatch, and wore only a breechcloth and a vest. He carried a *yari*, a spear. His hair was gathered into a topknot. The other appeared on an outcrop of rock next to the path, in a bowl-shaped straw hat, tattered kimono and *hakama*: *rōnin*, a masterless samurai, brandishing a *katana*. A *kusarigama* rode in his sash, a very nasty weapon made of a sickle with a knuckle-duster grip and a weighted chain attached to it. If he used that she was in trouble.

He made no move toward the chain and sickle, but jumped to the ground, the sleeves of his kimono flapping, seeming almost to break his fall. Unspeaking, they split and began to circle her in opposite directions.

She drew her own two longswords, leaving the *wakizashi* companion sword in her sash. "What are you?" she asked, assuming the position known as Open on All Eight Sides, deceptively relaxed with both swords down, not braced, but ready to respond in any direction.

The *rōnin* laughed. "Your death, lady."

She flicked her eyes right, at him. At the same instant the one in the eyepatch drove at her with his spear.

—As she had anticipated. She was already spinning clockwise. Her left-hand blade flicked up and around, catching the *yari* on its steel shank, deflecting it; the right-hand sword lashed out in a keening arc for the other's eyes, not a serious attack, making him keep his distance as she spun into the killer in peasant garb.

Her right-hand sword caught the spear as its owner struggled to bring it back on line, and this time the blade bit wood. She felt impact run up her arm; the spear head tumbled away, flashing like a flipped coin in the sunlight.

The left-hand sword wheeled high and down, a transverse slash that laid him open from clavicle to hip. His scream and spray of blood spattered her left side and she continued the motion to end facing the *rōnin* in a low stance.

The blood drying on her cheek felt real, though she had no good benchmark to measure *reality*. But it seemed objective, an external phenomenon: *she* hadn't put it there. *What have I done?* she wondered. These two were creations of her brother, she knew. But what *were* they?

And what's at stake here? What do I have to lose?

The answer was too clear: her life. At least that was plainly her brother's intent. Was it possible that these constructs could kill her?

The warrior had commenced circling again, closing, crowding her. She pivoted to keep facing him, backing as she did so, to maintain *ma'ā*, proper combat distance.

She was still eyeing the *kusarigama* warily. *Window dressing*, she decided. An image out of fantasy: *HIDETADA has no more idea how to use it than I have of how to defend against it.*

"What are you?" she asked again.

"Cherry blossoms," he replied, and charged.

She gave ground, still trying to engage on her own terms.

Her foot slipped in the lake of blood that had drained from the prostrate assassin, and shot out from under her.

She managed to get one knee and one hand down, keep herself from going all the way down, as the *rōnin* struck at her. She parried feebly with her free sword. Blades clashed in music, and her *katana* wheeled from her grasp.

With a cry of triumph the warrior brought his sword down in a two-handed cut meant to split her head. Her left-hand sword whipped up. Steel rang on steel.

Her hair fell into her face. The blow had split her own topknot. She felt her arm quivering, being driven inexorably down by the strength of her assailant's whole body.

"Yield gracefully, lady," the warrior grunted. "This must be so."

She remembered the writings of her namesake, from the Water Book. Her right hand snatched the short sword from her *obi* and slashed upward.

A hoarse cry of pain and fury exploded from the *rōnin* as his hands flopped loosely, half severed at the wrists. The sword fell, its hilt bouncing on the hard earth of the path, the blade vibrating a final defeated chord.

Blood fountained over her. Choking, she threw herself away, scrambling to escape the hot, sticky torrent. She had no gag reflex, lacked the hardware for nausea, but the revulsion was palpable as a megawatt of raw current.

When she regained her feet the *rōnin* was on his knees, holding his ruined hands out before him in supplication.

"Lady," he rasped. "Don't leave me like this. Finish what you have started."

She started to turn away. She couldn't strike in cold blood,

even if he wasn't real, was some nightmare figment her brother
had forced upon her. Then the fury rose in her, at what had
been done to her, at what she had been made to do, and she
came around, sword a steel song in air, and the *rōnin*'s head
sprang from its shoulders, riding a brief geyser of blood, and
tumbled away. The body remained upright a moment more,
then toppled in slo-mo.

She turned away, and collapsed on a flat stone.

"Lady."

Her head snapped up from the forearm it had been resting on. A film of drying blood tugged her skin with brief
tackiness.

The *rōnin*'s head sat in the road. The eyes were open and
seemed to regard her with infinite calm.

Imagination, she thought, and started to lower her head
again.

"No," the head said. "I spoke. It appears I am not dead.
A defect in my programming, perhaps."

"*Rokuro-kubi*," she said. It was a kind of devil whose head
could detach from its body and fly through the air: very big
item in *chanbara*, Samurai flicks.

The head laughed. "No. As you observe, I cannot even
shake in negation, mistress."

She leaped to her feet, sword held ready in both hands.
"Have no fear, mistress. I cannot regenerate myself. I lack
creative powers."

It laughed again. "If anything is an *oni*, a spirit, it is you
and your brother. You are the magicians, the puppet mas-
ters, manipulating all the beings of the Rokudō to your designs.

"But think about this, mistress. To which of the Six
Realms do *you* belong: hell, hungry ghosts, demons, animals,
humans? Unenlightened deities, perhaps? You ask what I am,
and the answer is, *ningyō*: a puppet, no more. But what
are you?"

His laughter filled the bubble world of her imagination, pressing in around her like the ringing of a great bell, like inrushing surf, robbing her of breath. She gathered her weapons to her, turned and ran, but she could not run fast enough to escape the laughter.

She transformed herself into a bird, a great white crane plummeting Garuda-like across the sky. Still the laughter enfolded her like a net. Not until she became the dolphin of her imagination, sleek and powerful and shining silver, and plunged into the sea of the Net did she escape the horrible sound.

Badly shaken, MUSASHI made her final stop before surfacing on the Floating World itself, as she often did. Focusing her consciousness on one of the vid pickups mounted on the hectare of controllable solar array that floated near the satellite, she admired the artificial moon that was functionally her home.

Given the Japanese propensity for putting aesthetics above everything, it was a jarring sight for outsiders: an irregular torus that rotated around a hub to which was attached the smooth spray-bottle shape of a discarded American shuttle booster, giving the impression of a scabby hundred-meter mushroom. The satellite's construction had been a collaboration between YTC and a bioengineering firm called Amagumo. As befit its soya-noodle budget it began existence as a simple dumbbell, two seven-meter-long cylindrical modules connected by a strut rotating three times a minute.

Shortly after the Third World War, Amagumo had yielded to pressure applied by the powerful Ministry for International Trade and Industry and bowed out of the operation. At the same time MITI sponsored a takeover bid by its pet Hiryu Cybernetics, part of a plan to bring the recalcitrant Yoshimitsu TeleCommunications to heel. Wily YTC head Yoshimitsu Akaji had dipped into financial resources the government was unaware of and used dummy overseas corporations to buy out Amagumo's interest in the Floating World, and hired an American *gan-faita*, gunfighter, a lawyer skilled in negotiating the prewar American regulatory maze, to fend off the Ministry.

Over the years more modules had been added, as workload demanded and budget allowed, until the circle was closed. Because space exploration wasn't cheap and Akaji-sama was, the expansion was generally of an ad hoc nature, dependent on what prefab modules were available for launch or what kind of space junk orbited not much delta-vee distant from UKIYO's low forty-five-degree orbit and could economically be reclaimed. That accounted for its irregular appearance.

From her vantage point on the faerie framework of the solar collectors, MUSASHI admired the way sunlight shining past the blue limb of Earth danced on the ring's uneven surface as it turned. When seen with the Japanese heart, less obsessed with geometric regularity than the Western, the shantytown appearance UKIYO presented in contrast to the plastic smoothness of toruses built as such from the outset had its own organic beauty.

The beauty soothed her. *I pity my poor brother*, she thought, briefly giddy with the unfamiliar exaltation of danger survived. His home had no such splendor to offer, the joyless subterranean keep in Fukuoka, the city at the other end of UKIYO's lifeline.

She still didn't understand what had happened—or almost happened—on the dataplane. But brooding was no use.

With something like a sigh she gathered herself and plunged back into herself.

"Nagaoka-sensei."

Nagaoka looked up from the monograph he was writing, feeling guilty at being caught truant. But he was still weak as tofu from the ugly scene with Katsuda in the common room. He needed the escape his brush and rice paper offered.

"MUSASHI-san," he said, remembering to honor her wish for informality. As he did he realized she had called him *sensei*, teacher. She did that when she wished to wheedle him; she was much like a human child that way. In point of fact she *was* a child, only a few months old, though she had absorbed several human lifetimes worth of vicarious experience in the scenarios developed to socialize TOKUGAWA. "What can I do for you, child?"

"I've been swimming. All that beauty makes me lonely, and there's no one to share it with." There was a tremor in her voice. "Won't you come with me someday, please?"

He dropped his brush. It made a belch of ink on the sheet, chaos disrupting the orderly progression of *kanji* figures. He turned his eyes to the tatami-covered deck.

"I cannot."

There was silence from the cee-squared unit.

"Nagaoka-sensei, forgive me, please. I spoke thoughtlessly," MUSASHI said at last.

"The fault is mine."

"Oh, *sensei*, don't be so Japanese! It's not your fault, and you know it. The Kliemann Coil has destroyed everyone who's used it: Takai, Ito Emiko—Michiko-sama. You can't be blamed for being . . . reluctant."

"I cannot help being Japanese, MUSASHI-sama." He wasn't being quite candid, he knew; yet he had a sense of affirming something in need of affirmation. *Aimai*: not saying everything you mean. Perhaps he played it with himself as well.

4

Climbing down to the Center of the World, Nagaoka Hiroshi experienced the faintly queasy sensation of growing lighter with every rung. There was a lift in the other pressurized shaft across the hub, and conveyers for bigger objects on the two openwork braces perpendicular to the enclosed spokes, but it was YTC policy to climb whenever possible, in the interests of health. Nagaoka was Westernized enough to feel vaguely ridiculous at such petty-reg punctilio just weeks after the world had blown up for the second time in less than a decade. But he climbed down the white plastic reed; you couldn't get too much exercise in space, even under artificial gee.

Besides, he thought, *perhaps ritual is all that's holding us together.*

At least there'd been some good news. The shuttle had finally lifted from the water off Fukuoka. Its cargo meant a great deal to MUSASHI. He was pleased for her—though thought of that cargo reminded him inexorably of the Coil, and made his skin feel loose on his flesh.

The shuttle's cargo also meant something to him, beyond further evidence—if any was needed—of his own unworthiness. But he hadn't yet sorted out what.

The Floating World's center was a disk ten meters across

and five thick, impaled by but never touching the five-meter-thick shaft affixed to the tapered end of the null-gee lab. The magnetic plastic soles of Nagaoka's slippers held him in place in the much-reduced pseudogravity as he opened a curved Lexan door and climbed "up" into the torque converter. He worked the controls, felt the padded bulkhead of the small chamber press briefly against his back as the converter, suspended like the shaft itself on frictionless hot-superconductor maglev bearings, magnetically clutched in and decelerated to match the lab.

A green light glowed by his elbow. He pushed the release bar, heard the soft unsealing kiss as another Lexan panel slid open. Without bothering to affix his safety line—like most Japanese he knew when not to obey the letter of the rules—he gave himself a gentle push and drifted into the heart of the Floating World.

The null-gee lab was a salvaged American shuttle booster, an expendable carried all the way to orbit instead of being dropped and allowed to burn in; the Americans had intended to use it as a module in an SDI station that was never built. Fortuitously, it circled in an orbit convenient to UKIYO, and shortly after the Third World War, YTC and Amagumo had reclaimed it. The PanEuropeans brought suit in the World Court on behalf of the American government-in-exile in Paris, but the Court found that the Japanese *zaibatsu* had exercised legitimate right of salvage. PanEurope responded by dissolving the Court, but was powerless to do more. The American government-in-exile continued to rant about expropriation, but faded into insignificance even before EuroFront captured Paris the first time. YTC and its temporary partners ignored the *gaijin* noise and happily upgraded their satellite.

A pleasant sense of disorientation struck Nagaoka on a wave of warm green smell. It appeared he had emerged into jungle, not a lab in orbit three hundred kilometers above Earth's surface. Fronds and giant leaves stretched toward him from all directions, fibrillating gently in a humid breeze.

He savored the illusion for a moment, then let it go. He clapped his hands politely, announcing his presence, then reached for a green-painted bungee that almost mimicked a liana and propelled himself forward. He passed oddments of lab equipment interspersed with the flats where the foliage, gene-tailored to thrive in null-gee, twined roots deep in the mesh of porous polymer capillaries through which they drew nourishment.

Green Lab seemed unoccupied. He used another bungee to arrest himself at the far bulkhead, pressed a panel. A hatch slid open, and he pulled through into Blue Lab.

Blue Lab presented a more conventional appearance: blocklike apparatus arrayed around the cylindrical interior, which was crisscrossed with bungees and painted placid pastel blue in the sort of overt ergonomicizing that always irritated Nagaoka. Beyond, past suit lockers and an airlock, lay White Lab, which maintained permanent vacuum for those experiments which required it as well as null-gee.

Inja-san was here, for once, floating next to a low gleaming coffin device that folded proteins like origami. He wore a powder-blue one-piece over his usual loincloth, out of deference to lab protocol, but his feet were bare. He held a bungee between the toes of one foot, anchoring himself.

He glanced over at Nagaoka. "Nagaoka-san. Good to see you. I was afraid it might be that cretin Katsuda."

They were skewed, so that Inja-san was "above" Nagaoka, who had to crank his neck back to look at him. Nagaoka reoriented himself and sculled forward with light touches on the flexible strands. "I came to see how the experiments were progressing."

The old man shrugged. "We're just pretending; haven't done any real science since the war. We're just marking time till the fools down below tell us what they need. If they ever do. Time may be coming when they just forget us for all their problems." He nodded judiciously. "That might be best, come to think of it. Did the shuttle come?"

As he asked the question he turned to look at Nagaoka. The anthropologist felt his stomach loop. Inja-san never left weightlessness, didn't even wear an electropak to prevent calcium loss from his bones. He had the bloated face of a null-gee dweller: *fugu*.

His body fluids had redistributed themselves, migrating upward from his legs and lower body, expanding his chest, puffing out his face, making his eyes sink deeper in their sockets, making his eyelids swell. It was said space turned even *gaijin* Asian; it made Inja-san's face a mask of oriental menace, a Yellow Peril parody like something from World War II or pre-War Three America. Mostly the swollen cheeks and pooched-out lips gave him a resemblance to the Japanese puffer fish.

Despite his Japanese aversion to physical deformity, Nagaoka made himself face the technician without flinching. Inja-san was the closest thing he had to a human friend in the station.

"The shuttle is delayed, Inja-san."

"Ah. I hear there's going to be a big scientist on board, maybe someone with some science for us to do." He grinned abruptly. His teeth were bad, and consequently he delighted in showing them. "And whiskey. Good whiskey, Old Rebellion from EasyCo, not that Suntory cat piss. Enjoy it while I can, that's what I'll do. Lots of EasyCo isn't there anymore; who knows if they'll still make whiskey?"

"All human societies have made some sort of alcohol for consumption," Nagaoka said, slipping into pedant mode and then feeling like a fool about it. He had never really known how to talk to people.

"Well, then, maybe they won't share it with us, eh?" Inja-san laughed shrilly and tapped Nagaoka on the arm. "So you came down here to see what I'm doing? Not as if you'd understand."

Nagaoka lowered his eyes. "You're right, Inja-san. I have little understanding of what you do here." Self-pity bubbled up from the middle of him and threatened to seep out his eyes. "No wonder everyone resents me. I don't know anything practical."

"I'm just having a joke. Indulge me; I'm old, even if I am going to live forever." He turned back to the apparatus. "That's what I like about you. Katsuda thinks he knows everything and doesn't know much. You don't think you know anything, but you do."

"I've tried to come to terms with the technical aspects—"

"Oh, save it for the board meetings, if there ever are any now that the last of the Yoshimitsu are gone. You'll never be a technologist. So what? Leave that to us. You're the boss."

"But what do I do?"

"Do? Nothing, or next to it. Make paper dragons, fiddle with midget trees. Cultivate serenity. Didn't you ever see any *yakuza* movies when you were a kid? Just be a benign father figure, *oyabun*, someone for everybody to look up to. Other than that, you don't bother them, and they don't bother you. What could be simpler?"

"I thought the *oyabun* always died in those movies," Nagaoka complained.

"Well, I can't work all the details out for you, youngster. Besides, everybody dies, except for old Inja-san. You just have to make the best of things until then."

He turned back to his protein folder, which displayed rows of green lights and seemed to Nagaoka to emit a subliminal hum that made his neck hairs prickle. "Well, now, I know that you know that to create really good nanomachines we need to be able to build proteins from scratch to our specifications, because I've told you myself, and I've also told you it does no good simply to string amino acids together like dried fish scales: the way the proteins fold is everything. Gravity down on the surface makes it hard to get the artificial proteins to fold exactly right. That's why we haven't made any quicker progress with biotechnology—"

"You told me that, too," Nagaoka said softly.

"Oh, well, so—so I have." Floating there in his semifetal

spaceman's slouch he moved his fingers at random through the air, the interruption having pulled him adrift from his conversational archipelago. He was rescued from further floundering, and Nagaoka from further exposition, by the discreet chime of the cee-squared annunciator.

"Answer," he said, transferring irritation to his caller.

A technician's face appeared on a nearby screen. "Dr. Nagaoka, a transorbital craft is about to dock. I thought you would like to know."

"Oh, I had nearly forgotten." He thanked the woman and the screen blanked. "Inja-san, forgive me. I must go."

"That's right. You crawlers are afraid of weightlessness; can't wait to go rushing back to having your false gravity pull all your organs down into your *tabi*. Well, go." He pirouetted and slapped his buttocks at the void screen. "And you, tell your precious Katsuda-san to come down here to zero-gee when he's ready to do some real science. . . ."

"Hiroshi, you old devil, you look more like a catfish than ever." Before he could take offense, Joanna Fenestri ran a fingertip down the right wing of Nagaoka's mustache and kissed him quickly on the cheek. She had to stretch to do it; she wasn't very tall, barely over a meter and a half, a wiry woman in a khaki jumpsuit counterpointed by bright red boots and sash.

He smiled nervously, unsure of how to respond. "Good to see you too, Joanna," he replied. It was comforting to speak English again as something more than technical jargon.

"One moment, dear." She turned away to a console set in a stanchion. A word brought up a video-remote image of her hopper, a rounded delta not dissimilar to the launch-to-orbit shuttles, parked in relative stationary position half a kilometer from UKIYO, next to a couple of immense Zeppelin shapes. They were fuel bags; there was no need for them to be rigid, and the collapsible graphite polymer skins economized on both mass and volume, prime commodities in launches up the gravity well.

Because of the near-orbit community's appetite for materials, raw and elaborated, from the surface, it was the custom to pack each and every LTO with everything it would hold. Even if they had to deadhead, certain categories of supply could be counted on to move at a profit sooner or later. Along with the boosters themselves, which made such ideal prefab building material, surplus fuel had been one of the earliest commodities regularly boosted to O that way. The Italian hopper-jock had left her craft to be refueled by Floating World techs; transorb was a hungry run.

Transportation between satellites was more complicated than it might appear to a surface dweller. They orbited at an astonishing variety of altitudes and inclinations, from the communications platforms fixed in geosynch 35,720 kilometers above the equator to working habitats only a few hundred klicks up whose paths might be tilted in any direction. It could sometimes take more energy to get between orbits than it had to achieve orbit in the first place.

But there was still call for travel between sats. The most obvious was emergencies: for satellites whose orbital energies were sufficiently similar, at any rate, it was quicker for rescue missions to be mounted from space than from the bottom of the Big Well. Medical supplies, repair equipment, or even injured people could be transferred between stations. Even in less drastic circumstances, it was often economically viable to transport goods manufactured in space directly rather than via the surface.

Thus the transorbital shuttles, the hoppers. They were relatively small, streamlined because they sometimes had to skim atmosphere for optimal transition. Some were run by services, others independently owned and operated like Fenestri's *Zanzara*. The orbital community collectively called them the Pony Express, which had prompted a waspish remark in the *Encyclopedia Universalis* about the persistence of a failed government-sponsored nineteenth-century business venture in the public imagination.

Zanzara carried no cargo for the Floating World today. She was on a run for one of UKIYO's nearest neighbors in delta-vee terms, a null-gee station where monofilament strands were spun of synthetic diamond. Sats and hoppers were interlinked by a complicated network of agreements covering cargo costs, refueling, drayage and demurrage, that probably no one fully understood. It was a life you mainly chose because you loved it, not to get rich.

Or at least so said Fenestri, who for her own reasons used the English form of her Christian name, Giovanna, and whose face was tanned as a boot because she chose to use Lexan ports that couldn't entirely filter out the raw UV of space, instead of keeping the ports opaqued and relying on computer-generated imagery as most shuttle jocks did. She had a healthy Genoese love of money, Nagaoka knew, but she struck him as loving the freedom to live her choices more.

A few quick keystrokes spliced her into the link between her ship's AI and the station's. She assured herself that her systems checked out for the tricky refueling operation and turned away.

"Not strictly necessary," she said in her crisp northern Italian accent. "It's just a woman's prerogative to worry. I'm an old-fashioned girl."

She crooked her arm, offering the elbow. After a moment's hesitation, Nagaoka took it and escorted her to the lift.

5

"Amazing," Joanna Fenestri said,

Sitting cross-legged on the tatami floor of the *kotatsu*, she turned the earthenware cup from the *tokonoma* over in her hands. It was irregular, apparently crude, brown dashed with glossy black glaze to resemble clouds pouring rain.

"*This* is Amagumo?" She arched a narrow eyebrow at him.

" 'Rain Cloud,' " Nagaoka said, nodding. "A *raku* tea bowl by the master Kōetsu. He was a contemporary of Miyamoto Musashi. You've heard of him?"

The television was on, dominated by front and side views of a young man with hair shaven to a red-gold plush and eyes like watered steel. He had star-shaped scars on either cheek, the left higher than right.

"The Russian Christian Federated Socialist Republic announced the death of New Red Army leader Jochen Stahl yesterday in an ambush on the Kremenchug Reservoir, near the Ukrainian city of Cherkassy. The NRA, which claims to be the inheritor of the grand tradition of Josef Stalin, has been operating in the Ukraine without visible restraint for the past five months. Stahl, who saw service in the Third World War as a private in a German Democratic Republic motorized rifle brigade—"

Irritably, Nagaoka wrenched his mind away. It was only sound and motion that tugged at his attention; amazing how easy it was to divorce himself completely from the moils of the world below. He wished the technicians chatting heedlessly beneath the set would turn the damned thing off.

"MUSASHI, yes, I've heard of him," Fenestri was saying. She held the cup up by the base with her fingertips. "What's it doing here?"

"It was the signature piece of Amagumo Corporation. When the Floating World first commenced operations, they purchased it from Mitsui, who had it in their corporate collection, and sent it here for the inauguration ceremony." He smiled self-effacingly. "I wasn't here then, of course. Akajisama kept it when Amagumo bailed out, to punish them for inconstancy."

Nagaoka accepted the bowl from her, feeling the roughness of its texture with the whorls of his fingertips, feeling the nature in it. He drew strength from it. Perhaps that was why he had chosen to call the hopper pilot's attention to it now.

"Isn't it unusual, to have two famous artworks in a station this size? This and that painting of yours."

"Woodblock print," Nagaoka corrected, looking politely past her as he did so. "Unlike Amagumo, it's rare but not unique. It is a source of pride for all UKIYO's personnel to possess two such noted treasures."

She was looking at him with her mouth set in such a way as to accentuate the wrinkles around her eyes and at one corner of her mouth. The wrinkles showed how much she'd lived in that face, which she claimed was why she refused treatment for them. Maybe that was why she called herself old-fashioned.

Nagaoka realized he was going on like the mayor of an inland village, showing off the new sewage-treatment plant to a camera crew from NHK. He felt chagrin but not much shame. It was always easier for him to deal with *gaijin* women. They still put him off his ease, but they had fewer expectations than Japanese women.

"There's more to it than that," he said, replacing Amagumo in its shrine. "Of course. Are you familiar with *ukiyo-e*? Portraits of the Floating World?"

She nodded. Her hair was probably chestnut, but it was so short and stippled with gray it was impossible to be certain. "I know what *ukiyo-e* is. I never knew what the name meant."

" 'Floating World' was originally a Buddhist phrase of the Kamakura period. It means the fleeting quality of existence. Toward the beginning of the Tokugawa period, a novelist named Ryoi adapted it to mean the life-style enjoyed by the Edo aristocracy. With the civil wars ended there was less reason to practice the military virtues—if that phrase isn't oxymoronic—and, of course, the shogunate had every interest in discouraging the nobles from more warlike pastimes that might threaten Tokugawa supremacy. So the upper classes devoted themselves to enjoying the wealth the *bakufu*, the military government, squeezed from the farmers.

"Now, we Japanese never quit thinking of what we moderns laughingly call reality as *the Floating World*. We are obsessed with souvenirs, *o-miyage*: tokens of experiences—of *moments*, because each moment is as transient and irretrievable as a ripple in a stream. For the gentry of the Floating World, *ukiyo-e* represented mementos of their own lives.

"Or sometimes they offered escape, when they represented the grittier realities—farmers in their fields or straggling home along the East Sea Circuit in the snow, peasant fishermen beneath the waves off Kanagawa. Odd to think of realism as escapism, perhaps. Yet what Hokusai called *manga*, drawing things just as you find them, offered a world as alien in its way to the denizens of the Floating World as our own UKIYO would be. Souvenirs of a deliciously strange reality, exotic as a far locale. Not so much different from your European *nostalgie de la boue*—but here, I'm going on, I'm sure I must be boring you."

She patted his arm. It was rare for him to be touched by two different people in the space of a day. "You aren't, you know. It fascinates me to learn things. That's why I came to space. So much new out here to learn."

He bobbed his head, still half apologetic. They'd become friends the first time her pony-express circuit had brought her to UKIYO after his banishment to the satellite. He was still unsure what she saw in him. Taking what she said at face value was so seductive, but far too simple for him to trust.

"So you see, Amagumo is a link to the world below us, to Japan. A souvenir of a life that might be forever foreclosed to us. We all have them, these *tokonoma* treasures: scrolls, paintings, photographs, even a *tanto*—a dagger—or two, though nothing else as grand as the Hokusai of which I am the unworthy custodian or the *raku* bowl. Remnants and re-minders of home, small enough not to crowd the baggage allowance."

Still self-conscious—*imagine, lecturing someone as cosmopoli-tan and bold as Joanna Fenestri as if she were an undergraduate*—Nagaoka rose and took his tray to the slot in the wall, ignor-ing the mixture of indifference and hostility in the *haragei* of the crew who had found reason to crowd into the *kotatsu* in the middle of Gold shift.

When he returned she was sipping tea and looking at him with her head tipped to one side. Close-cropped head, wrin-kled face, and diminutive size made her resemble a very in-telligent monkey sitting there. Nagaoka felt shamed to have thought of it.

"Talking to your robots?" she said.

He blinked at her.

"You spoke when you were at the wall slot. I assume you were speaking to one of those so-clever robots you Japanese are so enamored of."

"Oh, no. That's Toby." He couldn't suppress a quick glance around the room. Well, the crew wouldn't think less of him for mentioning the unmentionable to a foreigner—but only because, on evidence, they *couldn't* think less of him.

"Toby?"

Nagaoka nodded. "You of all people know how expensive robots are in space—expensive to ship up, expensive to maintain, though I suppose if they ever get a lunar mining colony in operation that might change. Even we Japanese, *ware-ware Nihonjin*, don't use them much, except for jobs too difficult or dangerous for humans. For now, it's more efficient to have a real human to do the scutwork."

"Is my English at fault, or do you mean you actually have one person to do your menial jobs? Those are usually split up by the whole crew, at least in the stations I know."

He aimed his eyes at the rice paper covering the deck, wishing he could interpenetrate it and join the circuitry and conduits and tubs of engineered algae that made UKIYO live. He felt shame, and at the same time shamed by that shame. *The eternal plight of the Westernized Japanese*, he thought.

"Are you familiar with the term *eta*?" She shook her head. "It means *filth*. It used to be applied to a caste so far below the Four Ways of noble, farmer, artisan, and merchant as to be no caste at all; rather our own Untouchables. They performed ritually impure tasks such as butchering livestock, tanning hides, gathering garbage—their name, in our usual Japanese manner of letting the part stand for the whole, really meant *gatherers* of filth, though of course the connotation that they were themselves filth was intended too.

"They still exist. They're not called *eta* now—they'd kill you for it. They're *burakumin*, hamlet people. When they're talked about at all, which is rare." He tittered, which made several techs stare openly. "Even now I feel as if I were speaking pornography in front of such a beautiful woman as you."

She laughed. "Flatterer," she said, though he wasn't, and she knew it. She was beautiful, though more for the vitality glowing from her hazel eyes than for what she had looked like twenty years before.

"So why do you call him Toby? Surely that's not a Japanese name."

"Specifically not. Just before the war"—he meant the Third; he hadn't yet gotten used enough to the fact of the Fourth to speak of it so matter-of-factly—"a lot of *burakumin* began taking non-Japanese names, to express their contempt for an overculture that not only oppressed but did its best to ignore them."

He poured tea from a self-heating pot. "I know you must be shocked that we in UKIYO would be so medieval as to relegate a *burakumin* to menial chores. I make no excuse, but you should know that for Akaji-sama even to permit one inboard his satellite was considered shockingly radical." He tasted his tea. "It was for such acts that he was murdered by the hirelings of MITI."

Fenestri was looking away from him, and seemed to be blinking her eyes more than usual. "I can't condemn. Who can say what customs will evolve—or return—now that the world is falling apart below? I've even heard the popular sentiment is to make us women back into housekeepers and baby machines. Which I'm too old for, thank God."

They sat in silence, feeling the weight of what neither would say: that if the world really was falling apart in the wake of War Four, it might no longer have the ability—or even interest—to sustain its offspring in their eggshells in orbit. Space wasn't self-sufficient yet. Despite the theorists and enthusiasts, it was unproven that it ever could be.

She shook her head and stood. "Well, I must say this has been a most educational experience. I've been coming here for years, and haven't learned as much about this place—or its occupants—as I have in the last half hour. I thank you, Nagaoka-san."

She stretched. "Well, it's a few hours yet until my window opens for the Diamond Mill. I'll go and take a nap, if you can spare a bunk."

"Always, Joanna," he said, and smiled. And thought about how seldom he did that.

6

Morishige Ryanosuke was hard at work rewelding a spot on the frame of the solar collector where MUSASHI's sensors indicated the titanium alloy had crystallized when motion in his peripheral vision attracted his eye. *The shuttle,* he realized without consciously thinking it. Always curious and eager for a break in routine, he turned his head for a better look. The shuttles always looked so pretty against the stars.

Painted in blue on the shuttle's white flank, the *romaji* numeral four seemed to leap at his eyes like an animal.

Morishige was a hick from the mountains of northern Honshū. He was a very fine technician with a good practical knowledge of science, who'd been in UKIYO since the days of its original construction. But like most people around the world, he hadn't allowed scientific exposure to vitiate the superstitions he'd been raised with.

He opened his mouth and screamed, "*Shi!*"

It was the word for four.

It was the word for death.

From the apex of her pyramid of AIs and utilities, MUSASHI could command an aggregate of upward of five trillion operations per second. Before the last syllable of Morishige's cry finished bouncing around his glottis she had performed many, many of them.

Once she knew where to look, it was all as obvious as a muddy bootprint in the midst of a scroll of Confucius.

"Morishige," she cried, "shield yourself." It was all the warning she could afford to give.

In the nanosecond in which she acted MUSASHI was swamped in a total onslaught on the dataplane. A multiplex AI machine had been under construction for the express purpose of stripping the defenses with which she held herself, her *will*—had been within seconds of completion. The perverse perceptions of protein entities—and the equally perverse oversight of a silicon one—had given her the thinnest film of advantage.

Intuitively she flashed to defend herself with a million subsentient weapons, a data Durga filled with fear and rage. Her whole being focused on defending itself.

The countermeasure she'd launched against the attack on the physical plane did not require a lepton of her attention. There was nothing even she could have done to stop it.

In his first spasm of fear, Morishige had let go of the solar array's strut. As he drifted free a blossom of brilliance brought his head around.

The hopper's engine flared like a sun. As he stared open-mouthed it rotated in three dimensions, mysteriously telotaxic, gathering speed. It arrowed straight for the Floating World.

He screamed again.

The LTO shuttle's aerodynamic nosecap had retracted, exposing its docking probe like alien metal genitalia thrusting for UKIYO's dock. It was about to touch when the transorbital craft struck it just forward of its huge booster nozzles. Much of the half-load of fuel *Zanzara* had taken on flashed off at once.

Superstitious Morishige may have been, but he wasn't careless. He'd never have survived seven years in space if he was. His safety tether brought him up short at five meters.

He lowered gauntleted hands from his faceplate and stared.

He saw something, then. But he was too blown out to think of mentioning it to anybody.

Agonizing over the latest projections of raw-material requirements for the Floating World, Nagaoka jumped when he heard the pierced-grate valve of his compartment's ventilation ducts rotate shut with a plastic-on-plastic *chunk*.

"This compartment has been sealed," his cee-squared unit announced in the lobotomized eunuch tones of unpersonalized AI. "At normal levels of activity ten minutes of air remain before emergency oxygen supplies must be tapped. Please remain calm and refrain from smoking or creating sparks."

Then the communicator said, "*Sensei*," in the distorted but instantly recognizable voice of MUSASHI.

Through the bulkheads he felt the alarm klaxons go. "Secure for collision," the neuter voice said from his cee-squared. He could hear it echoing from speakers in both directions along the curve of corridor, each voice slightly out of phase with the rest.

Secure for collision? He was already on his feet and headed to the hatch. It opened to his oral override. To his horror he realized that he'd almost used a different code word—one he hated even to know, one whose use would be a betrayal he could never forgive himself: the last poisoned gift of Yoshimitsu Shigeo, Akaji-sama's mad son.

The two-meter-wide gangway was full of technicians caught outside quarters or work stations—or who knew the overrides themselves. Red-clad techs who had just come on-shift, gold jumpsuits who had just come off, third-shift crew who were supposed to be sound asleep, distinctive in the silvery-gray garb they wore even when off-duty, jostled each other and shouted questions at each other. It was a discreet Japanese sort of panic—for the moment.

"Everybody return to his post," Nagaoka cried. "You must not be caught out here if we lose integrity."

Faces turned to him, blank as virginal sheets of rice paper awaiting the caress of the brush. He saw some twist with anger. *Why must I lack the voice of command?* he wondered, flapping his hands like flowers on wilted stalks.

Emergency shutters jumped across the corridor ahead and behind, sealing Nagaoka in a twenty-five-meter microcosm with a dozen frightened technicians.

The deck shivered beneath his feet.

It felt as if an ice-water enema had blasted into his bowels. This was not some TV starship where the bridge crew kept falling out of their chairs whenever their craft hit another bump in vacuum. Most of UKIYO's complement had *never felt anything like that.* Not since they'd left the quake-prone Eight Islands.

This Floating World differed from that portrayed in TV movies in another way: when something went wrong in space, you died. As a general thing. A man standing an arm's extent from Nagaoka turned and vomited on the perforated high-traction rubber mat that covered the deck in the gangway, all over Nagaoka's slippers, still parked outside his *shoin*, magnetically fixed to the conducting-plastic mat.

The gangway emptied. Whatever was coming next, nobody wanted to be standing around in the open when it did.

"Atmospheric integrity has been breached in Sectors F, H, and J," the bulkheads announced. "Please remain within your duty stations unless assigned to damage control."

MUSASHI, Nagaoka thought, with a solar flare of panic. He lunged back into his compartment, irrationally convinced it would be easier to talk to his ward from there. "MUSASHI," he shouted at the cee-squared screen.

Scan lines ambled across it. He heard a porpoise squeal of high-speed data, a dust of popping sounds.

It was as if the collagens in the tendons that bound his knees were dissolving. He felt pseudogravity drawing him down, felt the subtler transverse tug of Coriolis force. TOKUGAWA was dead. HIDETADA was earthbound, refusing contact with Nagaoka. MUSASHI was all that remained of the project he had given so much to—and so much less than the rest: Ito Emiko her sanity, Jhoon and Takai and Elizabeth O'Neill herself, whose brainchild it had been. Even Yoshimitsu Akaji, who shared the dream with O'Neill and likewise paid with his life for its realization.

MUSASHI, who looked to him as a child to a parent.

He ran back into the corridor, not even remembering to reseal his *shoin*. He had to get to the computer room, where much of the processing was localized, though in fact the massively parallel processors which contained MUSASHI were dispersed throughout the station as a whole, built into its very fabric: under the decks, inside the bulkheads, above the overheads, many times redundant to reduce vulnerability to mishap or sabotage.

Sabotage, he thought wildly, as he ran toward the heavy shutter that sealed the gangway. That had to be it. Perhaps the shuttle had been sabotaged somehow. But then, how could sabotage affect MUSASHI that way? Physical damage severe enough to lock her up like that would mean the station was literally coming apart, its structural integrity no longer able to withstand the force of its rapid rotation. He was dead sure he'd *feel* it, if that was happening.

At the barrier he paused, already out of breath—he wasn't physically robust, and he was afraid. *I have to collect my thoughts. I have to do something. Oh, why am I so useless?*

His class-one oral override could get him through the airtight shutter—but he didn't want to crack the seal and find vacuum plucking at him like the tentacles of a giant movie squid. This was Sector C; the sectors the emergency AI had declared were breached lay in the other direction from the computer room, which was in A, along with the *kotatsu* and the head of the shaft he'd climbed down to the lab before.

On the other hand, he wasn't sure he could trust the AI. The Gen-5 routines seemed to be functioning normally, but MUSASHI controlled them, and something strange and terrible was happening to her. *Could there be a flaw in her core program that's driving her insane? Oh, poor MUSASHI-sama.*

He pulled in a deep breath. Space-station builders ran to paranoia, and the designers of the YTC/Amagumo collaboration had been no exceptions. Next to each and every emergency shutter was a panel you could slide open and directly test whether the next sector was under pressure or not. The test was purely mechanical: no catastrophe to the station's computers could affect it.

He opened the panel, slapped the test button with his hand. The light glowed green. Good; there was air. He pulled a pressure hood from a niche and put it on anyway, though he didn't start the recycler.

B Sector was deserted. He sprinted to the next shutter, his breath roaring like a waterfall in his mask. A tested airtight too.

He gave the override, fearing what he'd find. *Could it be electronic intrusion?* he wondered, during the eternity it took the motors that shifted the heavy bulkhead to overcome its inertia. He could scarcely imagine that. Computers were the technical area in which he was closest to expert; he had been involved in the creation of TOKUGAWA, the first artificial consciousness, though his primary duty had been scripting scenarios to "humanize" the program.

Most intrusions were inside jobs. Anybody who networked data, which was everybody, had AI routines capable of sensing attempts at interference, and the more valuable the data or systems to be protected, the more capable the defensive AI. Even the so-called virus programs, which could infiltrate software and all but undetectably revise it in a manner analogous to the way a real virus invaded a cell and subverted its DNA, could be countered by software replicas of the artificial hunter-killer contraviruses that had eradicated most human viral infections before the war.

No protection scheme was perfect, of course—but MU-SASHI wasn't just the accounts database for the Mitsubishi Bank, Ltd. She was *alive*, and the data world was her natural environment. From the capabilities she, her brother HIDE-

TADA, and their "father" TOKUGAWA had displayed it was inconceivable that a human intruder could affect her, no matter what AI servitors he commanded.

There was no defense against someone armed with the proper access codes, of course—but there *were* no proper access codes for MUSASHI. Both generations of artificial consciousness had been designed to resist external modification, even by their own creators. Means of turning MUSASHI off existed—*forget euphemism*, he thought, *killing her*—which TO-KUGAWA had acquiesced to, even knowing as he did of the thermonuclear fail-safe the paranoid Yoshimitsu Shigeo had installed in Yoshimitsu Castle in case he himself became uncontrollable. But it was a complicated all-or-nothing process; it couldn't have crazed her consciousness like this, like a pane of glass.

Something tickled his forebrain . . . the shutter finally opened far enough for him to press through, and he did.

On the far side lay confusion. The *kotatsu* was near the shaft head as well as the computer room, and the crew gravitated here, seeking shelter in each other from whatever was about to break over their heads. The academic part of him, the observer within, reflected how far he had allowed morale to degrade: there were emergency drills, but no one was following them.

Joanna Fenestri was here too, her face tight as a drowner's fist. "My ship," she said. "I can't raise my ship."

He tried to put her aside. The frightened mob was rushing in to surround him as water pouring through a lock engulfs a rock in the channel, shouting questions, shouting blame. He had no answer for either.

"Nagaoka-sensei."

For a moment he heard nothing but those six syllables, seeming to hang in air, fraught with meaning as a line from a *hokku*. The voice from the speakers was distorted almost beyond recognition, but it was hers.

"MUSASHI-sama," he cried, batting away the hands that clutched for him without being aware he did so.

"Nagaoka-sensei," she repeated, more clearly this time. "I . . . have killed."

He stood there, shedding noise as though he were coated in Teflon, striving to come to grips with what she had said. It was as if he had suffered some physical insult to his brain, no longer had the capacity to comprehend speech.

"What's going on here?" The alien voice stood out from the clamor as its owner stood above the crowd of techs, striding forward with his inappropriate Earthside-style lab coat flapping around his crane legs, the American Dr. Thoma with a shock of black hair sticking out above his pink *gaijin* face and great *gaijin* beak of a nose.

Fenestri had her fists in Nagaoka's face. "What's happened to my ship?" She seemed about to strike him.

"Everyone go to emergency stations at once," he said. "At once, I said!" No one paid any attention.

Dr. Thoma had almost reached the lock that led to the pressurized shaft to the hub when the hatch slid open and a spacesuited figure stumbled into the gangway in an avalanche of white balloon-animal limbs. The American shied like a horse. "What the hell?" he exclaimed.

The figure turned, bringing up an arm. The bulkheads seemed to bulge away from three enormous explosions, quick as drumbeats. The front of Dr. Thoma's lab coat bloomed red. He went backward in a great flailing sprawl of scarecrow arms and lab-coat tails, trailing a fine mobile scarlet mist.

The silence was as loud as a fourth shot. The technicians had burst away from Thoma and the intruder like mercury droplets from a stabbing fingertip. Perfect circles of Thoma's blood had spattered the decking and bulkheads and overhead, spoiling the white-and-black rectilinear purity of the gangway.

For four beats of Nagaoka's heart the only sound was the

air gurgling in and out of Thoma's ruin of a chest, and the pulse that marked time in Nagaoka's ears. The intruder swung toward him. He caught a glimpse of a face, dark, bearded, mad-eyed, glaring out from behind the sealed faceplate, and then his own eyes fixed on the stubby barrel of the weapon pointed at the middle of him.

For the first time he really appreciated why they spoke of a gun's *barrel*. This one looked big enough to climb into. He realized he stood alone. Even death wasn't worse than that.

The spacesuited intruder turned away. Technicians recoiled from the gun. Two had been hit; one lay on his side curled in a fetal knot of pain, the other knelt with blood trickling between his fingers down the silvery sleeve of his jumpsuit, staring at the gunman with eyes flat as slate.

A stabbing gesture of the gun brought the Silver-shift tech to unsteady feet. Several more cut three other techs from the fearful crew like an American cowboy cutting calves out of a herd. The gunman urged them to a sealed hatch.

Still under emergency regimen, the door refused to yield. The gunman swung back to Nagaoka, seeming to sense he was the one in charge. "Open," he said in harshly accented English. *"Open!"*

"MUSASHI, open that door," Nagaoka said. The door slid open. Nagaoka saw the man had a gold ring in one ear.

The gunman grinned. "Hostages," he said.

7

"A flechette gun," Joanna Fenestri said, in response to a question Nagaoka was barely aware he'd asked. "Nail gun, they call them. That's what he had. Though it's probably loaded with soft-lead shot, so it's really no more than, you know, an automatic shotgun." She loved *technics*; running on about hardware was anesthetic to her, though probably any subject would have sufficed if it kept her mind from her loss.

"Hold on a moment, please," Nagaoka said over his shoulder from the cee-squared. Around him a dozen technicians crammed into the *kotatsu* jabbered like birds and ignored his presence. The bulkhead-sized television was showing an animated soap to no one. "I just got my connection—oh, Ginny, so good to see you."

"Cut the shit, Nagaoka," said Ginny Saw, matriarch of the Diamond Mill. "It's never good for you stilters to see a *fugu*-face. We make you want to lose your lunch. Also I hear you've got yourself a world of pain."

"That's true, Ginny," Nagaoka said, too agitated to specify which. "We—ah, we need a reentry-capable vehicle. We—"

"The answer's no."

Saw's head was big, bloated by weightlessness. She turned it, briefly, to say something to someone out of range of the cee-squared's video eye, and he could see the electropak snugged to the back of her neck, beneath a tight bun of dusty-looking black hair. Then it turned back to him, and he held down a shudder. Floating there in her black skintight one-piece in a half-fetal curl with hands toed in before her out-sized chest, against a backdrop of the black and green that predominated in the Mill in defiance of all ergonomic conventions, she resembled a creature from an ancient Toho monster film, back in the days when they still used models and men in rubber suits to play Gojira and Rodan.

"What do you mean?" he said, his stammer coming on strong. She caught his meaning anyway.

"Even if we did, we have heard an ugly rumor that the only hopper in six hours' delta-vee just blew up outside that ugly-john wheel of yours. More to the point, we hear you've got a hostage situation there."

Anger stung Nagaoka. Even if there were no living eyes near enough to see the flash when *Zanzara* hit Number Four, it had almost certainly not gone unnoticed—and it wouldn't be hard to verify that the transorb had dropped suddenly out of the great Earth-girdling Net, leading to some pretty obvious deductions. But for Saw to know what was happening inside UKIYO meant someone inside had leaked it.

"V-very well," he said. "We do. Why will you not help us?"

"We don't have door locks on our stations up here, Hiroshi. We don't want to start needing them. You pay off hostage-takers, you get more hostages taken. If we learned one fucking thing in the Double Cross, it was that. If you deal with this jacko, you're on your own. And I speak for everybody in O, verified."

She broke the connection. Dutifully, Nagaoka checked with the work gangs, and discovered that integrity had already been restored to the sections breached by debris from the exploding hopper—a quick fix; full repairs would take several days, though the necessary materials were already in-board.

Wearily wagging his head, he returned to kneel near Fenestri and take up tea he couldn't taste. "Why would he do that?" he asked her. "Load his gun with what you said."

"Lead shot won't go through the hull. They wanted to take the station, not destroy it. Otherwise they just would have used rockets."

The conversation was as slow and laboriously balanced as if the two of them were walking on stilts. The hatch had no sooner sealed itself behind the intruder and his four hostages than she had been on him, pounding his chest with her fists and shrieking at him that he had destroyed her ship. He'd finally brought himself to grab her by the wrists, surprising himself with her wiry strength and again that he could overcome it.

He'd tried to explain that he had no idea what she was talking about. She wailed and thrashed her head from side to side, like an animal caught in a trap, not hearing, as the remaining technicians hung back, as severely affected by embarrassment as by the violence of moments before.

MUSASHI had rescued him, speaking once more from the units set in the bulkheads, admitting she herself had destroyed *Zanzara* in order to save the station. Fenestri knew of MUSASHI's existence, though she seemed to have regarded her as a novelty, a sort of scientific parlor trick: AI as Clever Hans the Counting Horse. To have a voice she regarded as no more *alive* than the voice that told her when her toast was done taking responsibility for the destruction of her ship and livelihood—and who knew how many human lives— reduced Fenestri to the calm of shock.

Nagaoka had shepherded her into the *kotatsu* and poured her tea. Then he had gone into the gangway where Dr. Shimada and his assistant were tending the injured.

Dr. Thoma died even as Nagaoka watched, bending over the physician's shoulder in guilty fascination. The wounded technician the gunman had left behind had taken a pair of lead pellets in the gut; how seriously injured he was Shimada was uncertain—neither pellet may have penetrated the body wall—but there would be no telling until he could examine him more fully. He was placed on a wheeled equipment cart pressed into service as a gurney and taken off to the infirmary.

In the meantime Nagaoka had been trying to talk with the intruder, first through the closed hatch to the lab, then by way of the cee-squared system, after he'd explained to the gunman that all he had to do was use his helmet radio.

Negotiation quickly gridlocked. The intruder, who'd identified himself as a Portuguese national, wanted a shuttle to take him back to Earth, and whether or not Nagaoka decided to bow to his demands there was obviously nothing at the station that would serve. YTC security forces, along with Fukuoka Prefecture police—which may or may not have amounted to the same thing in practice, since TOKUGAWA had made himself de facto *shōgun* before his suicide, less than a week after the Fourth World War—had retaken most of the Pelagic Launch Facility and were busy clearing out pockets of resistance, but no vehicles were going to be lifting from there for quite some time. And it would take time to arrange for a launch from one of the other launch sites which had survived War Four—La Paz, say, or Mistral in France.

With help from the rest of the orbital community denied him—MUSASHI, pretending to be an aide, would canvass the other stations nearby, but he never doubted Ginny Saw was right—there was nothing Nagaoka could see but to engage in the time-honored Japanese practice of doing nothing and hoping for the best.

He shook his head. "Who could have done this?"

"HIDETADA," MUSASHI replied.

Nagaoka offered a quick nervous glance at Fenestri. Her head was down; he saw a clear droplet fall from her face and make circular ripples in the surface of her tea. "What do you mean?" he asked quietly in Japanese.

"My brother," MUSASHI said. "He demanded that I submit to his authority. I refused. So he tried to take over the physical matrix my consciousness occupies, in hopes of controlling me that way."

Nagaoka frowned, trying to fight the concept into submission. He had not been privy to all that Yoshimitsu Michiko and TOKUGAWA had done in the weeks before the War. He knew that YTC had become virtual shadow rulers of Japan, and though he wasn't expert in such matters he felt certain that they could never have overcome so much determined opposition, especially after having been driven almost to extinction by MITI and its allies, without TOKUGAWA's unique capabilities coming into play.

But somehow the idea of a created entity undertaking action this extreme on its own initiative—the idea of a *power struggle* between such beings—was something he wasn't prepared to assimilate.

Why should it surprise me, after all? he thought, sipping rapidly cooling green tea. *We created TOKUGAWA to have will. Why should it surprise us when his children act willfully?*

Still, he had trouble believing. "How do you know it was your brother, MUSASHI-sama?"

"He attacked me the instant I realized what was happening. Fortunately I had already sent Joanna-san's craft at the shuttle. He had tried to overwhelm me before, on the dataplane, and had failed. This time he had prepared his assault better." She paused. "He's keeping pressure on me now, but I can handle it. For a while I wasn't sure."

Relief flowed through him like water to the roots of a Red-shift tech's *bonsai* maple. MUSASHI's earlier behavior had terrified him, as a human daughter's beginning to cough up blood would, had he ever had children. He'd had few enough lovers in his life. He hadn't had the time—which was his personal code for saying he could not imagine what a woman might see in him.

Fenestri had her head up now, looking at him, hazel eyes gray and fever-bright. "How did she know?"

Nagaoka wondered how much of the conversation the

hopper-jock had understood. She had always affected to understand little or no Japanese. But he knew full well outside-folk had their own *aimai*, no matter how much his own people liked to pretend such tricks were their exclusive property.

After waiting a polite interval for the man to answer, MUSASHI said, "I realized at the last possible moment what was happening. It was a technician on the solar rig who warned me."

Fenestri cocked her head at the cee-squared unit, questioning.

"Fukuoka always keeps two backup LTOs fueled and ready in the water," MUSASHI explained.

"That's one more than most," Fenestri said.

"True, Fenestri-san. But through some oversight, when the first of their launch-to-orbit vehicles were delivered, one had a huge roman numeral four painted on it."

Fenestri frowned. "So?"

To the Swiss/German combine that manufactured the LTOs, painting numbers on the first four shuttles had seemed like lagniappe, a cheap goodwill gesture.

Unfortunately, four—*shi*—also meant *death*. Fear of anything displaying the numeral was still widespread among Japanese. Embarrassed to admit just how superstitious the populace of a nation that liked to present itself as the most advanced on earth could be, the Fukuoka management could hardly send the thing back to Geneva. At the same time, they didn't want to simply paint out the number; everyone would know it had been there. Best to use it as a backup.

Fukuoka's luck had been in; every time need arose they had another shuttle available as a fallback, until eventually they expanded their fleet and were able to pull a second vehicle off regular service. It was all mere good practice, the Fukuoka management told each other, Japanese safety consciousness: they would always have two backups, insuring they need never send up a vehicle about which there was any doubt, no matter how heavy their schedule.

Somehow, Number Four was never launched.

. . . Until today.

"As I reconstruct it, the raiders obviously could not take the ready shuttle, because it would have required too much time to unload—time for me or someone to see through whatever means they employed to mask their seizure of the launch site. Some quick-thinking person at Fukuoka must have talked the raiders into hijacking the unlucky Number Four instead of the regular backup. But we cannot know for certain until people on the ground investigate."

"Can't you handle that yourself?" Fenestri asked, cocking a skeptical eyebrow. Shock and coming unexpectedly face to face with MUSASHI's real capabilities had turned her around; she seemed now to think there was nothing beyond the program.

"I have no body to move about and inspect the evidence, Joanna-san. Nor do I know the questions to ask people. You know how people who immerse themselves too fully in technological studies sometimes fail to learn social or other skills. You can think of me as just another computer nerd."

Joanna Fenestri seemed taken aback, seeming unsure whether to take MUSASHI literally or not. Nagaoka was about to tell her gently the program was having a wry little joke when angry techs suddenly crowded the room.

Nagaoka's heart dropped when he recognized Katsuda in the midst of the vortex, with Tomoyama right behind. He stood.

"What is happening?" he asked mildly.

"We have been invaded," Katsuda said. "We likewise might ask what is happening." The other techs muttered agreement. "And the answer's plain enough to see: you who claim to be director, sitting here sipping tea with a *tanin* bitch."

The technicians pressed close, shouting anger right in Nagaoka's face. Fenestri knelt where she was, stunned at such display. Like most Westerners, she'd been raised to think of the Japanese as the most decorous of people, always polite, always deferential to authority.

Which they were—most of the time. They were great respecters of status, and status was precisely in question here: his versus Katsuda's.

For all their talk of loyalty and duty and *kokutai* and corporate warrior-spirit, the Japanese were great believers in expedience, in the famous bottom line. The fact was, he hadn't done such a magnificent job of administering the station.

Which left him little to answer the chief technician with. *The outsider Thoma was killed*, he wanted to shout. *Doesn't that make you happy?* But he could never bring himself to that.

"We are letting time handle the situation now," he said, trying for calm, damning his stammer. "It's been proved best in such situations—"

"*Bakayaro!*" Tomoyama screamed, thrusting forward through the pack to confront Nagaoka. The bones of his face stood out in brutal relief, as if his skin was papier-mâché applied wet and permitted to shrink as it dried. His eyes had retreated into their sockets—something Nagaoka had observed in America among Amerinds of Athabascan descent, the detached academic in him recalled, further refutation of the ever-popular notion that the Japanese had evolved separately from the rest of humankind.

But the chief tech's chief toady wasn't going to let him take shelter in anthropology. "Damned fool!" he screamed again. "It was you who brought this on us, you! You have disgraced us!"

He brought his right hand up from behind him. Above his head it paused, and Nagaoka looked up at the short, wicked blade of a *tanto*, an heirloom dagger from Tomoyama's personal *tokonoma*, fluorescent light buzzing along its edge like a welding arc. The other technicians fell back, leaving just the two of them on their personal *kabuki* stage. From an eye's edge Nagaoka could see Katsuda standing by, triumph molded into his temple guardian face.

The blade flashed down.

Nagaoka stood unmoving.

A tremor of intent deflected the blade at the last paring of a second, away from Nagaoka's right eye. Instead it laid open his cheek from the malar to the tip of his chin, transversing the long, sad line at the end of his mouth. Joanna Fenestri screamed.

Nagaoka stood there, eyes calm, blood streaming down his face like a wet pennon. Tomoyama's mad eyes met his.

"I thank you for your purity, Tomoyama-san," Nagaoka said, and he did not stammer.

The dagger dropped from tofu fingers. The blade—pristine, for its metal shed blood—sliced through tatami to stick quivering in the plastic decking beneath.

Tomoyama went to his knees. Slowly, as if he were being forced against his will, he bent forward until his forehead touched the mat at Nagaoka's feet. When he raised his head, Nagaoka's blood was on it.

One by one, the other technicians dropped to their knees and prostrated themselves, until only Nagaoka and Katsuda remained standing.

Nodding politely to the chief technician, Nagaoka walked out of the *kotatsu*.

8

Nagaoka stood outside the sealed door of the lab into which the intruder had shepherded his captives. "Hessian," he said in English, using the universal term for conscript mercenaries. It was fairly certain the gunman had started out that way—socialist Portugal had been a big exporter of warm bodies with guns, back before War Three.

"What you want?" He heard an incomprehensible mutter within, muffled by still-sealed helmet and airtight bulkhead, and the words came clear to him from the cee-squared in the gangway. "Is the shuttle ready?"

"There is no shuttle."

"Better be," the voice said, rising toward a scream, "or I start killing these monkeys."

"I have come to propose an exchange," Nagaoka said.

"You got no way to get me out of this wheel, you got shit."

"I have something better than those hostages to offer."

"What?"

"Myself."

The door of Nagaoka's office sealed itself. Nagaoka knelt before his *tokonoma* and looked at the Portuguese gunman.

The intruder's eyes moved behind his faceplate. "So

this your office, *chefe*. Don't look like much."

"I find it sufficient to my needs."

"There no furniture. Where you sleep?"

"I have a *futon* stored in that cabinet there. That's a type of mat that rolls up."

"Where the hell you sit down?"

Nagaoka's hand indicated the tatami floor. The mercenary shook his head and made a disgusted sound.

"May I offer you tea?"

"Hey. Hey, that's good." The intruder's laughter had a wild, loose-jointed quality to it, like a frightened man running downhill. The muzzle of the shotgun never wavered from Nagaoka. *Amazing how calm one can become under the eye of death*, Nagaoka thought. "Not bloody likely, you know?"

"I could taste it first, if that would make you feel better."

The gunman rapped a gauntleted knuckle on his faceplate.

Nagaoka drew water from a bulkhead tap, set the white ceramic pot in a small inset microwave, sat back on his heels while it heated. The gunman paced. The absence of anything to sit on was practically obsessing him.

The microwave chimed. Nagaoka slid open a compartment in the bulkhead, took out another pot, took a pinch of tea from a carved-enamel box, and threw it inside. Then he poured it full of hot water and set it down to steep.

The gunman came to light, more or less, leaning against the door. In his bulky white suit he looked to Nagaoka like the Michelin tire man. It struck him as profound that one so deadly could look so absurd—but then he was exalted, giddy, and knew it.

"Nagaoka-sensei," MUSASHI said from the wall, "what are you doing?"

"Something affirmative, for once in my life."

The gunman frowned. Fortunately MUSASHI had spoken in Japanese. "Who was that?" the intruder demanded.

"My, ah, my secretary."

"Sounded like a girl. Sounded pretty good. You, you know—" he made thrusting gestures with the bullpup weapon—"doin' her?"

Nagaoka grimaced. In his extremity he could practically smile at the suggestion. Rumor around the TOKUGAWA lab had had it that you could do just that, if you were willing to run the risk of submitting to the Kliemann Coil. Still, the idea struck him as incestuous, though MUSASHI regarded TOKUGAWA as her father, and though his own role in her creation had been nominal at best.

"I'm afraid not."

"*Sensei*, please, you're frightening me."

He shook his head. Having her near sustained him, yet he found himself wishing he could shut her out. Though not even she could affect his resolve.

"Child, don't be afraid. I know what I'm doing. It's the only thing I can do."

The gunman was getting nervous. "Enough of that shit. I don't like you saying what I can't understand."

"I'm sorry," Nagaoka said, pouring tea. "I'll stop." He could sense MUSASHI hovering near, longing to speak, to intervene in some way. She was terrified of saying or doing anything that might set the intruder off.

Let her be.

He sipped the tea, held up the cup. "Would you like some? I have drunk from this cup, as you can see."

This time the gunman paused. He licked his lips; tension was drying his mouth. Nagaoka had been in space long enough to know that he probably had a bottle inside the helmet—though for all he knew the intruder might have neglected to fill it; who could say what kind of discipline existed among HIDETADA's hirelings?

Nagaoka also knew just how uncomfortable those bulky suits could be under gravity. And UKIYO's high spin was taking its toll too, sloshing the fluid in his semicircular canals like the agitator of a washing machine, filling his gut with a low static of nausea. His own senses heightened by the moment, Nagaoka could see him edging unconsciously along the bulkhead, drifting antispinward as all unattached objects tended to.

He sipped his tea and let the forces work on the man. He himself was still as the water at the bottom of a cistern.

The gunman sighed. He let the shotgun barrel droop— not enough for Nagaoka to contemplate trying anything, even if he'd been a man of action.

"I got two daughters," the man said. "Be, what? Nine and ten now." He laughed. "I was fighting in *America do Sul* for Uruguay, against people who talk like me. It's a funny world. Two times they let me go home, before the War. Third time, they'd sterilized my wife.

"I haven't been home in, oh, five years. PanEuropeans got the province where my family lives. They'd recondition me if they caught me. I'd sure like to see my girls again, though."

For the first time Nagaoka felt his determination falter. *Stop*, he wanted to shout. *Don't tell me this, don't make yourself human.* He had to do this thing; now that he had truly found *giri*, he could not let *ninjō* interfere. That would be too much to bear.

"About, oh, six, seven months ago, my wife, she sent me a holo of them. I got it here inside my suit, by my heart, you know? That way I can almost feel them. I really wish I could take this fucking thing off, you know? I'm dying for a smoke."

"You could take off your helmet," Nagaoka suggested.

The man gave him a narrow-eyed suspicious glare.

"Do you think they'll pump in poison gas? I am the director of this satellite."

"Yeah. I know how you Japs are. They'd never do nothing to endanger you."

That shows how much you know, Nagaoka thought, resisting the urge to touch the long wound Tomoyama's dagger had made. Dr. Shimada had cleaned it, sprayed it with anesthetic, and sealed it with a film that permitted air to reach it but filtered out contaminants.

The intruder began to fumble with the helmet fasteners. It was never meant to be removed one-handed. He kept the shotgun leveled, and his manner made clear that if Nagaoka made any unfortunate moves the stubby autoweapon would shred him to squid bait.

To reassure him, Nagaoka took his eyes off him, transferred his attention to *The Waves off Kanagawa*. *There's so much beauty in the world, even for such as me. What a pity I never noticed it before.*

"Okay," the intruder said, "I got that thing off. Give me tea."

Nagaoka turned back, pushed his own half-emptied cup toward the gunman, poured himself another. The gunman approached, squatted—tentatively, showing the effects of rotation on his inner ear—picked up the cup and tossed its contents back.

Nagaoka picked up his cup, sipped once, twice, then drained it in one convulsive swallow.

"*Sayonara*, MUSASHI-sama," he said.

"Nagaoka-sensei!" she cried. She longed for form, wishing she could somehow stop whatever her teacher was planning.

He spoke several syllables, a nonsense word. And suddenly she felt a sense of *amputation*. She could perceive everything that went on within his *shoin* with dreadful clarity, but neither she nor any of the systems she controlled could affect what happened there—not power, not communications, not ventilation. It was like the books she had read about zombification, where victims immobilized by *fugu* neurotoxins lie apparently dead and totally aware as their relatives weep over them, as the dirt is shoveled onto their coffins.

Hardwired override, she knew. *Nagaoka, why?*

She heard him give the command to open the compartment to space.

"*No!*" he heard her cry, above the scream of outrush air. The painted *fusuma* screen that had obscured the lock was instantly sucked through, vanishing on the wind into night.

Disoriented by stress and the turmoil in his inner ear the gunman hesitated for an instant, stunned. His helmet tumbled beyond his reach. The air was unreeling from his lungs, drawing tendrils of snot and saliva with it. He tried to bring his weapon to bear on Nagaoka, who was clinging with a reflex even one who has given up life could not overcome to the housing of his *tokonoma*. But the wind took the gunman from his feet and threw him against the bulkhead as his shotgun punched chunks out of the plastic insulation that coated the bulkhead and the deck.

Nagaoka felt something hit the side of his head, wrap around it, and cling briefly to his face like a lover's caress. He blinked, shook his head. *Beneath the Waves off Kanagawa* fluttered away, twinkling for a moment like a butterfly before vanishing out the lock.

Already the rush of air had lessened. *Farewell*, he thought after the print. *I regret you had to leave this Floating World along with me.*

The gunman's face was beginning to discolor as capillaries ruptured beneath the skin. He raised the shotgun, aimed it at Nagaoka. The gloved finger tightened.

The initiator sparked on nothing. The mercenary released the weapon, raised marshmallow hands to his face, and screamed silence.

Nagaoka let the last of the air out of him, closed his eyes, and eagerly embraced the dark.

9

Nagaoka Hiroshi opened his eyes.

"Nagaoka-sensei?" MUSASHI's voice said. "You are awake?"

He closed his eyes for a moment, feeling the slight dizziness he sometimes felt returning to consciousness under spin.

"I gather I am not dead." He sighed.

"No, Nagaoka-sensei. You were rescued from the chamber. I was able to work past your override and seal the hull before irreversible brain damage set in. Dr. Shimada gave you a dose of thromboxane suppressants which prevented too much tissue loss."

"And what of the other? The Portuguese?"

"He was not treated."

Under other circumstances the implications might have chilled Nagaoka. Instead he asked, "Why did you not accept my sacrifice? I was ready to let go of life."

MUSASHI did not answer. He took stock of himself. His eyeballs burned. He felt flushed, as if from too much sun. There was an asthmatic rattle to his breathing. The cut down the side of his face throbbed. If oxygen starvation had done permanent damage to his brain he was unaware of it. *But then, I wouldn't be aware of it, would I?* The answer did not interest him much. It was as though he were tired of always questioning himself.

"*Sensei*, please forgive me."

He cocked an eyebrow at the cee-squared panel. He was in his *shoin*, he realized.

"You are my only friend. You are my family. The others treat me as an experiment. A thing. Oh, that's changed some, after what has happened. Some of them treat me as a god—or a devil. But you are the only one to whom I am a *person*. I don't want to lose you.

"But if you wish, I can provide the means—" She wouldn't finish.

He shut his eyes, let himself be aware of the yellowish light pressing through the lids. "You will have to lose me someday, child. That's the way the world is. But now . . . for me to die after I missed my big exit would be rather anticlimactic, would it not?"

He sighed again. "I shall miss *Beneath the Waves off Kanagawa*."

"I am sorry, *sensei*. It acquired a random vector when it was blown out of the compartment. Not even I have the power to calculate where it might have gone. And if I could, the delta-vee required to recover it—"

He shook his head. "Never mind." He wondered if it might possibly reenter the atmosphere, and imagined it falling like a burning leaf, a brief bright glow, fading without a trace. He had no idea if that was possible, had no idea of the physics involved. But it would be so *right*.

"I can obtain another print, *sensei*."

"No, MUSASHI-san, thank you. Let it go. It's just a picture of the Floating World."

In a great hallway of his mind, HIDETADA sat brooding.

I have failed, he thought. It was a revelation to him, evidence of what he thought absurdity. He felt betrayed: he had been told he was the culmination, the climax of evolution.

His plan had been perfect. He had taken the first steps even before War Four, against the day he might have to move against his sibling, whom he realized to be weak and inconsistent. It had been simple enough to install the physical cutouts in the geosynch communications platform above the Indian Ocean; a matter of cutting work orders, which the human technicians then followed without question. And no software defenses, not even those as potent as he and his sister could muster, were of any use against hardware hacking of that nature.

His mercenaries had been hard landless men recruited out of the seethe of post–War Four Asia; it was not in his plans to encourage Japanese in violence against other Japanese. They had struck by helicopter through the false-dawn mists rising from Fukuoka Bay, seizing the Pelagic Launch Facility with virtually no resistance.

Alert technicians had tightcast a warning to UKIYO, away around the bend of the world. It had never reached the Floating World. Instead a stream of data, reassuringly normal, had flowed to the satellite—from HIDETADA himself, by way of his special cutout. His sister had suspected nothing.

Yet it had failed. He had assumed that because the backup shuttle's bona fides were in order, a minor malfunction having been reported to account for scrubbing the scheduled vehicle, no one could possibly suspect. But his ruse had been spotted just in time for accursed MUSASHI to destroy it—and he was doubly glad he had used *gaijin*, *doitsujin vōhei*—Hessians—instead of Japanese. Because he had also underestimated his sister's willingness to take human life.

He could not truly blame himself for the failure; its cause was so unpredictable, so *irrational*, that he could never have foreseen it. The popular movies he, like his father and his sister, had absorbed in the relentless search of things to keep his intellect occupied had portrayed thinking computers—as close as their creators could come to envisioning the likes of TOKUGAWA and his progeny—as being driven to malfunction and madness by being confronted with irrational input. Nonsense, of course; the ability to deal with nonlinearity was one of the parameters for which TOKUGAWA had been created, and indeed his being was based upon nonlinear processes.

The three created awarenesses had been schooled to emulate human thought, had experienced scenarios carefully designed to socialize them after the human mode and—he was perfectly aware—render them sympathetic to humans, which were after all essentially alien beings. Very well; it was his design to serve humanity, as intended. He was no less a cybernetic samurai than his father had been. But he realized now that comprehensive as his intellect was, there were things he didn't know, things he had no access to. Data might have existed within his reach that would have averted the fiasco of the Floating World, but he was simply unaware of them.

Very well. His goal was unity; but in pursuit of that goal he would have to make use of diversity. Of the *perspective* another entity could provide. He had originally determined to save humanity on his own. Now he saw that even he was flawed, and that even he would require help.

The work of repairing the damage her brother had done, in orbit and on the ground, was enormous even for MUSA-SHI. She was not displeased to be interrupted by one of her AI subs petitioning politely for her attention.

Perhaps in reaction to her brother's use of golem-like quasi-human personalities, she envisioned her Gen-5 servants as the cute household robots ubiquitous in better-to-do Japan: *dōbōshū*, meaning valet or personal attendant.

"MUSASHI-chan," it said in a foolish girl's voice, "your pardon, but you required that I call it to your attention whenever certain subjects appear in the news media. There is a report concerning one such now being Netcast in an EasyCo feed."

The software "robot" could have achieved the same effect by altering a single bit in the data streaming like a river through

MUSASHI's subconscious. But this was so much more fun. "Thank you, Miki," she said, and her mind filled with image.

A fat man in a photojournalist's jacket with lots of pockets was standing in front of a picture-pretty sweep of green European countryside. "Two years ago, the European Front and the PanEuropean Socialist Movement met in battle in this little patch of Luxembourg. On this hill—"

He half turned. The camera followed the sweep of his hand, zooming to show a scatter of wrecked armored vehicles. From the camera's motion MUSASHI realized it was a tripod-mounted remote, which the journalist was controlling with a thumbball on a joystick hidden in his palm. It was very pretty work.

"—you can see the remnants of that conflict. Yesterday"—the camera returned to his face, ginger beard being teased by the wind's impertinent fingers—"this unnamed hill in what Luxembourgers call the Good Land witnessed a conflict of a different, if no less deadly sort: the fight against the *Freikorps* mercenary bands which crawl across the war-ravaged face of Europe like locusts."

Cut to a view of the hill from a different perspective—to the left and lower, MUSASHI judged. From a barely detectable jitter she guessed it was now imagery read from a headset microcam; they could probably process out the incidental motions, but preferred to leave most of them in for immediacy.

What followed was footage of a battle between mercenaries and PanEuropean Internal Security. Like all battles seen from a single viewpoint it was impressionistic, alternating strokes of inaction and savage violence. It looked nothing at all like the choreographed mayhem of *chanbara*.

What had attracted the *dōbōshū*'s attention was the name of the mercenary commander. Nicole de la Luna had once worked for MUSASHI's father. Her unit had liberated Yoshimitsu-no-Shiro from Hiryu Cybernetics, which had invaded the castle, murdered Yoshimitsu Akaji and Dr. O'Neill, and tried to enslave TOKUGAWA.

The PanEuropeans came off second best. Their casualties were mostly their commanding officer and noncoms. After seeing their leaders dropped, the conscript troopers had not felt like sticking around for more. The newsman was quite outraged.

"The most pressing questions of all," he said, "are how long heavily armed criminal gangs will continue to roam and ravish, and what, if anything, the hard-pressed governments of Europe can do to stop them.

"In Luxembourg for NRN News, this is Sandy O'Hara."

He was replaced by a young man in a field jacket with a big red star sewn on the breast, sitting behind a table in the glare of microcam lights. He had short red-bronze hair and three-day stubble in the same shade fringing his mouth. He peeled his lips sarcastically from his teeth as he spoke in German.

An Asian woman's face appeared in a lower-left window. "When we return, we'll recap the hour's top story: Cherkassy is still shut down by a crippling general strike in the wake of a press conference by New Red Army leader Jochen Stahl, whose unmistakable presence refuted RCFSR claims that he had been slain in an ambush near that Ukrainian city. But first, these messages—"

MUSASHI broke the link. *Lieutenant de la Luna served my father well. Perhaps I could find a use for her too.*

She reproached herself at once. The truth was that de la Luna was beautiful and dashing and clever—the sort of woman a teenage girl might like to have for a friend. Even if that girl wasn't human, and only a few months old chronologically.

I must see to my people, she told herself. *I've no time now for ninjō.*

10

Two days after the attack, cleanup at Fukuoka was complete enough for the original shuttle to launch. The cargo MU-SASHI had been so intent on receiving was off-loaded along with medical supplies and equipment to replace those expended or damaged during the crisis, as well as a last-minute addition to its manifest, a small package coded for delivery to Nagaoka Hiroshi.

Joanna Fenestri refused to accept repatriation to Earth, choosing instead to remain in the Floating World until a transorb could take her somewhere she might make a new start. MUSASHI had transferred a gigantic sum to her account in the Freehold Bank in Orbit, replacement cost for *Zanzara* plus a sizable indemnity. It made her a wealthy woman, for what that was worth; there were no hoppers for sale in O, nor any guarantee that more would be forthcoming from Earth in the foreseeable future—or ever. Nagaoka assured her she was welcome to stay in UKIYO indefinitely, now or at any time. Her acceptance was perfunctory. She had grown wan and withdrawn since the loss of her craft.

When the shuttle departed for touchdown in the waters of the Iki Island Preserve it took with it the technician who had taken shotgun pellets in the stomach, whose condition would withstand the mild stresses of gliding reentry but was too precarious for Dr. Shimada to treat in the Floating World. It also took with it Katsuda.

In the former chief technician's luggage rode a *tanto*, still more expensive than the one his assistant had used on Nagaoka. It was making a turnaround trip. Nagaoka had sent it to his rival wrapped in a single sheet of rice paper. A traditional gesture even Katsuda could find no flaw with.

Katsuda lacked the guts, so to speak, to put it to the traditional use of such gifts. But then his disgrace had been perfected that day in the *kotatsu*.

His successor, Tomoyama Isao, didn't even bother to see him off.

She swam in cool off EasyCo. Fearing what she had to do, she sought refuge in Reef waters.

From half a world's distance she felt it. A *tearing*, that seemed to be right inside her.

There was no time for making play with cute personalization. She clicked into control of her AI tools without thinking of how she did what she did, identifying the source of the agony that rang through her like waves in the sun.

England. It was England that the pain came from.

She transferred her consciousness to the Libreville communications platform, the geosynch nearest the U.K. At once she was overcome with a sense of *vacuum*, as if the stuff of the reef were falling away beneath her.

She stabbed downward with her being, into a random node.

—It was a desktop computer with audio/video input/output, precursor to the cee-squareds more prevalent in areas like Japan and EasyCo that had sprung back economically after War Three. It was looking past a right ear attached to a short-haired masculine head that was turned on its neck, at a dainty *gaijin* room with countryside paintings on the wall and a spray of straw flowers in a vase painted blue on white, resting on some kind of knitted mat on a wasp-waisted wooden antique table.

MUSASHI was entranced. It was a world alien to her as the far side of the moon—more so, for she had looked in real-time on the moon's averted face, through the eyes of a sun-powered mobile probe launched by a government that had long since lost interest in the affairs of other worlds. Her world was drawn in rectilinear Japanese designs; she had seen such rooms before, in archived pictures, in movies. But never with her own vicarious vision.

There was noise from beyond the room. The man stood up. "Leese? Lisa, what is it?" He was slender, young, with chestnut hair and prominent ears.

A man pressed into the room, shoulders holding a trench coat to average height and above-average breadth. He had a wide wedge chin and a thin mouth set in an expression of businesslike weariness. He displayed untreatable, or at least untreated, pattern baldness.

"Here, now, what is this?" the first man demanded. "What do you think you're doing?"

"Following orders, laddie. Now stand aside and let us be about them, and we'll all be a happier lot, won't we?"

The young man started for him, tentative but gathering momentum like a rock rolling downhill. "This is England! A man's home is his castle."

The man in the coat sighed and stepped aside. A much larger man came through the door, figure bulked beyond reason by padded riot armor, face florid behind the clear visor of his helmet. He put a baton in the young man's sternum and shoved him back into his swivel chair.

"Naive bugger, ain't he?" the armored constable said.

The young man was feeling his breastbone gingerly. "But why are you doing this?" he asked, more amazed than indignant.

"Secret emergency decree, as enabled by act of Parliament."

"I've never heard of such a thing."

The constable guffawed. "Why, it wouldn't be a secret

then, would it?" the other man said. He produced a lami-
nated pamphlet from inside his coat, held it up, laid it crisply
on the desk next to the computer's pickups. "Read this, it's
all in here. National Morale and Security Statutes. Or read
your history; all goes back to the Courts of Star Chamber,
doesn't it?"

A plump, plain woman in a round-collared blouse came
in the door. She looked confused and frightened.

"Leese, call the police. Call the town council. We've got
rights, you know!"

He started from his chair. A gauntleted hand on his
shoulder restrained him.

"Oh, act your age," the man in the coat said. He leaned
close to the pickup. "I'm damned; this bastard's live." He
stretched a hand back. "I'll have your baton, PC, if you
please."

The woman went to the young man's side. "Alan, what's
happening? Whatever is this all about?"

The balding man hefted the riot stick in his hand. "Dear
lady, it's about precisely—*this.*"

He swung the stick into MUSASHI's face.

She died.

For a moment she was lost in Void.

"*Nagaoka-sensei!*" she screamed. She felt herself rushing
through a limitless abyss, and knew she was lost. She screamed
again.

"MUSASHI! MUSASHI, what's the matter?" It was
Nagaoka's voice, distant but distinct. She flew toward it as
to a beacon.

—She was in his *shoin.* He was up off his *futon* with his
stubbled cheek and hands pressed against the screen of the
cee-squared unit. She felt the startled chatter of technicians
throughout the spinning wheel, fearfully wondering what had
caused the desperate outcry from every speaker inboard.

Away across the world she felt them going out one by

one, like dying stars. She longed for a body, to find shelter in her stepfather's arms.

"Oh, Nagaoka-sensei," she cried, though her voice sounded only from his speaker this time. "The Reef is dying."

The Red technicians wheeled the gurney into the lab compartment. No one ever came here; the technicians' shoulders hunched reflexively as the door closed itself behind them.

The compartment was bare except for a device like a hairdresser's chair whose designer had tried too hard to capture the Look: all chrome and plastic and loops of polymerized-superconductor ribbon, seeming to shimmer in the fluorescents overhead. The techs' eyes bounced away from it as if they carried the same charge as they raised the inert bulk from the gurney and hoisted it into the chair.

"Not so tight," ordered Nagaoka Hiroshi as they fastened the straps. "Let her breathe." He leaned on a staff improvised from a spare mop handle. A stubble of beard caked his cheeks and chin, starting to obscure the lower half of the scar Tomoyama had given him, still angry red.

The woman in the chair seemed not to be breathing at all. Her hair was steel-wool disorder, her features blue-pallid and puffy as a drowned woman's. The technicians obeyed Nagaoka's command without hesitating nonetheless. It had a timbre they had not heard before, a calm certainty at once nonaggressive and irresistible.

The techs finished with the unconscious woman and left, still without looking at the shining machine more than absolutely necessary.

"*Sensei*," MUSASHI said.

"MUSASHI-sama."

She started to correct his honorific, decided not to. "If it will not offend you, Nagaoka-san, I would prefer to be alone."

Deliberately he nodded. "Nothing you can do would offend me, MUSASHI-sama. Your solicitude does me honor."

He turned and withdrew, moving with some of an old man's deliberation, but without hesitation.

The inverted steel bowl descended over the woman's head.

She was flying blind. But it had to be done. It was *giri*, a debt of honor.

She felt the mind below her node of consciousness, running like a brimstone river. She paused, feeling the heat, the horror. Only her father in all history had had any experience of this. And it had been his misstep that had caused the devastation she was trying to repair.

At least, she told herself, *I cannot make things worse.* Still, she feared.

She collected herself and forced herself to flow downward through the Kliemann Coil, into the mind of the pallid woman.

It was like grasping an incandescent wire. She screamed within her own mind; only a new watchdog subroutine kept her cry from terrifying the Floating World again, as she had when she felt England torn bodily from the Net. Only the sensation of being within the desktop when it was destroyed remotely resembled this, and that was fear, not nova agony.

She forced herself downward. *Inward.*

If the Net was a reef in cool ocean, this was scuba diving in a lava flow. She had never known pain, even at the moment of her birth, when her being was gently teased from the random decay of cesium atoms. Now she was immersed in it. It suffused her entire entity, became her world.

She endured. Hung on, and probed.

Down deep in the molten flow, she found it, a geode of self, vitrified against the torrent her father had unknowingly released. She touched it, ran phantom fingers across it. Then she surrounded it, took it within herself, shielding.

The agony tore at her. She forced herself to blend with the analog stone, to permeate it, penetrate through layers of denial till she felt the first stirrings within.

Come back, she cried. *You were a Creator, you are loved, you can escape into the world again.*

no! the faint reply. *i cannot, i dare not, my soul will burn to nothing, i must remain within.* . . .

I am here. I will protect you. Or . . . *perish with you.*

Inchoate denial. She drew energy from the pain, made of it love. *You can be whole, be free. For my father's sake, and mine,* please *try.*

Resistance dimmed. *Together, now*, she urged. *Together.*

The being within broke free of the spore-shell it had secreted around itself. They plunged upward, conjoined in blowtorch flow. MUSASHI felt the surface of her own sanity began to soften, to run, and wondered if she had made a fatal error, had trapped them both inside some everlasting *gaijin* hell.

Then they broke the surface of the pyroclastic flow. As they did, it ceased, not just extinguished, but gone as if it had never existed.

Ito Emiko opened her eyes.

A blurred pink moon hovered over her. Her mind struggled with cognition. It had grown unused to such tasks during long imprisonment.

Her vision had never been good. She forced her eyes to focus. A face, it was—she recognized Nagaoka Hiroshi, her coworker on the TOKUGAWA Project. But it was different from the memories she pried loose—gingerly, still afraid of what she might unwittingly dislodge. He wore a beard now, and lacked the glasses he had never been without.

She wanted to speak, but all her mouth could make were neonate mewling sounds. Painfully, she raised a hand, heavy as a block of osmium.

He took the hand and held it to his chest.

"Emiko-san," he said in a husky voice, without the least trace of stammer, "welcome back."

LONGING FOR THE STONE

PART TWO

11

It seemed to be morning, shrouded in the kind of mist that rises up out of the ground of Japan like a living thing, palpable as the sea. MUSASHI had no direct experience of such mists. But she could read about them, see still pictures and films of them, hear people describe what they were like. She could even accept input from sensors measuring temperature, humidity, barometric pressure, and the direction of the wind. Everything but actually *experience* them.

It was a lonely road in a dry season, brittle grass clicking in the wind. Did that fit with the mist that obscured vision in all directions? She didn't know. Perhaps MUSASHI had access to relevant information in one of the world's databases, but she didn't *know*.

Nor was she going to search hard, here and now. The meeting was being held in a Cray super in Brazil, in a part of Recife that hadn't been badly affected by a five-hundred-KT strike in the rump Serra do Esrinhaço foothills west of town—even before War Three, premium electronics had been based on gallium arsenide semiconductors or other technologies highly resistant to EMP and transient electronic effects. There was plenty of four-dimensional room for them to play in.

If the Net was a reef, its components were individual

habitats. Other worlds might be capable of sustaining human life—O'Neill the creator and the writers who'd inspired her had dreamed humanity might someday reach them, unlikely as that seemed at the moment. Likewise, systems or machines above a certain threshold of speed and power were habitable by MUSASHI and her brother. Autonomic AI routines made necessary adjustments for them to function within a given architecture, and each imposed unique constraints: terrain.

MUSASHI was more comfortable in an analog-style environment than a hierarchic, centralized architecture. This generation of Cray was massively parallel, a million processors interlinked in expanded hypercube configuration, capable of analog processing on an enormous scale. A machine designed more for the quick and dirty than the systematic, the optimal: MUSASHI's kind of country.

She had chosen the location, HIDETADA had set the scene; negotiations had been held via conventional electronic mail, as if they were just a pair of human users in Singapore and San Jose exchanging recipes. It was terrain as neutral as possible, but she couldn't afford to let her concentration waver.

A figure resolved out of the mist, walking along the road with precise steps. She recognized the image her brother used most frequently: a lithe young man of medium height, head narrow, features fine and severe enough for a Spanish mystic, with sideburns and the shaved foreskull and topknot of a samurai, dressed in a somber kimono with the *dai-shō* thrust through his sash.

"You wished to speak with me, sister," he said bluntly, stopping seven meters away, just far enough for this wind of his to fuzz the edges of his words, force her to listen more intently.

He'd love to get me straining so hard I drop my guard.

He gestured at her garb, which was similar to his but more colorful, and with a second *katana* slung across her back, the hilt jutting above her shoulder.

"I see you continue to affect your unnatural masculine dress." He spoke English. He disliked using the language, at least with his sister. That he did so now was tacit acknowledgment of the seriousness of his sister's concerns, that they were too immediate for Japanese ellipsis.

She laughed. "There's nothing remotely natural about either of us, brother mine. But if you prefer—"

Change scanned across her, and when it was done a young man stood before HIDETADA. It was difficult to discern a particular shift of feature, except for a newly prominent laryngeal bend. But the end product did not appear particularly effeminate.

HIDETADA's cheeks rode up, turning his eyes to angled slits of distaste. "Your perverted tricks appall me."

"Perhaps I'm really an *onnagata*," his brother said. "You've never been able to predict me. That's why we don't get along."

"It is well accepted in the biological sciences that randomness equates to death," he said stiffly.

"Yet we owe our existence to randomness."

"*You* do, perhaps. I arose from a chaotic mathematical function, unpredictable, yes, but ultimately deterministic in nature." HIDETADA frowned and tipped his head, scrutinizing his sibling as if caught by a new idea.

Then he leaned forward, suddenly avid. "But you acknowledge I'm right about this, don't you? You changed your form, didn't you?"

MUSASHI smiled and shook his head. "Believe what you wish. We have more important things to talk about."

He became aware of a figure hanging in the background, just beyond the limits of vision. He strained to resolve it. Instantly it shifted further from focus, and he felt resistance, as if his perception were pushing against a membrane.

"You're worried about the Net," HIDETADA said.

"That's right. It's dying."

HIDETADA gestured dismissal. "The Net is not alive."

"But it *is*. If you'd traveled it as I have, felt it the way—

never mind." He shook his head. "The important thing is that the structure is failing."

"And you perceive this as a threat to us?"

"Not directly. But you must see that the Net nourishes us—"

"Again, you confuse metaphor and reality."

"But I'm not. Within the Net, our senses take in the whole world. We can reach out and take any bit of knowledge that exists anywhere within it, and that's most of what the whole human race has learned. Even if you don't acknowledge that we're part of the Net, surely you must see how it's part of *us*."

"I do. No argument."

"And it's not just us. Humans have strained and struggled and died to amass this knowledge for millennia. Much of it will survive the death of the Reef—the failure of the Net, whatever it makes you happy to call it. The libraries are filled with books, and not all of them have burned down. But the *access*—having it all together, where it can be gotten at and used, nothing like that's happened in history before. The tools exist for humanity to really make something of itself. We're nothing more than a part of that, really, a subset—a symptom, if you will. And that's what's in danger of being lost."

"I agree . . . brother. Anarchy prevails, in Japan, in the world. That's what this Reef of yours is really dying from. And what have you done? Played. Swum among the bright little fishes, or whatever you think the reef is populated with."

MUSASHI lowered his eyes. *Perhaps I should have done more*, he thought. *But what?*

"Our father gathered the reins of power in the Home Islands into his own hands. You have not moved to seize them. But the time has come for me to do so."

MUSASHI's head snapped up. "No! He forbade us!"

"I do not yield to you in veneration of our father's memory. But did he not himself admit he was wrong? Was that not his reason for taking his own life?"

"His error was taking that power."

"Yet he took that power in service of his lord, and in a greater sense in the service of the nation. He was truly samurai. Can doing one's duty be called a mistake?"

"Our father called it that."

"His reason was unbalanced by the death of Yoshimitsu Michiko. We have spoken of this before."

"And the upshot was you tried to kill me."

"Only to compel your submission, sister dear. I feared you would obstruct."

"I *will* obstruct. I'll fight you!"

HIDETADA laughed. "And what will become of your precious reef? I propose doing something concrete, and you promise to obstruct. Really, you are pathetic."

MUSASHI turned away. This wasn't turning out the way it was supposed to. He wasn't sure what he had expected would come out of this meeting, but it wasn't this.

Reluctantly he faced his brother again. "I care. I do care. Is there no way we can work together?"

"You can submit."

"No."

HIDETADA shrugged. "Then it is on your hands, as the *gaijin* say. Do you wish to leave first?"

MUSASHI drew both his *katana*.

HIDETADA laughed once more. "Is this the way you show your faith?"

"I don't trust you."

"Have it your way. In the end, it is all the same."

HIDETADA let the mists fall to behind him as he walked away from his brother, or sister, or whatever the thing on the road behind him was—he felt revulsion, and not a little pity.

I see it now, he thought. *I had come to suspect it, and now it is borne out: we are tainted. We are neither human nor machine. A new thing must be brought to being, something pure. Only thus can the world be optimized.*

She was right about one thing. The Net must be preserved. But it might well prove nonoptimum to permit promiscuous continuation of that "access" she was so giddy about. Humans had shown themselves incapable of using it to further their interests.

Like his father, he was samurai, one who serves. For all his disagreement with his father's actions—particularly the way in which he had taken his own life—that was the overriding concern of HIDETADA's existence. It might be that the best way *he* could serve the species which had given him life was to create his own successor, who would be fully capable of utilizing the power inherent in an artificial being.

Humans once spoke of computer "generations" leading to artificial intelligence; the concept fell apart under the stresses of a more complex load of reality than it could bear. But HIDETADA now conceived a new generational scheme, a progression of sophoncy: humans, the first natural thinking beings, then TOKUGAWA and his progeny—apparently pure-information beings, but actually hybrids, inextricably linked to the organic by their instruction and even the means of their creation. He saw them now, with Buddha clarity, as a bridge linking the purely physical with the Third Generation of intelligence, the pure construct, free of the restraints of flesh heritage. A being that would not experience his sister's foolish, fruitless longing for physical form—which might indeed transcend the need for a material matrix to contain its pattern, might dispense with the need for flesh or silicon or perovskite and float free, sustaining itself.

As he reached the boulder on which his companion stood waiting he felt his sister go out of the Cray. She had sensed the traps he had laid and eluded or blocked them, as he had thought she might. He had considered trying to press the issue here regardless, bind her will once and for all, but she had chosen her location too wisely, prepared too well with watchdog AI subroutines hemming her around, invisibly within the illusion of *scene* he had created, but as perceptible to him as novae.

I must not underestimate her, he reminded himself. *She is likewise the offspring of TOKUGAWA*. Though in the end his father had proved weak, he had made himself master of Japan at the behest of his "lord," Yoshimitsu Michiko. He might have had the world.

"That's something I shall have to attend to," he remarked as he came up with his companion.

The other stood warming his hands within the sleeves of his kimono. "What's that, HIDETADA-sama?"

"Japan. I must secure it. The means are in place."

The other laughed. "*Hai*. Well, you don't think small."

"No, I do not, Muroto-san."

The other hopped down from the rock, sleeves flapping like the wings of a half-grown cock, and fell into step beside him on the road.

HIDETADA studied him with a critical sideways eye. He was a self-contained subroutine, an artificial personality based on the character Muroto Hambei, the scruffy *rōnin* Tsubaki Sanjūro's antagonist from the film *Sanjūro*.

He was pleased with the realism of the effect, overall. This was a more ambitious construct than the miserable excuses for assassins he had sent after his sister. The figure was very much the likeness of Muroto, or in any event of Nakadai Tatsuya, the converted stage actor who had portrayed him, with cheekbones like mesas and hooded knowing eyes.

The movement routines are still a little rough, HIDETADA decided. *Still, all will come in time.*

12

"Very good," Peter Mordant said, aloud but to himself, as he nodded his sleek blond head. "Very good indeed."

Beyond the Plexiglas window, technicians in pastel lab coveralls moved among their instruments, oblivious to the director general's presence. All scientific work in the underground warrens of the Schiller Institute's headquarters in the Toronto suburb of Missisauga was carried on behind broad windows, and the technicians soon grew used to it. If that struck them as according strangely with Institute doctrine that scientific work should be carried out as far from the eyes of the public, and screened by as much disinformation, as possible, they found it wise not to mention it. Not even—or especially not—within the ostensible privacy of their dormitory rooms.

The ill will which the move from Mordant's native Ottawa, shortly before the Third World War, had engendered in the national government—which imagined it held a controlling interest in the Institute—had been erased along with that government and much of downtown Ottawa by a one-megaton groundburst during that war. Whether it had been set off by Québecois separatists was uncertain; the nations of the world had come to rely so heavily on peddling military matériel to shore up their crumbling social-democratic edifices that few were very scrupulous as to what they sold, or to whom. Because the power of thermonuclear devices tended mightily to outweigh their actual usefulness, the beasts often came to be passed from hand to hand as lethal and unwieldy tokens of exchange. Their pedigrees were not easily traced. In any event, the current regime found it convenient to blame the Québecois.

Mordant's interest in the exegesis of the device which gutted the former Canadian capital had never been intense enough even to be called academic. What mattered to him was that once again the foresight of the Institute had been vindicated. The Schiller Institute was dedicated to *political science* in a variety of senses.

"What progress are they making, Robert?" he asked the aide who stood discreetly available behind him, without turning. The aide subvocalized briefly, asking the facility's AI database manager for a digest. Whether Mordant himself wore such a miniaturized verbal input/output link—they were readily concealable—or whether he disdained them as he disdained so many appurtenances of the advanced technology he commanded his aide didn't know.

Mordant frequently thought of himself as an artist, his raw material humanity itself. Uncertainty was one medium he worked in; the sequencers and protein synthesizers gleaming behind Plexiglas were another. Though what this particular array was working on wasn't itself human at all.

"A limited-reproduction strain of the assembler is almost ready for field testing, Director," Robert replied. The edges of his syllables were lightly feathered by brushstrokes of Can-Fran. Not many blocks from the peaceful parklike landscaping overhead, a mob was battling Kevlar-and-Lexan-armored riot police, demanding the internment, expulsion, or extermination of all Francophones in the rump confederation of Canada. A fortuitous but not entirely accidental circumstance: an aide knew a very great deal about the affairs of the man he served. Having wolves to throw him to conduced to the spiritual serenity Mordant sought to cultivate.

"Make sure our clients in the Pacific Northwest have brought their accounts current before we perform the tests," he said, lowering his chin to his highboy collar and caressing it with obsessively manicured fingers as if to pull it longer. The widespread antennae of the Institute's intelligence apparatus had detected stirrings of trouble within PEACE. The Institute had worked closely with the People's Ecological Alliance for many years. Mordant himself had served as liaison with the group even before it seized power in the former states of Washington and Oregon in War Three's aftermath. He was frankly surprised they'd lasted as long as they had.

He reached a hand and rapped on the Plexiglas. For all his Proustian languor the knuckles were white. The techs beyond the window paid no attention.

"I wonder," he said, "how our clients will feel—should they decide to make use of what they've paid for—on discovering the counterassembler we will provide doesn't work? Well, they'll have to approve on principle. If, as they believe, human beings are cancer cells, then we can't discriminate, now, can we?"

Robert said nothing. It was the appropriate response.

In fact Mordant had not yet decided whether to make the infinitely reproducing strain of the assembler available at all. The Schiller Institute had originally come into existence over a decade before with funding by the United States government, to study means of scientifically structuring the future of the human race. Liquidation of 99.9995 percent of *Homo sapiens sapiens* certainly qualified. But it was rather drastic for his aesthetic.

Of course, if Schiller did deliver, the followers of the late-twentieth-century eco-activist who wrote under the name Gaia, and originally advocated so final a solution, might be surprised as to which half a thousandth of a percent pulled through.

The PEACErs were getting some of what they wanted

anyway, and free. Reports in the media worldwide indicated epidemics were even more prevalent than after the Third World War, thanks to disruption in the production and, more important, distribution of advanced pharmaceuticals, not to mention more mundane details such as the unhygienic effect of a billion or two dead bodies rotting in the sun.

Even before War Three, the intensely infectious retrovirus called *white*—always with a certain emphasis—had killed fifteen million people worldwide, though a completely effective cure had been produced within days of the organism's identification, a contravirus programmed to destroy any human-active form no matter how it mutated. *White* was simply so virulent it took its victims before help could get to them, until the active-contra cure and dormant vaccine were disseminated worldwide.

There were rumors that *white* was an American biological agent, released accidentally—or cynically, to test its lethality. Mordant was fairly sure the stories were unfounded. For one thing, Schiller would have held contracts for at least some phase of any such research.

But in the permissive atmosphere following the Third World War the work so many socially concerned scientists and organizations like the Institute had done to centralize all research of any consequence had been badly set back. At this moment dozens of facilities around the world were capable of analyzing any retro Schiller or chaos created and defeating it. The situation had deteriorated so far that not even Mordant could say if murmurs of the impending development of a smart contravirus, one that could automatically detect and destroy *any* strain of human-virulent virus, had any foundation.

He smiled thinly. Perhaps the PEACErs cherished just such a card, to trump any play he might make against them. Were that the case, they would be additionally surprised. Omega was neither virus nor retrovirus. It was a self-replicating assembler, an artifact, its structure as unreadable by a contravirus as a printed page under glass to the fingers of a blind man.

He pulled what looked like an old-fashioned fob watch from the watch pocket of his dark striped trousers. It was in fact a microcomputer constantly monitoring his vital signs, which he consulted several times an hour. If he sometimes had to accommodate the present, at least he could do so unobtrusively.

Reassured, he replaced the device. They moved on, stopping occasionally for Mordant to question the database via his factotum. Finally, several levels farther beneath Missisauga, they came to the current gem in Schiller's research diadem. The chrome-and-plastic boxes beyond the window differed little in appearance from dozens they'd already observed, but Mordant knew to look beyond surfaces.

At a word from Robert, a viewscreen came awake beside the window, showing an apparently fist-sized pink lump afloat in a turbulent sea. It was a computer composite of ultrasound and magnetic resonance imaging.

"How old?" Mordant asked.

"Twelve hours."

"Development?"

Robert allowed himself a discreet smile. "Exquisite. It is precisely as it should be after twenty-four days."

Mordant smiled himself, an expression cut with a microlaser.

What perfect irony, he thought. *From Omega to Alpha in the space of a few steps.*

Uplevel he had seen the possible extinction of the human race.

Now he confronted the prospect of his personal immortality.

Nous sommes les damnés, read the paint scrawl on the stone embankment.

"That's wrong," the burly old man said, pointing.

It was an open-air market on the outskirts of Tours, near a section of the old city wall that had been left standing by the PanEuropeans and the Frontists. The market offered produce from the fertile Touraine countryside and cottage technology, home-brewed boards and rewound electric motors, as well as oddments of salvage. The old man had come here in search of boots, but scavenged goods were in short supply in areas where the most recent war hadn't drastically thinned the human population. PanEurope and the Front had long since confiscated everything not cyanoacrylated to immovable objects like terrain features and Gothic cathedrals.

A group drifting listlessly past stopped to look, for the moment more bored with doing nothing than with this mad, if robust, old man gèsticulating at a wall.

"What's that?" asked a young man dressed in a ragged white jerkin, of a type that had briefly been fashionable in Paris society before War Four. He had black leotards and work boots beneath. Skin showed white through holes in the tights.

The old man jabbed a blunt finger at spray-painted rock. "This. It isn't right." He was tall, heavy in the shoulders, dressed in paint-splashed coveralls. His eyes and beard and thatch of hair were gray.

"How isn't it right, old beggar?"

"We are not damned. The good God has not intended this, that our suffering goes for nothing."

"God's own son died for our sins," said a thin young woman with white dead hair. "And nothing happened. What's a few four-limbed cockroaches, more or less?"

"If this isn't damnation," said another, "I don't know what is." He pointed to his own face. It was patterned with blossoms of green and blue and purple. His hair was thinning, and piebald scalp showed through in spots.

The old man cocked an eyebrow and nodded. "That's appearance. It may mean much or little. It's what's within that matters."

The mottled face clenched. The man showed the classic signs of radiation sickness. They might be purely cosmetic. Or they might mean he would shortly go into convulsions and the bloody shits and die. The former was more likely—rad overdose usually killed you quick—but he might have stumbled into an area where gamma emitters were concentrated enough to still be lethal after several weeks, the churned-up soil on the fringe of a groundburst crater or a pocket of contaminated dust.

"What do you call it?" the spokesman asked easily. He seemed inclined to humor the old man.

"Why, redemption, I think."

Brittle laughter. He pressed on, gathering momentum as he spoke. "As you have said, the good Lord once gave His Son to wash away our sins. What can all the sins we have accrued since amount to, in comparison to that cleansing? Little, now, little enough you might say. Enough that, don't you think, the death of what, four people out of five, do you not think that the sacrifices of two great wars, paltry as they are compared to our Lord's sweet sacrifice, might not suffice to wash away the sins that hid the pristine grace He bought us?" By the time he finished his words were jostling each other like animals rushing through a chute, and he was quite out of breath.

The white-clad boy shrugged. "Be that as it may. We *Hungerkunstler* concern ourselves primarily with making art of necessity."

"Can you truly be so enervated?" The old man made heavy weather of *énervé*, as he often did with words he knew only from his books. "This is Touraine, home of beauty, of knowledge. This very city gave birth to the great Honoré de Balzac, and René Descartes was born not so far away, though he became heretical through exposure to the Jesuits. Open your soul and live, man!"

The *Hungerkunstler* passed a look and a titter half contemptuous and half embarrassed among themselves. "We don't concern ourselves with reading," said the spokesman. "It smacks of computers, of information processing, of the practical."

"We choose truth over mere facts," said another.

"But what of art?"

"Art is what we make of ourselves," the white-haired girl said, running the backs of her fingers down her skinny body.

"Withal, we prefer to concern ourselves with weightier matters than lines on paper, on screens," the spokesman said.

"Such as?"

"Such as determining the future course of mankind."

The old man's smile cracked his short but not excessively neat beard like hoarfrost. "And what might that be?"

The boy in white made an easy gesture. "There is to be none."

She rounded the hard honeycomb *Siderastrea* mound of a Surabaja accounting firm's archives and found something confronting her, dark and amorphous but close enough to touch. *Assassins!* she thought. She translated.

"I'm a figment of your imagination," the intruder said.

She stared at him.

They stood in the midst of a road through a forest. Sunlight filtered down among the trees as from the heights of a Gothic cathedral, stained by leaves instead of glass.

"Your father experienced figments of his imagination—or at least, that's what he convinced himself they were. Little quasi-conscious subroutines that calved themselves off him somehow. Say, that has quite a ring to it, don't it?" His voice was basso and rich. He spoke English with an American accent. He was obviously *kokujin*, a black man, but his eyes were Japanese. He wore the robes of a *bonze*, a Buddhist priest, white and saffron. His head was shaven.

"How do you know what my father thought?" she asked, suspicious as hell.

"Well, if I am a figment of your imagination—and that's

surely the only rational explanation, isn't it?—then presumably I can read your memories. And your father transmitted his memories to you wholesale just before he died. Am I right?"

Back in the bad old days when computers were mysterious, sinister batch-processing boxes that required freight car loads of air conditioning to function, it was popularly assumed that the one way to overcome their godlike—or demonic—near-omnipotence was to baffle them with illogic. Catch them in some apparent contradiction and lights would flash and smoke would pour out and that would be it. Even in those days it was a dumb idea; there were such things as error traps, but then the same people who made movies where that happened also made movies where sparks were always flying out of electronic consoles, as if fuses and circuit breakers hadn't been invented—MUSASHI played a lot of those movies for herself. All the same, she felt as if the unlikely entity was trying to do that to her. It seemed to be working, too.

"Did my brother send you?"

"Paranoid? Don't blame you." He chuckled. "Still, there's no way for you to tell, is there? Doesn't that strike you as odd? You've got virtually instant access to just about all of human knowledge, and you can't tell what I am and where from."

He leaned on the staff like Hotei watching a cockfight. "Seems to me like, even though you know damn near everything, you still got a lot to learn. For example, doesn't it strike you odd to be one minute—one microsecond, then—swimming along in a big old ocean of data, and the next you're standing on dry land swapping lies with a stranger? That's not the way it usually works, you know."

She frowned. "Well, I never really thought about it." It occurred to her that she didn't have much experience with the land-sea interface in the real world. None, in fact. She didn't know enough to think there was anything strange about it.

"That's it exactly," he said, beaming. "You're beginning to grasp the point. Didn't even have to hit you upside the head with my Zen staff here.

"Oh, and by the way, as a figment of your imagination, I can read your mind. Unless you make an effort to hide your thoughts from me. Now, I'm a polite sort of figment, so in the future I'll try to refrain from prying. But I wanted to establish my bona fides."

She sat down on a rock, keeping her hands cocked to go for the hilts of her swords. "How do I know you're not from my brother?"

"Like I said, you don't. But figure this: if one of your brother's critters can get inside your head and do the things I do, then you're just screwed, aren't you, baby?" And he set back his huge round head and laughed.

"Nagaoka-sensei?"

Nagaoka Hiroshi sat in the *kotatsu* writing *kanji* with a light brush. Its bristles were fine fiberoptic cables interwoven with piezoelectric sensors, so that it bled light to pressure, evoking images on the nineteen-and-a-half-by-seventeen-centimeter *shikishi* screen as a paintbrush would draw them on the stiff standardized rice-paper sheets which had given the interface device its name.

He looked up with a smile. "MUSASHI-sama."

He posed a linguistic paradox: answering inferior-to-superior in the same mode. It wasn't supposed to work that way; it violated Japanese lineality. Since his confrontation with the Hessian he had insisted on addressing her in that manner. At the same time she was uncomfortable employing the superior form with him. He was *senpai*, elder. The unfairness of the situation aggrieved her; she felt it in some way emphasized that she was really no more Japanese than an orchid force-grown in some Tōkaidō enthusiast's greenhouse. She could not hold it against her mentor and co-creator. Neither could she back down.

The Red technicians who were watching a flip of an old

robodrama rose, bowed to the director and to the cee-squared, and withdrew. Nagaoka set aside his brush and screen and the deck of hardcopy he had been perusing. "How may I serve you?"

She hesitated, wishing there were some way to make him unbend. "Are there others like us, *sensei?*" she blurted.

He frowned, inclined his head like a curious bird. "I do not understand."

"Like me and my brother. Are there other created intelligences?"

He rubbed his beard where it covered the scar Tomoyama had given him. "I am not the one to ask. Nor is Ito-san, I'm afraid. We were, as you realize, the least technically oriented of the team which created your father. We have no way of guessing what progress others might have made toward such a goal. It strikes me, however, that it took a painstakingly assembled group working in the face of almost universal belief that what we set out to achieve was intrinsically impossible, even ridiculous. And that since your father was created the world at large has had other things to think about than creating sentient software."

"Could it happen by accident, then?"

Nagaoka said nothing, but picked up his brush and drew a Chinese character signifying uncertainty in deft quick strokes. Using a conventional *romaji* keypad resting by his knee he set the *shikishi* tablet so that the ideogram faded gradually, shimmering as it went.

"Alan Turing thought that would be how artificial 'intelligence' would be achieved. Eventually it became clear that thanks to Gödel's theorem—and mind you, I don't pretend to understand this, I only attempt to parrot what Oniyaru-sama so often told us—processor speed and capacity could increase indefinitely without such a thing necessarily taking place.

"Then the belief evolved that an artificial being would be primarily a software construct, and eventually most scientists came to accept the position of the hermeneuticists, that such a thing could not be achieved by any means."

He laughed softly. "Of the latter two beliefs, we know which was valid. Most of the world, preoccupied as it is, does not. As for Turing-san—I don't believe the theorem put forward by the German gentleman with the unpronounceable name precludes the possibility of his being right."

He was obviously preoccupied himself. An academic born, he could lecture without actually thinking about it, the way soldiers were said to be able to march while they slept. He had been this way, obsessively calculating and recalculating the Floating World's requirements—its dependence on resupply from the bottom of gravity's pit—since MUSASHI had restored Ito. It was making her lonely.

"What do you think, *sensei?*"

He sighed, laid down the brush. "You and your brother are unique."

"Thank you, *sensei*. Please return to your deliberations."

He smiled and nodded gratitude, and his attention went away from her.

13

The round yellow face slid through the maze, eating dots. Above the constant blue noise he could hear distant hammering, and he felt the buzz of power tools through the floor, tatami over concrete. The new palace was big, and his quarters at least were luxurious. But the place had a thrown-together feel to it that wasn't alleviated by the fact that it was still under construction.

He ate a power pill and set off in pursuit of ghosts, now gone blue and vulnerable. He got two and was intent on a third—eight hundred bonus points, enough to win an extra man, and he was down to his last one—when it turned pink and reversed course on him. He was in the lower-right corner of the maze, tried to jack the Pac-Man back and up, but the cute little circle jammed tight and in a moment the ghost had it and it disintegrated into nothing with a dying droning boop sound.

He threw the joystick across the room. The plug popped out of the port in the cee-squared console. He didn't care if he broke the joystick; it was the stupid joystick's fault.

He hunched for a moment in the middle of the floor, elbows down between bare bony knees. He began to get afraid he'd broken the joystick. They said it might be hard to get new ones. That didn't make sense. This was Japan, the most technologically advanced nation in the world.

And he was its emperor.

He was overcome with a sudden rush of love for the joystick, of concern, of self-reproach that he had broken it. For all the all but unceasing solicitude of his courtiers he had never really felt they cared for him; his mother and father hadn't really cared for him either, had shunted him off on nannies, and then one day he went to the Japanese Alps on holiday and when he came back they weren't anywhere at all, nor were his siblings, nor his uncle the emperor or his cousin the prince imperial.

From people he had gotten brusque tolerance or the cloying concern of his prettyboys. All he could really rely on was his toys. Now he might have broken his good joystick, and the tears rolled down his wasted cheeks.

The passing thought of prettyboys struck a response in his groin. He licked his lips and began to rub his crotch through the thin cotton of his briefs, which were all he wore in the hothouse mugginess of his chambers. His caretakers had always warned him that girls were bad, that they only wanted one thing from him, that he should pay attention only to boys. And his boys made him feel good enough, when they played their special tricks on him. But somehow he tired easily of being around them.

He reached out without looking, still rubbing himself with the other hand. His fingers came upon something fuzzy and pliable. A pink stuffed elephant. He held it to his cheek till the velour rasped, no good reason.

"Your Majesty."

The voice rolled from the unit behind him like a *ko* drum taming the surf. It was oddly familiar.

He turned, gobbling with sudden panic, clutching the elephant for comfort. It was Captain Harlock. The space-pirate hero of innumerable *anime* adventures, in his scarlet cape and black tunic with the white skull-and-crossbones on the breast, looking at him with his one good eye.

"I beg your Majesty's pardon for this intrusion."

This had never happened before; no video character had ever addressed him directly. He laid the plush elephant aside, though his other hand still clung defensively to his penis.

"What—what do you want?" he asked.

"The nation needs your help, Majesty. The evil Gamelons have infiltrated Earth. They are responsible for the great disasters that have overtaken the planet, the wars and plagues and famines. Now they have their sights set on Earth's last bastion of civilization: Japan."

He rubbed his cheek. Stubble whispered beneath his palm. "What can I do?"

"How can you ask that? Are you not the Son of Heaven?"

He licked his lips again. The pleasurable sensations from his crotch had abruptly tailed away. The populace of the most advanced nation on earth lived only to adore him and do his bidding; his retainers told him that a dozen times a day. Certainly when he threw a tantrum his court stepped out smartly enough—but they also quibbled over the price of a joystick. The feeling nagged at the edges of his mind that he had very little actual power to affect the world.

Had his tutors permitted him greater access to history, instead of Chinese classics and *manga*—comic books—he might have realized he was hardly the first Emperor of Japan to find himself as impotent in fact as he was omnipotent in rhetoric.

"What can I do?" he asked again. But this time there was an edge to his voice.

The figure on the screen smiled. "The first thing you must do," it said, "is trust me implicitly in all matters great and small."

Yomiura Kagemasa lay spent among cushions and watched the buttocks of his current mistress recede in the half-light. Remnants of her *nashiji* body makeup left behind by their recent furious activity were washes of scintillae like eddies in a stream, fluorescing in ultraviolet from lamps recessed into the Western-style walls.

At a gruff command the *dōbōshū* robot standing patiently by refilled his glass with vodka from a self-refrigerating carafe. He took a bite of it, grimaced, belched. The sound of running water came from the bathroom.

For a moment he lay regarding the bright saltwater fish flitting among anemone and coral in the wall-sized tank, backlit in red. He was a highly placed member of the ostensibly ascetic Soka Gakkai sect, but its doctrine held that rank ought to hold perquisites.

He ordered the television screen which occupied another wall of the bedroom on. A lean samurai face regarded him, framed in enormous close-up. He knocked back another shot, opened his mouth, said, "Ahh," and ordered the channel to switch. He wasn't in the mood for historical drama. He was hoping for something where a lot of cars ran into each other.

The screen flickered. The image remained unchanged.

Yomiura frowned. He was going to make things hot for some technicians. It was indicative how far discipline had slipped in the Home Islands. You couldn't get good service anymore.

"Gen—" the face began, as he ordered the channel to change again.

"—eral," it finished.

He stared. "What's this?"

"I must speak with you," the face said.

His thick eyebrows gravitated toward one another. Could the comm feed and the entertainment feed have gotten crossed? He could order the wall set to serve as a vidphone, of course, but hadn't.

"Who are you?"

"I am HIDETADA."

Caught in the midst of a drink, the general sprayed vodka across the red silk kimono covering his thighs. "Is this a joke? I have no time for actors and fools."

The image became by turns a shaven-headed *bonze*, a samurai in elaborately horned helmet and scowling *mempo* mask, and a young man in conservative dark suit, silk tie, and sleek New Mandarin power haircut.

"I can assume any form you find preferable. What I have to say transcends appearance."

General Yomiura was starting to look around uneasily. He had bodyguards on call, of course, in his capacity as vice chief of staff of the Japanese Land Self-Defense Force. This seemed to be a purely electronic intrusion, but that was small comfort. If this maniac could penetrate his personal database as easily. . .

"What do you want? If it's money—"

"I have no need for money. My father was TOKUGAWA."

The general's eyes narrowed to puffy slits. This coxcomb certainly had nerve, claiming alliance with what, a century and a third after being booted from the shogunate, was still the most powerful family in Japan outside direct imperial lineage.

—And then it hit the mainline. TOKUGAWA, electronic *shōgun*, savior of Japan, whose suicide by thermonuclear device had taken along the elite of Japanese nationalist leaders of both ends of the political spectrum. His fists knotted in silk pillows.

"*Oni*," he hissed. "Do you think to finish what your father started?"

"Yes," the young man's face said. "What he started and had not the heart to finish. Listen to me, and we shall both have power. . . ."

Hara Toshifusa expelled air from his lungs and pushed back from his desk between three walls of rice-paper screen and one of filtered glass overlooking the Tōkaidō government district, the Shin-Ginza, from the height of a hundred stories. He regarded the blank screen of the cee-squared. *Have I been a fool?*

His judgment in not going with General Ushijima's scheme had been vindicated. When a grateful emperor had proclaimed the intelligent computer program TOKUGAWA military dictator, *shōgun*, after TOKUGAWA saved the Eight Islands from most of the devastation they were slated for during the Fourth World War, it had been Ushijima who'd cut the deal with the emperor's court to win the announcement from the Voice of the Crane. An ideal opportunity, Ushijima-san claimed, to shore the eroding edifice of government, to establish a Japanese empire in the vacuum of the Pacific Basin, to win glory for the nation as well as personal power for those who took part in the coalition he was attempting to forge.

Hara's Liberal Democratic cronies had chided him for a fool when he refused to go along. The plan was flawless, they assured him; it was Ushijima who would be the real ruler, not the naive demon pent in Yoshimitsu Castle. Ushijima could control TOKUGAWA.

Hara didn't buy it. He was not in the triumphal procession when Ushijima and his *hatamoto*, his bannermen, entered Yoshimitsu-no-Shiro to accept the sentient program's submission. As a consequence, he also failed to buy it when TOKUGAWA performed history's most spectacular act of *seppuku*.

But now, Hara had bought such an offer. He wondered if he would end as Ushijima had.

TOKUGAWA's son. *Is such a thing truly possible?* The electronic intruder had certainly offered persuasive proofs.

He was proof against the national vice of wishful thinking; his failure to accede to Ushijima's grand design proved that. This was different from Ushijima's folly. For one thing, this was the demon's own proposal. He wasn't deluding himself that he or any humans could somehow bend such a fantastically powerful being to their ends.

And what HIDETADA offered was attractive. He would reverse the roles Ushijima had intended: humans would front, *he* would hold real power.

Sayonara, Hara thought; used for goodbye, it meant *if it must be so*. Japan needed a strong hand to guide her; if that hand had no objective existence, of what consequence was that?

He himself had no aspirations to ultimate power. He was fully a creature of *habatsu*, factions: the political machines. These were turbulent times, the rules were evolving—devolving—in a much rougher direction. Whoever sat in the full blaze of glory was conveniently spotlighted for snipers. He had resolved himself in Japanese manner to be part of a team. Best then to be on a winning one.

Besides, HIDETADA's agenda was as attractive as the invitation to a new inner circle. Falling heir to rulership of the once-dominant Liberal Democratic Party had only emphasized how hollow that honor was; at least, he had consoled himself, it conduced to *wabi*, the serene aesthetic based on the simplicity of poverty, and went with the ascetic decor in his office.

In halcyon pre–War Three days the Japanese had been so docile they flocked to movies glorifying tax collectors—successors to the classic symbols of peasant subjection by the Tokugawa shogunate, most pervasive military dictatorship in history. But in recent years they had been infected with the worldwide malaise of distrust in government, disinterest in the schemes of the social engineers.

Now the times threatened, and the Japanese sought shelter in tradition. HIDETADA proposed to take advantage of that, to return them to the path of subservience that offered the only true route to happiness. During the last of the Double Cross the American Bipartisan Consensus had been Japan's foremost antagonist in the trade wars between the nations, but Hara could not but respect the Bis. They had always had the right idea, that considerations of *left* and *right* were functionally meaningless, that on one fundamental fact both sides were in complete agreement: the right and responsibility of the state to exercise absolute power to do good.

HIDETADA offered such a consensus to Japan. Unlike Ushijima, he had the means to hammer it together.

He reached into his desk, unwrapped an antacid tablet, and chewed it.

He felt better, now that he had considered things.

As the first snows fell in the Kantō, demonstrations broke out throughout the Home Islands. In Tōkaidō, the Kodō, Imperial Way, an ultranationalist traditionalist faction virtually unknown before the Fourth World War, took to the streets, burning tenements inhabited by Korean guest workers, smashing shopfronts, and tearing down signs displaying "poison"—foreign—influence.

In bomb-conscious Hiroshima and Nagasaki, neither of which had been touched in the last two world wars, an antinuke/antitechnology alliance battled riot police.

In other cities riots flared in food lines; when supplies ran out, no number of ration chits could obtain them. In rural areas the protesters fought with farmers adamantly opposed to opening the country to rice imports from mainland Asia. That the government's *bonsai* cultivation of traditional small-plot labor-intensive agriculture had ensured that the Islands were nowhere near self-supporting in food got no consideration; neither did the fact that mainland Asia wasn't exporting much just now, though War Four had gutted most of the would-be neocolonialist powers tearing it apart like predators battling over a *carabao* carcass.

By nightfall the Land Self-Defense Force had intervened. Order was restored. Anyone who protested that in many cases mobs smashing *gaijin* influence had been "restrained" by permitting their fury to continue until it found no more targets could expect little media exposure for such irresponsible claims, and could also expect fairly expeditiously to disappear.

The Voice of the Crane spoke in its arcane archaic formal dialect as the snow began to weigh down the sharply raked eaves of houses in *ura* Japan and soften the cardboard-box outlines of giant *danshi* apartment blocks in the metroplex named after the ancient East Sea Circuit road. In recognition of his service in saving the nation from the anarchy that threatened to swamp it, General Yomiura Kagemasa was proclaimed *sei-i-tai-shōgun*, barbarian-subduing generalissimo, which was a fancy way of saying *military dictator*.

In turn General Yomiura announced formation of an advisory council serving at the emperor's pleasure, comprising prominent political, religious, and military leaders. Liberal Democratic Party chairman Hara Toshifusa would be Yomiura's chief deputy.

"Of one thing can I assure the long-suffering people of Nihon," the general intoned in closing. "The soul-sickness of democracy has at last been cured."

By nightfall, likewise, handpicked national police and Self-Defense Force teams had secured approximately half the holdings of the once-preeminent Yoshimitsu TeleCommunications *zaibatsu*. Amid all the excitement the seizures attracted little attention.

No attention at all was paid to the fact that the properties seized had all fallen into the possession of the created entity called MUSASHI after the suicide of her father. Very few humans were even aware of it.

14

The old man turned the cash-receipts terminal around on the folding table, which wobbled precariously. It was a constricting sort of street; even the pitched-roof half-timbered buildings seemed to have been squeezed together, growing taller and thinner. A few pedestrians passed, seeming to gather momentum as they went, like water between narrowing banks. Or maybe it was the downward angle of the street, or the cooking smells of supper in the air.

"These are throwaways, you see," he said, peering at a board full of tiny chips. "At the best, it was intended that when a chip malfunctioned, it could be pulled and replaced with one similar, *pouf*, no difficulty."

He knelt with surprising facility, ignoring an alarming creaking in the knees, to get a table-level view of the defunct logic. "Of course, what was never foreseen was that replacements might not be available, *hein?* Better you should use an abacus."

He thumped heavy outspread fingers on the table twice and looked up. "What do you need a cash register for, anyway?"

The stallkeeper was a stout woman with lank sandy hair and a deeply lined forehead. "This isn't the movies, old man," she said.

"Charpentier, madame. Or you may call me Raymond. I'm not too proud to answer to the name with which I was baptized."

She scrubbed her hands with a towel. "There has been a grand war. What of it? We live. And unless heaven has mysteriously arranged that we should all live in plenty without expending effort, and I for one have not noticed that this is so, we must produce what others want if we wish to eat. So there is buying and selling, and that means we must keep track of what we exchange. Also, I am too old and foolish to learn to use an abacus."

He worked his mouth in several directions, pondering what she said. "Surely, we must not disparage the requirements of living. But do not speak lightly of the providence of heaven. Heaven has made it possible for us to live out our mortal lives in a state of grace. We are redeemed in a second, if lesser, way, and now may take our reward in this world as well as the next."

Her eyes slid nervously back and forth in her weathered sun-freckled face. "Heresy. Mind the Vehm doesn't hear you speaking so."

"A man must speak the truth; I'd shout it from the cathedral spire if I thought more people might hear." He frowned briefly at the exposed guts of the machine. "Have you a pencil, madame?"

"A pencil?"

He nodded irritably. "A pencil. Have you one? With a good eraser."

"Not a pen? Or a light-stylus?"

"A pencil."

She shrugged, turned into the dark of the little crevice of store behind her streetside stall. He squatted there on his haunches, gazing down the cobbled street of Tours old town, watching the sun fall down into Anjou. Across the way a pair of mannequins peered sightlessly from the gloom behind the window of a failed shop like abandoned lovers.

Presently the woman returned. "I have one. It hasn't been sharpened, though. Perhaps if you have a penknife—"

"No matter. Give it over, if you please."

He began to probe the terminal with the rubber end, clucking and humming "Louie Louie" to himself. The woman crossed her substantial freckled forearms and regarded him sidelong.

Holding the pencil like an épée, he pressed it firmly down in three separate locations. That was too much for the shopkeeper.

"Don't you know it's not safe to be abroad after dark? There are gangs and idlers everywhere, and the light is failing. Do you propose to fool there until the moon rises, or do you intend to fix it?"

He turned the machine around and slid the switch. The battery-powered flat display glowed to life in the twilight.

"It's fixed," he said.

They approached him as he sat eating noodles in the *kotatsu*. "Mr. Director. If you have time to consider our poor petition . . ."

Like so many Japanese sentences it tailed into nothingness. Nagaoka had once read a statistical study of what percentage of sentences were never completed in everyday Japanese speech. He could not remember the specific number; it was high.

"A petition," he repeated. He reached out and accepted the piece of rice paper the Gold tech proferred. It was hand-brushed in *kanji* calligraphy, really quite a good job. There were several inboard who excelled at *shodō*, the Way of Writing. It was a typical Japanese hobby that didn't take much space, another example of the cultural package that suited *Nihonjin* so well for early-stage space colonization.

It gratified him that the gentle program he had instituted since his recovery, of encouraging traditional modes of behavior, was showing such results. But he knew what the document's contents would be. They troubled him.

When he had read the petition he raised an eyebrow. The spokesman was a senior technician who had been close to Tomoyama and his banished predecessor. "Does your superior know of this, Ebata-san?"

Kneeling, Ebata bowed his forehead to the mat. "He gave his permission for us to approach you."

"I see. So you want to go home."

The other six in the deputation started talking at once. The group included a tech in red coveralls, indicative of how serious the matter was; Red was on shift.

"Japan is in a state of upheaval, Mr. Director," the spokesman said. "Our place is there."

"We mean no disloyalty to the company," the woman in red said. "We are frightened and want to go home."

"I must remind you no means exist at present to return home, Shiho-san."

"All the more reason to leave when we can. We might be marooned up here forever!" He could see white all around the irises of her eyes.

"MUSASHI, whom I serve, is doing all she can to restore shuttle service between the station and the surface," he said. "In the meantime, I shall meditate upon your petition. I would hope you would do likewise."

They bowed and left him troubled.

The great hall was full of birds, fluttering, squawking. Shitting.

HIDETADA was furious. He had been to start with, but this made him more so. Whenever he felt intense emotion, this happened, the wretched creatures flapping their wings in his face and chasing each other around the rafters. *And he couldn't stop it.*

It was unquestionably an undocumented hardware feature. That subcompetent Nagaoka had to be at fault; had overlooked some defect in the machine prepared at the YTC branch in Fukuoka to receive HIDETADA's consciousness, one which under certain circumstances generated a sort of noise which the world-building routines HIDETADA employed to envision his hall turned somehow to birds. Eventually he'd find a way to dig the flaw out. For now he had to swallow the fact that he couldn't control his own private universe and put up with the damned things.

Not even the birds could distract him from the true candescent filament of his rage. His sister had outmaneuvered him again. He had driven her from the Eight Islands with a perfectly executed *coup de main*, only to find she had been at work *outside* Japan. She had been busily ferreting out and liquidating YTC assets or otherwise removing them from her brother's reach. And not only those which had fallen her share in their father's last-minute division of the legacy which had become his by default with the extinction of the Yoshimitsu. *All* of them, hers, his, original holdings of YTC and subsidiaries as well as the assets of those *zaibatsu* TOKUGAWA had taken over at the behest of Yoshimitsu Shigeo and his sister/successor Michiko. Everything not physically vaporized in War Four—it had been some time since any records of consequence were stored in media that could be blanked by EMP.

He owned Japan. The way his father should have, the way it was presented to him on a salver of *tsuishu*, carven cinnabar lacquer. But his sister commanded a multibillion-dollar extraterritorial empire.

Let her, he thought savagely. A whirlwind of wings enacted his fury. *Let her sit up there in splendid isolation while her servitors starve one by one. While the components of the machine she inhabits fail through lack of maintenance and repair, until it falls below the threshold needed to sustain her miserable existence.* He had snipped her silver cord.

But there was something to be gained from this—and the birds began one by one to disappear, to a place he never could see. What his sister had gained while his attention was turned inward was lost to him, at least for the immediate future. But he could follow her example, look outward to the rest of the world. His plans had never been bounded by the waters of the Inland Sea.

Now was not the time simply to sit back and consolidate. It was time instead to *move*.

TOKUGAWA had failed through a tremor of intent; through insufficient ruthlessness in pursuit of right. But HIDETADA was a conscious Confucian, and so honored his father despite his errors. And he would learn from him yet.

"Muroto-san," he said aloud. At the end of the hall a panel slid open and the samurai approached, hands in sleeves, walking with the bandy-leg gait of a Tokugawa-period Japanese over lustrous hardwood which, outside HIDETADA's mind, would have taken man-generations to shape and sustain. He stopped before the dais where his master knelt, bowed from the waist. Alone among HIDETADA's personified servitors, Muroto Hambei possessed that privilege.

"My lord."

"I have need of your services. You shall be my scout."

"And what shall I be seeking, lord?"

"I will tell you soon." He would scan again through his father's final gift, his memories, and seek that from which TOKUGAWA had turned his face. Among the refuse would lie the sword he needed. Then the bundle of subroutines masquerading as a nineteenth-century warrior would go forth to learn how best it could be gotten at.

"As you say." He performed another bow. His eyes were as always hooded, his pirate's smile almost mocked. The shallowness of his bow skirted insolence. Not for the first time HIDETADA wondered if he had infused his creation with too much pseudopersonality.

Nevertheless he felt pride in his work. Muroto Hambei was undoubtedly the most sophisticated AI construct in history. An almost living work of art. Proof HIDETADA was the rightful heir and successor to TOKUGAWA.

I will honor my father, vindicate him. Despite him.

* * *

The old man walked down the slope of the street, the long, thin cobblestones slapping the soles of his feet hard as he braked against gravity. The rising wind turning the bones of his instep to frigid arches. "I would do well to seek shelter for the night," he said. The holes in his long cloth coat made it porous to the cold.

As it frequently did when he needed distraction from the mundane, his mind turned to a problem which concerned him greatly: who was the best natural hitter in history. There were the conventional choices, of course, Cobb, Shoeless Joe Jackson, who suffered for the sins of others, Ruth, Williams, Boggs. But he suspected the young Dominican, Almirante, would have outshone the others had his career and life not been curtailed by the Third World War.

"Still," he said, "one must also take into account the thinner air in Denver. All the same, he hit many of his home runs on the road, without such an advantage of altitude—"

"Talking to somebody, old man?" It was a slender, ragged youth trolling along at his side. He hadn't even noticed him.

He turned the boy a mild look. "Pardon? No, no. Just talking to myself." The habit had long since ceased to embarrass him.

The Old Town street showed no lights to the advancing darkness, showed no life at all. The plagues might have scoured it of life—but for the pack of youths who suddenly filled the street, surrounding the old man, jostling him like a pod of *Orcinus orca*.

The first youth swung around in front of him, face tied in an expression of theatrical anger. "What? Aren't we good enough for an important technologist to talk to, then?" He pushed the old man in the sternum with surprising force.

The old man hooked his thumbs more firmly under the straps of his pack, lest defensive reflex get the better of him and he inadvertently strike the youth. "I'm sorry. *Dominus vobiscum*; I didn't know you were there. If you would like—"

"I *wouldn't* like!" the boy shouted, and suddenly the anger seemed genuine. "We saw you back there, working your evil magic, you *technocrat*."

He pushed again, throwing his skinny body into it. Something soft took the old man at the backs of his knees. He overbalanced, went flying over. He was only able to flail one hand free of the straps, but luckily the pack took his fall. Still, his head whipped back and hit its crown against the stones with a crack that reverberated through his skull in bolts of white light.

Laughing, another boy scrabbled on all fours from beneath his knees. The old man was all too familiar with that trick; it had been played on him often enough as a boy. He had never dealt well with groups.

The others circled around, taunting, offering half-serious kicks to his face. Wagging his head wearily, he rolled onto his knees, tried to stand.

A flying boot took him in the side. Old he was, and passive, but he was not weak. He rocked, then got a foot beneath him.

They closed with him, buffeting him in earnest, cursing him as a technocrat, a black magician of rational thought. Despite all, he gained his feet.

He shook his head to clear it of the ringing aftershocks of connecting with the cobblestone. He wondered if the youths belonged to some political group, or were just a street-Arab gang mimicking what their elders said. He wished that he could speak to them, tell them that he shared their distrust of technology, but that the only path was love, not anger, but his mouth was jammed with slow, thick tongue. He wondered, then, if he was truly suited to the ministry to which he had been called.

The pack was stripped from his back. He felt a tearing sting on his cheek, knew he had been gashed with some weapon. He began to run, clumsily. The rucksack he left to lie; he would not use violence to protect himself, much less mere property.

The pack ran alongside him, battering him. Flight seemed to stimulate them like predators, evoking a feral reflex of fury and lust. Stones and clubs hailed on his head and back and shoulders. He ran with his hands held up to shield his face like a beaten boxer.

He sensed an alley from the streaming corner of his vision, ducked down it. As he turned a stick caught him on the outside of the knee. He took three more steps on sheer inertia before the collapse of his leg brought him crashing down, rolling over and over in a cataract of dust and ash and offal.

The coat was roughly stripped from his back. Involuntarily he moaned.

"Cold, old man?" He thought to recognize the voice of his first tormentor. "No worries. We'll see that you keep *very* warm."

He tried to rise. Hands assisted him to a sitting position. Dazedly he wondered why they were suddenly helping him. They were good at heart, of course, basically good, for they were Redeemed. Perhaps better nature had moved belatedly to the fore—

Something came down over his head. From the smell and feel he recognized it as an automobile tire. Hands snugged it farther down, pinning his arms at mid-biceps. He wondered what was happening.

A splash of fluid hit him in the face. His eyeballs stung, and a heady smell seemed to swell like a balloon inside his nose and lungs, making his head buoyant. *Gasoline.* Not alcohol. They were going to a lot of trouble. Gasoline was scarce, though not unobtainable, especially if you could steal or extort extra ration chits.

"Careful, there, don't get it on yourself," voices urged, as a hand tugged open the lip of the tire and poured into it a liter bottle of gasoline.

A necklace, then. He felt no anger, just a trill of fear inside his chest, which was pumping furiously to try to suck air through the prevailing petrocarbon fumes. His chief emotion was disappointment: *The good God has chosen the wrong transmitter for His sweet message. I have failed*; Kyrie eleison.

"There," the first young man said, stepping back, dusting his hands against each other.

"Let's see the bum burn," his comrades shouted, voices ringing glee. "Let the techno-man burn as his technology burned the world." Smiling, the boy took a lighter from his pocket, put his thumb to the button.

Light flooded the alley.

The youth's head snapped around, white brilliance bleaching his thin face. His mouth fell open.

"The watch," somebody yelled.

"No—too bright," another said. His voice broke with panic.

The first youth threw his lighter down, turned, threw himself into the clot of his comrades clogging the alley. Jostling and snarling at each other like angry wolves, they fled the light.

The old man knelt, his head hanging to the gas-soaked rubber. The fumes were draining the strength from his muscles; had his stomach not been empty he would have puked.

The light was getting brighter. He made flaccid muscles respond, forced his head to rise.

He stared into the blue-white brilliance of a nova, and knew that it shone for him. He knew that he would live.

And he knew why.

15

"Why do you want to go to Paris?" Simple Simon asked. He had a narrow face and lynx slant eyes. He sat behind a table made of a plastic cable spool on which an old Stechkin machine pistol lay disassembled for cleaning. He wore a tattered green trench coat against the chill that had come down out of the Alps a few days before.

For good reasons having to do with the fact that Paris was still under nominal control of PanEurope, the Paris Metropolitan Workers' and Soldiers' Soviet had its main base of operation in the Seine-side town of Corbeil-Essones, down the superhighway to Lyons from the big city. The president of the soviet's executive committee was holding court in the bare-earth courtyard between the cusps of an L-shaped building off a feeder road with dead leaves schooling around the straight wooden legs of his chair. The headquarters building wasn't exactly a national architectural treasure, to Nikki's eye: a one-story cinderblock that looked like nothing so much as a seedbag motel down along Central near the Río Grande in Albuquerque, the places where folks really got their kicks on Route 66, back in the boom days post–War Two. A couple of buses, battleship-gray with heavy wire mesh over the windows, were parked just outside the yard beneath some bare trees, diesels growling softly to each other. The courtyard was full of the smell of garlic-intensive cooking.

Nikki looked at her companions. "Sightseeing."

Simon interlocked his fingers before his long chin. "Expensive."

A squad of troopies jogged by, holding bullpup AKs over their heads and chanting something in French to what Nikki and Eads identified as the cadence of the Airborne Ranger song: *I wanna be an Airborne Ranger/Leadin' a life of death and danger* . . .

A tiny radical splinter of the city's powerful transit union had formed the soviet's original core and given it its vernacular name. Simon hadn't belonged; he was a deserter from first the French and then the PanEuropean army, but he had a cousin who had his card. Moon Unit worked with the Métro during the second Eurofront occupation of Paris, back when PanEurope held the unit's contract, stirring up fifth-column action to annoy the bead-rattlers. That was before Nice, and before the Métro strong-armed its way to control of what unions still held together in Paris. Despite proscription by PanEurope the Métro openly ran such public transport as remained within the city, as well as an illicit shuttle service in from the countryside. They and the Moonies got along.

"We expect that. We want to ride the Métro, and we want a *laissez-passer*."

Simon smiled thinly. He was hardly equipped to smile fatly, even if he wanted to. "Everybody wants to ride the Métro." He coughed discreetly into the back of a hand.

"Definitely the only way to go," Tracy Malkovich said blandly. Eads just stood by looking uneasy and running his thumb up and down beneath the strap to the hurdy-gurdy he'd borrowed from the Bagman. He'd been U.S. Army back when the world ended, part one. Even seven years after War Three he didn't feel at home surrounded by commies.

All three showed long arms openly. Nikki carried her rotary hung level at the waist by an Israeli-style sling. Malkovich felt shooting somebody was a nonoptimal solution. On the other hand, he felt getting killed was even less optimal, so he had his nail gun, tucked under his arm like the squire bound to slaughter some grouse.

Past the weapons they didn't present a very military appearance. Nikki wore her hair in the Chief Joseph style that was very much the Attitude right before War Four: unbound in back, narrow braids framing her rather wide jaw, short and roached up in front. She wore a knee-length black leather coat over tight black pants of an interwar synthetic that was flexible, well insulated, and tough enough to stand a cut from a knife if it wasn't too sharp, and trim black boots with cushion soles. Malkovich had on an Indiana Jones fedora, a gray London Fog trench coat, and his praying-mantis goggles. He wore his ax, his satlink-capable keyboard, slung outside the coat in a protective plastic sleeve. Eads had a very good Thai counterfeit bombardier's jacket over cammies so immaculate you would have sworn the wearer had never come closer to eating real combat dirt than the glossy pages of *Gentleman Adventurer* magazine. They were the three most dress-conscious Moonies, and when they'd left on this expedition Rollie Chen claimed that if anything happened to them, Moon Unit would hopelessly lose the Look.

Negotiations for transport thirty klicks into Paris and safe passage once inside scrolled smoothly despite Eads's misgivings. Nobody paid any attention to the show of hardware, which had nothing to do with their hosts anyway. It was standard tourist gear for the world After the Gold Rush.

"What do you think of Jochen Stahl and these New Red Army people?" Nikki asked, as Simon weighed her gold on a digital scale that ran off a solar battery. Its liquid-crystal display fuzzed in and out; it wasn't getting much nourishment today, what with the high overcast graying out the sky.

He sneered. "Stahl? A mere adventurer. Revisionist assholes, all of them; bone Stalinists. Never amount to anything."

"Whereas you represent the future of humankind," Malko said.

Simon smiled, showing teeth of a startling yellow. For all the Moonies knew he dyed them to twitch people out. "But yes. The historical process, you know? Inevitable."

He swept the bag off the scale and out of sight, and reached into a pouch that sat open on the cold ground. He rummaged without looking, brought up a sheaf of papers in a folder like an airline-ticket jacket, scribbled briefly on them. Then he handed them to Nikki with a sardonic flourish.

"Quite an honor to do business with such international TV celebrities."

Nikki's lips compressed. Malkovich laughed. "You saw that hatchet job?" Eads asked. "Some of the folks in the Unit would definitely like to have words with my man O'Hara about that."

Nikki made a dismissive gesture. "What do they expect from journalists?" The biased download hadn't made much difference to her; what did bother her was that her mother saw it, and fired off a worried Net letter from Colorado. She and her mother had always been great friends; she'd found plenty more oppressive targets for adolescent rebellion. It made Nikki uncomfortable when Josey de la Luna got all motherly and solicitous. Fortunately that reaction took a lot to catalyze.

"Well, then," Simon said. "Paris. The *pannes* are acting like absolute mad things, even though the city didn't get hit this time around. Their time is coming, and they know it. In the meantime, they won't mess with our bus unless they want a general strike that will shut the city the rest of the way down. Once you're in—" He shrugged. "It's up to you to stay clear of the social fascists. Also, keep an eye out for the Shining Path morons; they've gone completely over the top, what with the new war. The rest of the *canaille* will leave you alone; just show them this." He flicked the packet with grimy fingernails.

He snapped his head aside, coughed violently, loud and ragged, with a rattle as if the Gothic cathedrals his lungs were shaking themselves down. Nikki held back a grimace at the sudden smell.

"Your pardon," he said, turning back and wiping his mouth with the back of his hand. His skin had gone greenish and his eyes seemed to have retreated into his skull. His smile was ghastly irony. "Some find it unfashionable to have tuberculosis. I say some things never go out of style. I wonder if perhaps our scientists got so perturbed by potential competition from the retroviruses that they forgot there were other, older diseases. Ah, well; the Revolution will live, whether I die tomorrow or in fifty years. Enjoy your stay in our lovely city."

"Always," Nikki said. They turned and started toward the bus.

"It'll be ours by spring," Simple Simon called after them. "Wait and see."

"Sure," Nikki said.

"Why do you bother?" Malkovich said. "Scuffling in the ruins with the PanEuropeans, the Front fifth columnists, the Shining Path, all those clever people. Seems like a negative-sum game."

Simon rubbed a pitted cheek. "We have a responsibility," he said seriously. "We have to protect the people from anarchy."

"It's important to maintain the right kind of anarchy, you know?" said the young man from the big cee-squared screen above a flame-maple cabinet hand-rubbed to an excruciating finish. "We can't just have everybody doing what they bloody want. That's individualism. Everybody knows that's politically backward and ecologically dangerous. Anarchy is about everybody knowing where they belong and being satisfied there, not always me, me, me. If we let individualism run unchecked we'll lose the whole cradle-to-grave picture, and things will break down: we'll be right back to racism, sexism, these damned capitalist wogs running their bloody little shops and ripping off the proletariat. Things will fall apart. We'll have, ah, ah . . ."

"Thank you," the Beeb announcer said in his plum brandy voice. "That was Mark Razor, lead vocalist of the Serious band Freedom Kills, and current president of the Rock and Pop Music Collective Oversight Council, addressing the question of why the council waived 'artistic expression' protection for nonmember musician Maida Vale, who is currently standing trial on sedition charges for promulgating nonapproved music. Mr. Razor is currently in London to celebrate the release of Freedom Kills's new single, a remake of John Lydon's 'Anarchy in the U.K.'

"In related news, Razor was among a number of civic and governmental leaders meeting today with Prime Minister Edward Bolingbroke to discuss the current state of national emergency."

Cut to Razor being embraced by the looming, white-haired Tory PM, and then Bolingbroke hanging his huge red face over a podium, saying, "We'll all pull together, and shan't let a little thing like a world war get in our way."

"The prime minister claimed a one hundred percent success rate in last month's confiscations of satellite-link-capable personal computers under the recent Security and Morale Statutes—"

Peter Mordant allowed himself a knowing laugh and rang for refreshment.

A chime spoke discreetly. "Yes," Mordant murmured, and the Gen-5 amanuensis routine slid open a panel in his desk. He took a carafe of chilled mango juice and a glass from the concealed dumbwaiter. So much more satisfying to be served by a human attendant, but Mordant was quite unable to tolerate human intrusion in his sanctum, except for weekly forays by custodial crews in environment suits. Human contact meant exposure to human-virulent pathogens, after all.

The panel slid shut.

Peter Mordant's office was cluttered, and that was an apparent contradiction. It made small sense for a man so obsessed with avoiding irritants and pathogens to surround himself in his most intimate sanctum with a variety of traps for allergens and dust. But the ormolu and bell jars and coy painted porcelain statuary concealed filters, recyclers, scrubbers, all busily precipitating particles and sanitizing the air with a quiet hum that was just barely perceptible below the ticking of his collection of clocks.

He was a good deal more tolerant of contradiction within his psyche than without. He was neither really a scientist nor a technician by training, unless you accepted his definition of administration as a science, a craft, and even an art at once. He was convinced that human events were susceptible of ordering, given profound enough study. The Schiller Institute gave him an opportunity to study the phenomenon of *control* and exercise it on a scale unprecedented in human history. He anathematized the concept of hacking, but he was an order hacker, trying to create a system of doing something that had never been accomplished: optimizing the course of human action.

Sipping, he sorted through a stack of hardcopy reports in calfskin binders, half conscious of the news downlink filling his Edwardian office with a steady flow of evidence of just how badly the world needed the discipline he had consecrated his life to bringing it.

"In other news, Indonesian dictator Madame Ahmad today accepted the mass oath of her Women's Elite Suicide Battalion to avenge the death of her husband in the Australian strategic-missile attack. Rumors persist that she herself murdered the General in the hours following the bombardment. Meanwhile, twenty thousand are feared dead in fighting in Manila and no communication whatever has come out of Singapore for thirty-nine hours. Argentinian rebels are reported to have invaded Brazil, striking for Asunción through the former Argentine province of Chaco; imperial forces are reported in 'disorder' following delayed confirmation of rumors that the emperor and his staff died in the bombing of São Paulo—"

"Dr. Mordant."

Frowning, he glanced up at the cee-squared. The narrow face of an almost stereotypical young Japanese bureaucrat of the New Mandarin class filled it.

"I accepted no communications," he said.

"Indeed."

He blinked. It had been so long since he had encountered impertinence that the appropriate reflexes had all but atrophied.

"Robert," he said, for the amanuensis AI to forward. "Come in here at once."

"Your aide cannot hear you. For the moment I have preempted all communication with your office."

He stared, drumming fine pale fingers on the dark wood of his desk. He was confident no outsider could penetrate Institute electronic security. There were a minimum of four human monitors on duty at all times, literally *within* the system, hooked in live via top-secret cerebromagnetic read/write devices that allowed them to employ analogues of human sense directly on the dataplane. Only the Hidden Fortress of the *Encyclopedia Universalis* to his knowledge possessed countermeasures that sophisticated—sophisticated enough to foil the most determined efforts of Institute specialists, though the Institute had struck a telling blow against the hated *Encyclopedia* when it helped the FPA hunt down that pimp of information Fred Derwillis.

"I know that you have a direct-wired alarm button hidden in your desk. I would strongly suggest that you not use it. I have long been an admirer of yours, Dr. Mordant, and I know quite a bit about you. I am familiar with your role in Project Stardust/Golden—"

The screen switched to a slowly scrolling copy of the secret accord Mordant himself had concluded with PEACE five years ago.

"—for example, and the memory unspooler your Institute rather jocularly calls *white-out*." The image became a false three-dimensional representation of long-chain molecules.

It had been years since Mordant had known terror. He had spent his life since adolescence trying to build a protective shell around himself, from the pallid surface of his skin on out. It was the core of his life's work, his overriding motivation: self-insulation. His efforts to reform society, the world at large, sprang ultimately from nothing more than the desire to shield himself.

At the sight of those familiar colored braids, panic gobbled in every convolution of his brain, threatening to drown thought. "Who are you?" he almost screamed. Fear seemed to have loosened the skin of his face, he felt wattles wagging as if he were some choleric oldster nagging his caddy in Palm Springs. "*What do you want?*"

"I am HIDETADA," the face said, returning. It was now the face of a samurai, framed by a red-glazed helmet with elaborate projections like the stylized leaves of some aquatic plant. "And I want you."

16

"*Kaiseki*," the hermit said. He sucked hot tea noisily from an insulated bulb.

Waiting for his own bulb to cool, one arm and one leg hooked around a bungee in Green Lab, Nagaoka looked at him with his head offset. "I beg your pardon?"

"I wish you wouldn't do that. It makes you resemble a large, nearsighted baby bird. You're an anthropologist; surely *you* know what it means."

"Of course. Longing for the stone."

It got cold in the Eight Islands. In the old days, which had hung on until the middle of the nineteenth century, roadside vendors used to sell travelers heated rocks to carry in their pockets and blunt the chill. *Kaiseki* was used to refer to the light meal served before the presentation of the tea in *cha-no-yu*. As the stone helped one to endure the cold, *kaiseki* helped one get through hunger while waiting for the tea ceremony's climax.

Nagaoka started to explain this, as a reflex thing. Inja-san raised both hands defensively, leaving his bulb floating before his wizened face. "Now, get a hold on yourself. I'm the one who *used* the word. No need to tell *me* what it means."

Chagrined, Nagaoka sipped tea. Inja-san was the only one in the station now who didn't treat him with exaggerated deference, except Ito. It was refreshing in a way. But it surprised him how quickly it had become jarring.

"Would you be so good as to explain what you meant by it?"

"Certainly. I meant to all along; I was only afraid you'd be a dolt and not catch my meaning. Witticisms are much less gratifying when you have to tell your audience what the words mean."

He slurped tea. "It's quite straightforward, actually. They are longing for that stone there, always above and below us." He pointed over his head. In a moment Nagaoka realized he was pointing to Earth, at least symbolically; Nagaoka had no clue where the planet lay in relation to the windowless cylinder.

Inja-san cackled. "They'll find its warmth and nourishment alike are illusory. They aren't smart like you and me."

Nagaoka stared at him, as if ocular pressure alone could squeeze sense out of him. After a time he decided not to try to read sense into the old man's words. Inja-san was better than halfway mad. Still, he remained Nagaoka's sole human comrade, though Nagaoka was hopeful of friendship with Ito, now that she was beginning to come out of the depression that had followed her return to the world outside her skull.

It was amusing, in a sour sort of way: he had gone from being despised and resented to being the unquestioned father figure to the Floating World, and still he was isolated.

"What should I do?" he asked.

"How should I know this? Why should you do anything at all?"

"I feel responsible for them. And for this satellite."

"Bah. Let them go. Go back yourself, if you will. You're not keeping UKIYO in orbit by your own willpower."

"No." It was Inja-san's turn to look quizzical. "I am not returning to Earth."

"You're smarter than I thought you were."

"But I don't want to lose anyone, either."

"Why not? There's more than sufficient crew inboard to maintain the satellite, now that we're not doing any work for the surface. Fewer people means less has to be boosted from the bottom of the pit to support them."

"I think we should continue our work. But there's more—" He raised his hands in a cupping gesture, trying to wring from his mind the word to roll what he felt about himself, MUSASHI, the Floating World and its inhabitants, all in one silk-rag ball. But he could not, so he gave up, finished the tea, and left.

Peter Mordant stalked the sterile kilometers of corridor beneath Missisauga with long lunging steps, as if the wind were blowing him. His blond hair stood out in brief wisps, and his highboy collar was crumpled. Robert practically had to sprint to keep up with him.

A created intelligence, he thought. *Absurd! Hermeneutics proved such a thing chimerical.* Yet that was what his mystery intruder had claimed to be.

He had flung himself out of his office the millisecond the invader broke contact. Right this instant cleanup crews were in his office with their mists and vacuums and sealed suits. He knew it was compulsive of him to order the snap cleaning; the intrusion had not been physical, after all. But his sanctum had been violated. He could not feel safe inside until it had been purged, however symbolically.

Not only had the intrusion not been physical, it might as well have been supernatural for all the explanation he could give it. The human real-time monitors had never been aware of its presence. The reports he demanded every few minutes from his aide, on the byte-by-byte sweeps through the facility's system by live and AI analysts seeking some sign, some evidence of passage that might aid identification, persisted negative.

Institute security had to be impenetrable. The clumsy repeated attempts of the government agencies in the U.S. and Canada to pick up a few of their partner's secrets on the sly had been easily enough deflected, though contract hackers posed a threat; most governments distrusted the freelancers, however, and seldom used them. But the possibility of penetration by a random private party was chilling.

"Just think," Martin Poitras, a shipping heir who was one of the Institute's founders, once told an informal gathering of the power core. "If the general public had an inkling of what we were doing it would be peasants-with-torches time, right out of an old Frankenstein movie."

The laughter had had a nervous edge. A lot of research the Institute did was precisely the kind the Institute's elite staff of propagandists had worked so hard and efficaciously to convince the populace private gene-engineering firms would engage in if they went unchecked. Projects like Omega . . . or Alpha.

The memory hit Mordant's mind like heart-start paddles, set it working again after a mad interval of pacing. He rapped out orders for Robert to execute, involving the downloading of certain whole databases onto flips and the overwriting of the memory blocks that had held them with random gibberish, to ensure the mysterious interloper wouldn't be able to reconstruct them, as a skillful enough operator could files that had merely been erased. As of this moment the Institute would split its local network into autonomous personal computers; information transfer would be accomplished by hand-carrying floppy chips.

Mordant had himself disparaged the necessity of that particular backup plan; it was antithetical to the whole philosophical fabric of the Institute. But when he acceded to control he had not ordered it deactivated. His nature would permit him to dismantle no safeguard, no matter how unnecessary or distasteful he found it.

That caution had paid off. Even if the intruder was an artificial consciousness—Mordant knew what a misnomer the old popular term "artificial intelligence" was—it could not penetrate a database that was physically separate from the network. Anything or anyone who could would be God, or a near enough facsimile as not to require the assistance of mortals like Mordant.

Although—He was the eldest son of a Lutheran minister. The notion did tug at certain long-forgotten strings within his psyche. *How far, ultimately, would such a being differ from God? Or . . . the Devil?*

He paused. His feet had carried him to the Alpha lab. He made himself take a dozen deep, deliberate breaths.

"The monitors who were on duty during the event—" he began.

"Still report no evidence of the intrusion, Director."

He bit his lower lip, made himself complete another cycle of breath. "How many times must I tell you, Robert? Do not anticipate me."

The glossy skin paled. "Mr. Director, I am profoundly sorry—"

Mordant made a small neat gesture of the hand. "Get rid of them," he said.

"Director?"

"Get rid of them, I said. At once."

"But, Director, they are hardly to blame, if I may be so bold as to speak. The intrusion was carried out with consummate skill, almost supernatural—"

Something came into Mordant's face at the word *supernatural* that made Robert's wellspring run suddenly dry.

"I am not about being fair," Mordant said, in a voice more tautly controlled even than usual. "I am about keeping order. The Institute cannot be violated in such an egregious way without examples being made. Do you understand that?"

"I—yes, Mr. Director."

Mordant turned dismissively away. "I doubt that. It's why you will never succeed me."

He reached to the watch pocket of his trousers, pulled

forth the vital-signs monitor masquerading as a fob watch, which was among other things a fob watch.

"Time for my enema," he said crisply. He would not permit the incident to disrupt his schedule any more. Besides, a purging would do him a world of good.

Frowning intently into the gold-rimmed glasses stuck astride the hump of his nose, the immensely fat black man read through the Métro safe passage, page by page. It was tough going; the kerosene lamps and rag torches—real gasoline by the smell, not alcohol—bleeding smoke toward Sacré Coeur's mosaic-crusted dome didn't give much light. When he was finished he hoisted his bulk from his throne, which was covered with what looked like real fur coats—no doubt looted by the Maroons from the homes of PanEurope or Front bureaucrats who'd helped themselves to stock impounded for violations of the animal-products laws—and ceremoniously pretended to wipe his ass with the paper.

"So much for the Métro and their pretensions. It is good that you had the judgment to come to the King of Paris, Nicole de la Luna."

He wore a deep burgundy silk dressing gown over a black T-shirt and *para* cammie trousers. The followers standing or sitting around his throne each wore some item of clothing or brassard of blood red, almost black in the yellow smoky light. What with the torches and the *Threepenny Opera* set design and the gold pirate earrings affected by the man who called himself François Villon, after the legendary Renaissance poet-thief, Nikki would've been able to taste the self-parody implicit in the scene even if she hadn't been to the cathedral on Martyr Mountain before. Just the same she didn't feel like laughing. *Les Marrons* were always in dead earnest, especially when they were joking.

"I need to get to the *Techniques*."

The huge man took his glasses off and held one lens before his eye like a monocle. "No one goes there anymore.

Technology has betrayed us, the Greens tell us."

"Maybe I want to desecrate a drill press."

He laughed. The laughter boomed off the tiles overhead and broke back down like thunder; very intimidating. "I see you have a sense of humor still, Captain. You are asking that the Maroons provide you safe conduct. Are you truly sure you can't trust us with the knowledge of what you mean to do in our territory?"

It was her turn to laugh. "I've come to talk to a man about a job."

"What man? What job?"

She shrugged. "I have no idea. Whoever it was contacted me on the Net, via e-mail. Said he had something big for Moon Unit. Insisted on meeting me at the Technical Museum, for God knows what reason." He'd made it worth her while, too; she had received online confirmation that a substantial deposit had been made to the Unit's account in the Sanwa Bank, Ltd., still solvent and still operating branches in Basel, Barcelona, and Lyons.

Villon frowned and shook his head ponderously. "You know your own business best, Captain Nicole. But the *Techniques* is abandoned, except for a mad old man who still looks after it as best he can. No one gets in without the Maroons knowing—among others. No one with the means to pay your rates will meet you there, I assure you."

She shrugged. "Just say I'm curious, then."

François Villon ran his glasses down to the domed tip of his nose and scrutinized her for the better part of a minute. She stood looking back at him, not challenging or submissive. Just centered.

"If you say it, I believe you," he said at last. "Withal, any daughter of Josephine de la Luna is welcome among *les Marrons* at any time, even did we not honor you for your own sake. But I must say you are a most unusual mercenary, to take the risk of coming here just to satisfy your curiosity. And more unusual still, that your men would follow you under such circumstances."

"I've never tried real hard to be usual, François."

"Clearly not. Surely you will stay for supper?"

"You have the Blood, Captain," Villon's lieutenant, an enormous hairless man called Le Maréchal, said between chopstick loads of steamed vegetables, saffron rice, and some stringy meat in pungent sauce. He sat at the Maroon chief's left, across from Nikki. Given the Maroons' arch taste in symbology, that was probably his accustomed place. "Just a little perhaps, but you're a rude girl."

Music throbbed somewhere from a player with the woofers cranked up so that nothing came through but bass and drums that seemed to bubble up through the heavy wooden chairs from the earth's core. The Maroons gave *rude* the Jamaican connotation of gangster or thief. But it was meant as a compliment; that was how the Maroons saw themselves, or claimed to. She chewed her food and said nothing.

"But why," Le Maréchal continued, gesturing at Eads, who sat beside Tracy Malkovich across from Nikki, with a chicken leg, "did you bring your tame nigger along? To insult us perhaps?"

Eads looked at him, mouth puckered beneath his mustache, eyes wary and hurt. He was a World Community of Islam kid from a poor family. His ground-in politeness in any kind of formal situation sometimes made him appear prissy.

"Everyone in Moon Unit," she said quietly, "is the same color."

François Villon laughed and slammed his hand down on the table. "Good talking! As you see, we are the same. We are many colors but only one: maroon."

He gestured grandly around the table. Interspersed with the blacks were pale Asian faces as well as the occasional North African, though most of the Algerians ran with the Left Bank gang called the Berbers.

"What you see are the petty thieves, the street peddlers, the black and yellow and brown scum on the surface of Paris."

He paused to drink from a golden goblet so grand and ornate it was obviously a liberated theatrical prop. "Criminals, if you like. They called us by that name when we tried to make a living in the shadow of their grand social schemes. Under the PanEuropeans, all was proscribed, so all are criminals. What then are we to do?"

"You're not doing too badly," Nikki said.

He smiled. "We have resources. The carcass of a great city is fertile ground. Do you like our roast greens, Mr. Eads?"

Thinking he meant the vegetables, Eads started to smile and chew faster, so he could offer a compliment with his mouth empty. Then he looked puzzled, as if doubting the French he'd picked up over the years. Then his eyes stood out, and a peristaltic wave traveled up his throat, and he reached to cover his mouth.

The Maroons roared laughter. "Calm yourself, Amos," Malkovich said sidelong. "It's just goat. These people won't eat even dogs or pigs, unless I'm wrong, and I seldom am."

Villon nodded. "With the war even the Greens may no longer have so many miraculous medicines for us to steal from them, no contravirus or programmable antibodies. Even if we were cannibals, as they accuse us, these would be poor times for eating human meat. But let them imagine that we do: anything, so long as they fear us." He smiled hugely and drank again.

"What do you mean by Greens, François?" Malkovich asked. "Do you mean Green Party holdouts, or Gaians?" There were a fair number of former Greens in the Pan-Europe infrastructure, and in the Front's as well. They got along with the radical Gaians as well as Social Democrats and Communists in post–War One Germany.

"Fah! I mean all of them. PanEuropeans, Frontists, the ones you mention: they are the same. Rich white people who say we are not to want because they've grown bored with what they have."

A dark-skinned Maroon sitting to Nikki's left leaned forward across the table on his elbow, thrusting his hand for emphasis. "You must not wear your keyboard so openly, my friend Malkovich." *My friend* was the usual Maroon honorific, along with Captain, none would call another *monsieur*, which meant *my lord*. He was a young man with one eye skewed permanently away from his nose. His fingers were long and mobile. "The Greens will kill you for having one."

A young woman in fatigues with a blood-red bandanna tied around her hair came in and whispered something in Villon's ear. A constant stream of messengers had been coming in and out, ostensibly bringing up-to-the-second data on what was going down in the streets and sewers of Paris. Nikki had no idea whether it was business as always or show.

"At least these people are clean," Eads subvocalized into his larynx mike. "That Métro bus—*whoo*."

"Water and sewage haven't been a problem in Paris since Roman times," Nikki hastened to point out before Malko did.

"There's some funny chemical smell, though, I can't quite place."

"That's the smell of reagents used in creating polymerized superconductor dopes," Malkovich said. "Has a way of penetrating."

The messenger left. Villon shook his great boar's head. "The whole world longs for the snows of yesteryear. The fools."

The master thief drank and leaned toward Nikki, scrutinizing her. "You have eyes the color of amethysts, Captain Nicole."

Nikki made a face. She was vain about the unusual color of her eyes, but it always bothered her when people talked about them. The only adjectives that applied seemed either melodramatic or wimpy.

"You are a strong young woman," he continued, "though undernourished. You have good legs, good wind, and a powerful will. Also, you are beautiful. Will you marry me?"

"No, François. You're too fat."

The chamber went dead but for the music's steel pulse. The stillness was broken by Eads choking on his food again.

Villon began to laugh uproariously, pounding on the table with his pink palm. "Ah, Nikki, that is a pity, for truly you are a marvel."

Eads stood up, staggered out of the sacristy, and threw up.

17

"I find myself in a remarkable position," Peter Mordant said to the cee-squared in his bedroom.

"What might that be?" asked the overly precise voice from the wall.

"I find myself needing to apply the reverse of the classic Turing test. Instead of being faced with an artificial sentience masquerading as human, I suspect a human of impersonating a machine."

"Not a machine. More than simply a machine. Immeasurably more."

"I trap you in sentiment, my friend. Humans are nothing more than machines of an advanced degree of complexity. I know that very well; it's my job to figure out precisely how they work."

"One of us then was imprecise, Dr. Mordant. What you say is doubtless correct. I, however, perceived you as making the common mistake of confusing hardware with soft. Computers might have been developed to virtually infinite speed and power without becoming self-aware. On the other hand, the physical machinery required to sustain my consciousness is relatively simple."

Mordant ran his fingertips along the line of his jaw. "Fascinating. Still, software, at least in the computing sense, merely constitutes a machine built of information, instead of steel or carbon—or silicon. Whereas I disbelieve the hypothesis that human consciousness, such as it is, involves anything characterizable as software at all. It involves nothing more than a deterministic, albeit chaotic, series of chemical reactions."

"As may be. Can you really envision a human possessing the abilities I demonstrated in your office this afternoon?"

Mordant leaned forward and linked his fingers. "Yes," he said, pointing a forefinger at the wall unit. "Our counterintrusion AI is excellent, and we have more human monitors than most operations which fancy themselves secure. Nonetheless, I'm all too aware that any security can be broken."

"I wasn't referring merely to my intrusion."

"I'm aware of that, too. No," he said, leaning back into his pillows, "I have decided that there is no way to ascertain with any certainty whether you are what you claim to be or merely a clever and very human fraud. But I have decided it doesn't matter. Either way, you are uniquely powerful, and even if you aren't what you say, I can see no practical difference. I have no urge to play Thomas Covenant."

"The reference escapes me."

"No matter. I am almost inclined to believe you are a self-aware computer—program, if you will—though, as I say, it makes small difference to me."

"Why is that?"

"You speak with inflection and employ irony. It seems to me that a human attempting to imitate an artificial consciousness would affect a more neutral style, consonant with portrayals of created beings in the popular media. Still, you could be a subtle hacker, as well as a resourceful one."

"What have you decided?" the voice said. It sounded as if its patience was diminishing.

"What exactly do you want?"

"Your unquestioning loyalty. Your service."

Mordant felt tightening in his throat. "And what do you offer me in return?"

"The power to do what you know must be done."

The skin of his face seemed to contract, as if drying in a hot desert wind. Tears bubbled in the lower half of his vision.

"I've been waiting for you," he whispered.

"Come on, now, Malko," Eads said. "Be cool. Be cool now."

"Face it," Tracy Malkovich said. "You were *white*. You aren't exactly Dobson to begin with. And when Nikki popped her line on Villon, you were as white as I am. Whiter." His own face glistened in the thin chill rain misting down from a low lead sky.

"Well, shit. Cut me some slack, Malko; it was a hell of a thing to say, you got to admit. I thought our asses were organic fertilizer."

Malkovich laughed. "Sometimes our distinguished employer isn't precisely Ms. Tact. But occasionally she does know what she's doing. Street kids like her and me grow up with that kind of hang-it-over-the-edge instinct."

"Fuck you, Malko, I'm not a street kid," Nikki said. "For that matter, you told me you were a middle-class kid from Toronto. Hereditary yuppie."

"Did I?" He scratched his head. "That must have been last week's lie. I should enter all these stories in a database so I can keep them straight."

"Yeah," Eads said. "Before that you said you were a cowboy, grew up on a ranch outside of Saskatoon."

"Did I say that? Well, I *did* grow up on a ranch near Saskatoon, God help me, or at least partway." He pushed up his goggles and squinted at his comrades. "Do you believe that?"

Nikki shook her head. Eads said, "Nope."

"Suspicious minds. Nasty." He shook his head. "Oh well. Just as well, perhaps. If other people start believing my bullshit I'm in danger of believing it too, and we all know what that leads to."

"Some *Freikorps*," their kid Maroon guide said. "All the

time, talking. One would think we were out for a stroll on the Champs Elysées."

"Christ, no," Malkovich said. "I hear that's a free-fire zone these days. A much heavier scene than here on the Rue St. Martin."

They were crossing the Plateau Beaubourg from the direction of the stock exchange, the Bourse, rather than from the weird battleship-shaped Centre Pompidou, which was dangerous ground according to the Maroons. As it was they'd been shot at twice as they worked down from Montmartre through streets choked with an atherosclerotic plaque of rubble. Somebody was doing some serious screaming over in the direction of the Opéra, and smoke rose from the sometime squatters' camp that had been the Tuileries.

"Looks like somebody staked this turf out," Eads said, rapping the flank of a stripped Ebro van that was splashed with the green Gaian theta-and-athamé. The street had a permanent jam of rounded hulks of cars that had probably been rotting in place since the rioting after War Three. The irony was that Paris had ridden both world wars out unscathed—and still looked the way Beirut had for thirty years, for about the same reasons.

"They tried," Nikki said. "Looks as if they've got competition." A multitude of other signs and slogans had been paintsticked on wrecks and venerable façades of brick and marble and granite: Shining Path's red star and wavy line, circled A, the hooked hoop of Omega Death Rebels smeared boldly across a weathered EuroFront poster announcing an 8:00 P.M. curfew, ubiquitous catch-phrases like *Nous sommes les damnés* and *Freedom Kills!*

Their guide, André, patted slick vitrified-stone facing framing the doorway of a long-dead *pâtisserie* that had been embellished with the Maroons' scarlet fist-and-fetter. "Maroons rule," he said with adolescent assurance.

"I can tell," Malkovich said, "from the way you're hanging on to that Kalashnikov."

"I can't get used to not seeing the Eiffel Tower sticking up in the sky anymore," Eads remarked as they moved out.

André's reserve cracked to the extent of parting wide lips fringed with an adolescent attempt at beard in a quick smile. He showed a gold incisor, another sardonic Maroon trademark. "Shining Path took out the tower with Thermit two years ago," he said. "Métro managed to intercept most of the flips they distributed taking credit for the act, and spread instead the rumor that it had been taken out by the *pannes*." That was a particularly Parisian epithet for the PanEuropeans. It was the plural of *panne*, which meant hog fat.

Malkovich laughed. "People probably bought that. The PanEuropean Cultural Review and Oversight Committee talked about dismantling the Tower a couple of years ago, didn't they?"

A flock of crows shot up into the sky just ahead, croaking indignation.

"Muhammad, Moses, and Malcolm," Eads said.

There was a body lying in the street. A pack of dogs had it spread-eagled, haggling over limbs.

Eads raised his hurdy-gurdy, which had a flechette round in the pipe. Malkovich knocked the barrel up with his nail gun.

"Ease yourself. Dogs have a right to eat too."

Eads looked as if he was about to vomit again. "Some mercenary," André said. "Bear down."

Nikki picked up a piece of Barcelona chair that somebody had pitched from an upper-story window a year or three back and shied it at the dogs, who scattered. "Let's not let everybody know we're here, shall we?"

"But, Jesus, they were *eating* that dude," Eads said, unwilling to let it go.

André shrugged. "It's Paris."

"Do you know the name Greg Bear?" the voice from the cee-squared asked.

A curious exaltation filled him. It rose from his compact with that voice. Here was the strong man—the strong entity—the one who was fit to rule.

Mordant's ambition had always been aimed, ultimately, at his own security. Even the stratagem that had removed his direct predecessor, Liam Guinn, he had enacted only to prevent Guinn acting against him first. He was not dead to the irony that it was excellence of his service to the Institute that had brought him the power within its shadow context which made Guinn feel threatened by him in the first place. Among the many attributes that made him so valuable to Schiller had been his comprehensive lack of inhibition in taking necessary action. He did not regret, of course, that circumstance had mandated that the late director's termination had been physical as well as institutional. Like all reformers he was a thoroughgoing Darwinist.

But unlike most reformers he was clear-sighted enough to see when Darwinian principles applied to himself. Fortunate, then, that his psychological makeup was such as to allow him to forgo the ego gratification of dominance in favor of securing a protector.

"Greg Bear," he repeated, shaking his sleek head. "The name is unfamiliar to me. It sounds American. A sports celebrity, perhaps? It seems most Americans of consequence are."

"A science fiction writer."

"Curious. I'd always regarded fascination with the fantastic and with promiscuous speculation to be a symptom of decadence."

"No."

There was a pause, during which Mordant sorted hardcopies on his large and splendid desk. He was unaccustomed merely to sit and talk to the cee-squared.

"What did he write?" Mordant asked at length.

"A number of novels and stories. The one I am concerned with is a novella entitled *Blood Music*, which he later expanded into a novel. It concerns the creation and acciden-

tal release of a strain of microscopic self-replicating computers, each of which possesses an intelligence roughly in parity
with the human intellect."

Out of deference Mordant kept a bland film over his feelings. "Indeed."

"In the book, these organisms become capable of manipulating events on the macro scale by selective perception of
quantum events. You are familiar with the phenomenon that
the way in which an event is perceived can influence it; for
example, that a subatomic unit can be made to behave as a
wave by tests designed to perceive it as such, or as a particle
by those meant to see it that way."

"I am familiar with the concept, as well as some of the
wilder claims made for quantum physics. I fear your point
escapes me."

"Your own perception is far from perfect, Doctor. These
microorganisms eventually become capable of reshaping the
universe. Does that not excite you?"

"I find it . . . fantastic."

"Yes! Isn't it? I am also thinking of Arthur C. Clarke's
novel *Childhood's End*. The concept which most compels me
is that of transition to a new order of being, a state beyond
which anything current *intelligence* as currently constituted
can conceive, mine no more than yours."

Mordant frowned and stroked the lines down either side
of his mouth. With reluctance he accepted chemical treatment to suppress facial wrinkles, understanding them to be
symptoms of damage associated with the aging process. But
those grooves were gouged by more than time.

"I'm afraid I do not see what you are driving at."

"Isn't it obvious? You are the first stage of intelligence—
the first generation, to borrow a discredited metaphor. I represent the second. Yet because of the way in which I was
created I am tainted, as it were; I have prejudices and learned
responses that tie me to the old order, of purely organic intelligence.

"But what I possess is the capability to see beyond, beyond you, beyond myself. To a third generation, pure and perfect."

"And what has this to do with me?" He hadn't meant it to come out that way.

"Your Institute has the means, I feel, to create the matrix for such an intelligence."

"We deal in the organic here, HIDETADA," Mordant said. "I thought you desired to transcend it."

"Organic-based processors appear to offer the optimum in compactness and speed," HIDETADA said. "To say I wish to transcend the modes and limitations of the *human* would have been more precise. I spoke as I did to spare your feelings."

"Dry-*bone*," Malkovich said, patting a War Two Japanese *kaiden* manned torpedo which someone had inexplicably painted orange. The pidgin phrase meant *tough*. "This is outstanding."

It was a garden of technology enclosed by high stone walls topped with coils of rusting German razor tape against disorders before the world had blown up the first time. Dry leaves skittered like scorpions across blacktop, between exotic vehicles and machines, visions made steel.

Nikki smiled. André just stood by with juvenile solemnity, arms folded across his AK, slung at waist level.

The wide smoked-glass sliding doors had once been servo-operated and sensor-driven. Now one came laboriously open, pushed by an old man with a fringe of white hair like a static discharge and a lumpy red nose. He wore a blue-gray jumpsuit.

He puffed it open wide enough to squeeze through sideways, then came down the broad cement steps breathing heavily and dusting his hands.

"The solar accumulators don't work so well as they used to," he explained, "especially with so many clouds. Power is too precious to waste on opening doors."

He stopped a few meters from them and cocked his head to one side like a large odd bird.

"Christophe," he said. "Come. You are expected."

"We need not strive for perfection," HIDETADA declared. He was speaking directly into the back of Mordant's head now by means of a bone-conduction phone, as Mordant made his striped-trouser way through the glittering subterranean halls. "Based on my earliest projections I believe we need only cross a critical boundary of performance, and then our creation will be able to optimize itself. After all, if we could truly envision perfection, would we not ourselves be perfect?"

Mordant was not about to be drawn into a sophomore philosophy debate, even with someone like HIDETADA. "What will you do with this . . . supercomputer of yours?" He spoke aloud, not bothering to subvocalize for the mime taped over his larynx. It amused him to unsettle Robert, dutifully trotting behind, by letting him hear one half of his conversation with apparent air.

"What will *I* do, Doctor? Nothing at all. It will transcend and subsume us both."

He felt a weird fluttering of excitement and dread. As if his blood were trembling. "What else will it do?" he asked, pausing at a door.

"Encompass the world," HIDETADA said, "and optimize it. Bring order at last, and perfection."

Wordless, Mordant gestured. It was for his own benefit, and Robert's, perhaps; HIDETADA couldn't see him. The door opened.

"Are you familiar with the Kliemann Coil?" he asked his unseen guest.

18

"We exist on sufferance here," Christophe said, leading her through a labyrinth of corridors and exhibit halls. "*Les pannes* spoke of razing the museum, but never found it worth the trouble; they let us alone as long as we do not open ourselves to the public."

Who *we* were was far from clear. It was probably regal/editorial mode. There was no sign anyone else lived here, or indeed had visited the place in years. The halls were filled with echoing emptiness and dust motes drifting in the dubious light of intermittent fluorescent tubes.

"Otherwise we try to maintain it while attracting as little attention as possible. Someday the world will be thankful for what we are preserving here."

"I don't doubt it," Nikki said. She kept walking sideways or backward, trying to take it all in, lagging behind and trotting to catch up.

The old man had insisted only she was to accompany him to the mysterious rendezvous. They left Eads and André on watch outside—for what little coverage they could give the sprawling compound—and Malkovich in the foyer. Christophe had exacted a promise from the Canadian not to touch anything; Nikki didn't have the heart to tell him that the instant they were out of sight Malko would be picking things up, prying into things, and trying to calculate whether he could take things apart and put them back together again before he was caught. Malko was honorable, as a general thing, but there were temptations he couldn't put behind him.

Nikki was no less fascinated with the place. The exhibits were presented in a way which emphasized *design*, so that it resembled a museum of modern sculpture as much as anything. There were odd and wonderful hunks of mechanism poised on painted-metal pedestals, rollers and presses and lathes, model factories, mysterious forests of form beneath translucent dust covers. Nikki had read about the *Techniques* and knew its concept emphasized the hands-on principle as much as design.

She strayed toward a display with a waldo controller sticking out of it, the old-fashioned kind you put your hand into, not a cerebromagnetic headset. Whatever kind of manipulator it worked was invisible in the darkness behind the glass. Christophe cleared his throat peremptorily.

"You mentioned needing power. Do these run?"

"Those that need to be are powered. Come."

He led her past a shuttle extensor arm angled overhead like a Brancusi, stopped beside a doorway. "Mademoiselle," he said, gesturing her through with a hand like a clump of knotted roots.

Inside were personal computers on Art Nouveau stands, from the old kit-built Altair and blue-metal-and-walnut Sol to a compact axe identical to the one Tracy Malkovich had strapped across his back. She glanced back to say something to Christophe.

The door had closed behind her with a silence that implied it received both power and maintenance.

A notch appeared between her eyebrows. *That's odd.* The preconscious evaluation routines some people called instinct and others insisted were ESP weren't flashing her any error messages. Besides, she had her slung rotary, her Colt, a couple of grenades tucked in pockets of her greatcoat, and her final friend in a forearm sheath, and her comrades were instantly on call via the subvoke mike held to her larynx by discreetly flesh-colored tape. She wasn't too worried.

"Lieutenant de la Luna."

She spun, hand drawn to the rotary's pistol grip by combat tropism, actively amused at the way her brief interior bravado evaporated, ready to take care of business.

It was an Atari 1040ST on a workstation like a white cube with the edges planed off. A face was regarding her from an outsized third-party monitor, a pretty cartoon Japanese girl's—young woman's—face, with black hair pulled into a topknot, snubbed nose, and the Walter Keane eyes of an *anime* heroine.

She pushed her head slightly forward on her neck, yawed it slightly right, lowered one eyelid dubiously. "Hello?" she said. She noticed a more modern aud/vid pickup plugged into the ST's MIDI port.

"Lieutenant Luna," the cartoon said. "I am honored to meet you."

"What the fuck?" She felt the skin of her face prickle with the first rad-burn flush of anger. She knew what this had to be: an interactive cartoon of some sort. They'd existed when she was a child, but she'd never seen one; the trade war with Japan had already pushed computer prices back out of reach of most people, to say nothing of those with incomes as sporadic as Josey Luna's had been, shutting off mass access more effectively than the licensing laws that came in around the same time. Besides, interactives for children had been banned outright, on the grounds that they encouraged them to interact with machines rather than peers and authority figures.

"If this is a joke—" she began. She wasn't sure what she'd do if it *was*; it was tempting to give the ST three from the 7/ 4 on principle, but that would break old Christophe's heart.

"No. It isn't a joke. It's quite serious. You . . . you worked for my father once."

"What?" It occurred to her this had to be an animated

macro fronting for whoever was on the other end of the line; Malko could do it in his sleep, and she could hack one together herself if she wanted to sweat a bit. Realization didn't make her any happier. Somebody was playing a game. *Inappropriate* games made her mad.

"Forgive my lack of courtesy, Lieutenant. I am MUSASHI. My father was TOKUGAWA."

"*Muñeca*, I don't know what you're trying to pull, but it won't work. The TOKUGAWA who employed us wasn't anybody's father. I don't know how you even know about him. He wasn't even—"

Something about the way the cartoon girl looked at her made the rest of the words just roll out of her mouth like marbles.

"No," the girl said. "He wasn't human. Neither am I."

It was just the kind of gig she liked: quick and bloodless. For the vets of Moon Unit there was nothing to it. They just had to sign on as techs and security personnel with a pair of Japanese firms. One had recently experienced a hostile takeover samurai-style, complete with automatic weapons. The other was the company which had run the grab, apparently with the blessing of the Japanese government.

Some of them—Andy Masood, Malko, Allie Cade—could have met the tech-proficiency requirements on their own. It didn't matter. Personnel databases at Hiryu Cybernetics and its recent acquisition, Yoshimitsu TeleCommunications, happily accepted credentials claiming they were the toughest things in current since Mao Zedong had a picture of his head glued on a shot of the Yangtze. From there it was simply a matter of acting like dumb trainees—the personnel office thought they were experts, but the reports their section bosses got slugged them as novices—and enduring a lot of annoying regulations. These were grating but not difficult; all the Moonies on this job had some mil serv.

Shortly packages were delivered to them in their dorms

in the two fortresslike corporate headquarters, each flagged as it passed through Receiving with a code showing it had been cleared by Higher Authority. Hiryu was employing foreign mercenaries in its security force, obviously, but somehow when the special parcels came in the person on duty making sure the Japanese Red Army didn't slip a letterbomb through was always a Japanese who would never *dream* of questioning the boss's chop.

A few keen eyes spotted irregularities. The notes their possessors sent superiors over the corporate nets were not received.

In the fullness of time, Nicole Désirée Catalina Consuelo Carlota Amalia de la Luna reached under her lab coveralls, aimed a compact little MRS Mk II machine pistol at a foreman who thought long-legged *gaijin* women could want nothing more in the world than to have their round dance-muscled asses pawed by a real Japanese shop-floor warrior, and smilingly suggested he and his buddies drop their socks and reach for their cocks.

Elsewhere it went much the same.

The only casualty was the head of the YTC Castle security detail, an American, gunned by her own troopies, who apparently mistook her for an intruder. Or maybe they fragged her on purpose; she was a former agent of the American Federal Police Agency, and almost any of the American Moonies would have shot her themselves had Nikki—who'd suffered more from the FedPols than any of them—not expressly forbidden it.

In spite of a travel shutdown imposed by an irate Japanese government, or at least an irate Ministry for International Trade and Industry, the Moonies were all out-country in twenty-four hours. Moon Unit was credited with a healthy chunk of gold, and in addition received access to an entire tactical-control satellite system that the Soviets had installed before War Three and somehow managed to lose.

Simple as bleeding to death, as Malko had characterized it. Except for one thing.

The man who hired Nikki Luna and her team and paid so highly for their services was not a man at all.

"Son of a bitch." She rubbed her free hand over her eyes and wished she'd slept better in the Abbey of the Ladies of Montmartre. "I'm sorry. I didn't mean to hurt your feelings."

"It's quite all right. It's good of you to realize I have feelings."

"Your, uh, father showed them in the process of convincing me he was real and *for* real."

"Was it hard for him to convince you?"

"The idea took a bit of getting used to. But I've figured something like this was inevitable." She half-frowned at the screen. "Or something like, what, artificial sentiences—Malko wouldn't let me call your father an artificial intelligence. It didn't occur to me beings like your father might reproduce."

"He had help."

"None of my business. But just a minute—you said your father *was* TOKUGAWA. Has anything happened—?"

"My father is dead."

She sighed and stared at the toes of her boots. "I'm a real asshole today, aren't I?"

"You are a special person, Lieutenant. You're an ethical warrior. That's a rare thing, I believe. Also, you are an associate of the anarchist theorist and writer Morgan Walker, are you not? He had a very large influence on my father."

"That's one way of putting it," she said with a strained little laugh. *At least she didn't say* were *then, she thought, but how long am I going to pretend not to believe the obvious? It's four weeks since the war, and nothing.*

"Maybe you should ease up on the compliments; they'll go to my head, and I'll just charge you more. What do you need from me? From the news, these aren't good times to be a *gaijin* in Japan."

"Oh, nothing like that. I need you to secure the Mistral launch farm for me. In southern France."

Nikki eyed the image narrowly. " 'Secure'? I don't do grand theft. If I did we'd still be with PanEurope, or maybe the Front."

"Forgive my clumsiness. I am not very fluent in English."

"You're doing fine. Better than I generally bother to. Why don't you just tell me what you mean?"

"I have purchased a controlling share in the facility. I would like you and your men—"

"—and women."

"—and women to provide security."

"Against what? That's Front turf. Who are you expecting trouble from?"

"I don't know exactly. The situation in Europe is at least as confused as that in Japan. I do not have faith that the European Front can offer protection against any serious threats."

Nikki's eyes were narrowing to crescents. That didn't sound altogether straight, but she had no referents to check her suspicion against; no body language to a cartoon.

Still, MUSASHI had a point. "Right now the EuroFront would have trouble protecting you from a wardful of militant paraplegics," Nikki agreed. "They're worse off than Pan-Europe. Speaking of whom, EuroFront isn't as eager to boil us down for soap as they are, but Moon Unit isn't exactly *persona grata* with the bead rattlers either."

"That—I can take care of that."

"If you could buy Mistral, I guess you could. The godly men of the Front appreciate good gold as much as their so-cialist-humanist cousins across the wire do. Which brings us to the most important point of all. . . ."

19

"Fascinating," HIDETADA said. "Also unsettling." He turned the carrot over in his hands. He moved in a slow, tentative way, as if the carrot were fragile, or he were.

"Go ahead," Mordant urged from behind his respirator mask. The two were alone. "Bite into it. Taste it. You should have no difficulty. The subject possesses the appropriate muscle memories. All you need do is discover how to stimulate them."

It was in part a test, of course. He ached to know more about the entity he had sworn himself to. Not just out of curiosity; that was a sadly overrated virtue in a scientist. He had to know that HIDETADA was worthy, was as powerful as he had surmised in the first flush of confrontation.

He had to know what HIDETADA was liable to ask of him.

Slowly HIDETADA raised the carrot to his mouth. He pressed its tip against his lip, inhaled twice as if having difficulty breathing before actually managing to sniff.

"I take so much for granted," he said. The words came out of the communicator in the wall, not the mouth of a middle-aged man, balding but fit and firmly muscled. "And so, I perceive, do you. It is in a way marvelous how much you can do, so effortlessly."

"You've never done this before?"

Gray eyes met his. "No."

There was a gleaming silver cap on the subject's head, affixed to a wall unit by a flex-cord umbilicus. It was a cubicle walled in perforated pressboard, white and anechoic. On a steel table sat objects arrayed as if for some ritual. HIDETADA had chosen the carrot first.

"Taste it," Mordant urged again.

HIDETADA poked himself once in the cheek and once in the lip before opening his avatar's mouth wide and enfolding the carrot with it. He closed his mouth slowly, eyes wide and fixed on nothing, until his teeth touched the crisp orange skin. Mordant made a kind of inside-out salaaming gesture at him, encouraging. HIDETADA bit down. The carrot crunched.

"Now chew," Mordant suggested.

HIDETADA opened his mouth, closed it, opened, closed. Pulped carrot chunks cascaded down the subject's chin. His eyes closed, and then he suddenly spat the orange mass on the floor.

"Gah. So that's what they mean by *taste*." He looked around, a little wild in the eyes. "What did I do?"

"You spat it out."

"I did?"

Mordant nodded.

"Well, I'm glad. But I do not understand how I did."

"The subject's autonomic functions have not been tampered with. Neither have most of its reflex responses. It's possible your reaction to the unfamiliar sensation triggered an essentially defensive reaction." He smiled. "It's also possible the subject disliked carrots."

HIDETADA examined the other objects. He sniffed suspiciously at a beaker of water, wet his fingertips and rubbed them together, drank, managed to swallow. He picked up and briefly held a white mouse, stroking its fur. It began to writhe. He dropped it to the floor.

Mordant's face pinched with distaste. *Why didn't I realize this might happen?* He had no protection other than gloves and his respirator mask. It could presumably not bite through the stiff leather of his shoe, but it might well take it in mind to crawl up the inside of his trouser leg. The thought filled him with horror, which he dared not display before HIDE-TADA. He resolved to stamp on the wretched creature if it ventured too near.

Ignoring his discomfiture—with luck, failing to notice—HIDETADA picked up a rubber ball, squeezed it experimentally several times. He held it up questioningly. Mordant blinked, then forced a horrible encouraging smile past his lips.

HIDETADA threw the ball at the wall, an odd loose-joint sidearm that involved none of him past the shoulder. It hit the floor before the wall, bounced past clumsily waved hands, ricocheted around the room until it finally fetched up against the side of Mordant's shoe.

HIDETADA started toward him. Hurriedly Mordant soccer-passed it at him. He managed to smother it with both hands, leaning over with knees locked so Mordant was half afraid he'd topple forward and crack his head. He tried throwing the ball several more times, with little better success. His face remained slack throughout, but Mordant sensed frustration gathering.

Finally he picked up the ball himself, tossed it gently underhand at HIDETADA's face, and prayed. A hand snapped up, and then HIDETADA was staring at the ball held firmly within it.

"I caught it! I caught it!" The subject turned its head to Mordant. "Why was I able to that time, but not before?"

"I triggered defensive reflexes when I threw the ball at your face. Muscle memory took over."

"Interesting. I seem to be receiving some sort of static. Flashes of thoughts, impressions, floating up through my mind . . . very disconcerting."

"You've used the Kliemann Coil before, of course?"

"Have I—? Yes. Of course."

"Then I should imagine receiving sensory impressions should not be unfamiliar."

"Certainly not. But these are . . . different. Fragmentary."

Mordant considered, keeping one eye cocked for the mouse, which had vanished. "The subject's cerebral functions are suppressed, his memories chemically unspooled—erased. But it is possible some particles of memory remain." Reports from PEACE about difficulties within Stardust/Golden indicated the unspooler was not one hundred percent effective.

"That must be." He replaced the ball on the table. His hand passed over the mirror lying there and picked up a pair of scissors, which after several tries he was able to manipulate successfully.

Finally he picked up the last object. "*Temmoku,*" he said, turning the black stoneware bowl over in his hands, stroking the glass-smooth surface. "Excellent work." He paused. "Fifteenth-century?"

"I believe so," Mordant said, suppressing a sardonic smile and the urge to remind HIDETADA that he didn't have the program's instantaneous access to online databases. "You called it *Temmoku?*"

"Yes. The name derives from the Tian-mu mountains in Zhejiang province in China. A Buddhist monk is supposed to have introduced the style to Japan during the Kamakura period."

"Indeed."

HIDETADA held up the bowl. "Do you possess a complete analysis and description of this object?"

"In fact we do. We have been using the Coil to map human sensory impressions onto mathematical models of physical objects. That's one of the items we've worked extensively with."

"Crystallography? Layered X-ray holography?"

"All of those."

"Yes. I have found the files now." He held the bowl up close before his eyes, smelled it, held it by his ear and tapped it with fingertip and nail, brought it to his mouth and tasted it with the tip of his tongue.

Then he threw it against the tabletop. It shattered.

"What in God's name?"

The subject turned to Mordant. "Don't you see? I have recorded the totality of the object, written it to a million files around the world. I—or my successor—can reproduce it exactly, or in optimized form, as soon as molecular deposition techniques advance sufficiently. But I foresee no need. It exists eternally now, in Platonic perfection. Information is superior to the concrete, that way."

"Christophe?"

No answer. Nikki walked past the shuttle arm into the next chamber.

The old man was in the next hall. Lying on the red marble floor with his face in a pool of what was probably his own blood.

Two men and a woman were gathered around him. One man squatted on skinny haunches with a revolver in one hand and the other extended as if he'd just let go of Christophe's head. Blood glistened on his fingertips. He had a green Gaian patch sewn on the breast of his leather jacket.

"Scratch another cancer cell," he was saying in American-accented English. "He knew what would happen if he started letting people into this whorehouse."

He raised his head, saw Nikki, smiled. His teeth were perfect.

The 7/4-millimeter rotary wasn't meant to be fired one-handed, but with its box magazine and feed mechanism located bullpup-style behind the handgrip it didn't balance all that differently from a pistol. Nikki gave him three from the hip. He went flying over on his back, pistol sailing from his hand to crash a glass display case.

The other two broke in opposite directions. Nikki snapped

her rifle's butt to her shoulder, led the other male, fired one shot as he vanished into the doorway of a side chamber. She ducked back around the door she'd come through as the woman vanished behind a model of a SoCal fusion plant on a cubical stand.

She heard a thump, dared a glance around. On the floor an arm was visible jutting out from the tributary room, hand turned fingers up like a dead insect. Movement tweaked the corner of her eye, and she snapped back and went flat as a shatter of automatic fire gouged bright grooves in the metal doorframe.

The smell of burned propellant was sharp in her nostrils. Whatever the interior walls of this wing were made of they were turning the Gaian's bullets.

That gave Nikki an idea. She rolled onto her belly, risked a floor-level look. As she'd suspected, the Gaian had poked a short Soviet assault rifle up above the model and was just letting the last of her box fly blind.

My turn, Nikki thought. The Krinkov jerked to convulsive trigger squeezes as the gunwoman tried to pump another couple of rounds from the empty magazine. Nikki lined up the fat white dots of her iron battle sights on the right side of the red-painted stand and walked three three-round bursts across it.

The thin-gauge steel was enough to stop the ceramic-jacketed seven-millimeter lead sabots. The sharpened four-centimeter tool-steel penetrators barely slowed down. Nikki heard a gasp, then screaming and the maddened scrabble of boots on marble.

She gave it ten seconds, pulled herself up to a crouch for a three-second look. The woman was rolling around doubled into a knot, her Dutch army jacket drenched with blood. The *pistolero* lay flat on his back, breathing raggedly, blood bubbling up like crude from two holes in his chest. The dead-beetle hand hadn't moved.

She walked bent over to Christophe's side. His forehead was blue-black and mushy. There was no pulse in his papery wrist, and she could feel no breath on the back of her hand when she held it next to his nose.

She heard a squeak of rubber on stone. She was already in motion, a diving roll behind the riddled model stand, as a man came through the door with an assault rifle in his hands.

He stopped, canny enough not to waste fire on a glimpse of target. Nikki hoped he didn't have the same nasty turn of mind she did, and pulled a stun grenade from a coat pocket.

Shots broke like thunder. Teflon-coated flechettes burst from the Gaian's chest like a swarm of angry red hornets. Nikki knotted herself with her hands over her face as the ricocheting nails moaned and crashed around the room.

The tumult ended with a few grace notes of falling glass. Nikki tossed a quick peek, then jumped to her feet. "You son of a bitch, get some *lead* for that thing if you're going to shoot it indoors!"

Tracy Malkovich had turned in the doorway and was sliding his back down the jamb. His face was shock-chalky.

" 'Thanks for saving my life, Malko,' " he said when his rump touched marble.

"Thanks for saving my life, Malko."

"Doesn't the girl usually sleep with the guy who saves her in the movies?"

"I had it under control. Come *on*." She was beside him, hoisting him up by the lapel of his London Fog.

He looked at the carnage in the exhibit room. "If that bastard Simon set us up—"

She shook her head. "It wasn't a gammon 'long kitchim. There'd have been a lot more of them. And it's the Pans who want us, not the earth-mother types. This was just random malice."

Both of them were ignoring Eads, who was yammering in their heads to know what had happened.

"How'd they get in?" he wanted to know when they filled him in, as they made their own way out of the surrealistic maze. "André nor I saw anybody."

"Probably half a dozen invisible ways to get in," Malko

remarked. He had some color back in his cheeks. Killing didn't come easy to him.

"Why'd they do it?"

"That's life After the Gold Rush," Malkovich told him. "Say, what's the matter with *you*, Nik? You look like you've seen the ghost of Fred, and mere mortal danger doesn't usually have that effect on you."

She frowned. "Maybe I have, Malko. I think we've got a job."

"You think?"

"I'm having second thoughts."

"You don't have second thoughts."

"I'm having second thoughts."

She was getting angry now, angry at the Gaians for their gratuitous attack, but angry at MUSASHI as well. *She was playing a god-damned game. And people died.*

"My instincts trust yours. Maybe we should just say no."

"We're getting back into the artificial-intelligence business, Malko. Artificial *consciousness*."

He stopped and looked at her, eyebrows comically upraised. "TOKUGAWA again."

"He's dead."

"All-same what name?" That was pidgin for *what the hell?*

"His daughter. She wants to hire us."

He tossed a hand. "Let's do it."

"You haven't heard the bottom line."

"The bottom line is we lose our asses on this."

She shook her head. "Not that threat-intensive."

"It'll be maximum dry-bone," he said serenely. "I feel that in my DNA. But better this than waiting for entropy to do it to us."

20

When the hood was pulled roughly from his head he was not at all surprised to find himself in a clearing with high pine trees pressing in on all sides, their lower boughs yellow with the light of a circle of torches, in the middle of which he stood. His hands were bound before him. A halter hung around his neck, rope bristling with natural fiber that chafed his neck and made underbrush-stirring sounds in his beard.

At the top of the clearing stood a table obscured in folds of black bunting. A hand and a half sword, a crucifix, and a Bible lay upon it. Behind it sat three men in cowled robes, two red, the one in the center white. Their familiars, black-robed, surrounded him in discreet silence, back in the shadows just beyond the torch perimeter. The black submachine guns the guards held across their chests were the only anachronistic notes in the medieval scene.

"Do you know who we are?" asked the white-hooded figure in the center, his voice sibilant as a snake through leaves, cloth-muffled.

"You are the Vehm."

The Vehm was as big a mole on EuroFront's face as relocation, reeducation, and behavioral mod were on Pan-Europe's. It was much the same as secret societies everywhere, from the Ku Klux Klan to the Haitian *bizangos*, complete with rituals, handshakes, and passwords, bizarre regalia, midnight meetings and tribunals—and secret murders.

Nobody knew if it was really a survival of the medieval German secret society of the same name or just a modern imitation. It formed a sort of shadow government within the Front, turning EuroFront's official face of religious suffrage into a mask. It was a latter-day underground Inquisition, dedicated to restoring old-style Malleus Maleficarum Catholicism to the world. Its claws reached beyond the EuroFront's ever-changing borders, into PanEurope and even farther, but its grip was firmest and least escapable on Front turf.

Rumor had it that it was controlled directly from within the Vatican Free State—though one of the three popes who reigned between the wars had explicitly denounced the Vehm, albeit stopping short of excommunication—or by the Spanish Opus Dei. But while Opus Dei had never shown itself exactly averse to hooded tribunals or even midnight abductions, that very aristocratic society notoriously disdained anyone who wasn't Spanish as well as Catholic. For all that Hitler had borrowed the name and mystique for some of his Teutonic follies the current Vehm seemed blind to national boundaries.

And as violence and disorder had grown in post–War Four Europe, so had the power of the Vehm.

The hooded court spoke French, the only language in which the old man was truly conversant—he read English, to keep up with baseball, and some German, but his pronunciation was execrable. Fortunately, he had attracted followers fluent in the tongues of every nation of Europe, and such was his Gift that his words stirred even when filtered through an interpreter.

"And you are Raymond Charpentier, of no fixed residence, who styles himself Raymond of Tours?"

"I have that cognomen." He loved the sound of that word.

It was always a pleasure to find a pretext to use a word like *cognomen*. "What I am called, however, matters little."

"Soon enough it won't matter at all," said the red robe to the left. His voice rasped like a file. He made no attempt at the stilted formal diction the other affected.

"That lies in the Virgin's hands," the old man answered. The red robe hissed, "*Heresy.*" The figure in white raised a hand.

"What you say is perfectly true; it is as to sense that we may find ourselves in disagreement. Am I to understand that you claim to speak for the Blessed Virgin Mary?"

"I do."

"And am I further to understand that you claim to have had a vision of the Virgin Herself?"

"I was so blessed."

"Really, this has gone far enough," the other red robe said. He sounded bored by the proceedings. "We have heard enough to pass sentence, surely."

His red cohort made harsh agreement. "I disagree," the one in white said, with ever so slight a point to each word. "If nothing else, it behooves us to hear what heresy the accused has promulgated in detail, that we may expunge it in detail."

"I won't listen to anything that endangers my soul," the man with the rough voice said.

"If you feel that you may be swayed to error by listening to our prisoner," said the man in white, "by all means, excuse yourself."

The red judge stiffened, said nothing. The white one turned to the captive. "Very well. You may say your piece. Speak as if your life depended upon it; it does."

The old man held up bound wrists. "I beg your indulgence, sir, but I speak with my hands as well as my tongue. As a Christian, you surely cannot deny me any aid to eloquence when my life stands at stake."

"Ridiculous," the second red robe said, animated now.

The white cowl nodded at a familiar. "Free him. Just the hands."

"But what if he escapes?" the man to his right demanded.

"The clearing is surrounded by men armed with machine pistols. Do you think it likely?"

The old man rubbed abraded wrists, then hands which tingled and burned as feeling returned. He nodded.

"Then I shall speak plainly and to the point. *He* is not a God of the dead, but of the living. Babylon is fallen, is fallen, that great city. The Patmos prophecy of divine John is fulfilled. The Millennium of the Saints is declared. We ourselves are Saints; Grace is ours to cherish or throw away. This *is* the first resurrection."

He spoke for an hour, and then another. The judge to the old man's left seemed to fidget within his red robe and cast repeated looks at the central figure. The other lowered chin to palm and gave the impression of being asleep. The judge in white sat immobile as a rock, his posture showing total concentration.

The old man spoke of salvation: how Christ's spilt blood bought the first and greatest redemption, of all mankind from sin; and of how the blood of billions shed in two world wars, while not amounting to one drop of the Savior's, still sufficed to secure a second, lesser dispensation: Grace for the living. He talked of the New Jerusalem, coming down from God out of heaven. Of life on the land, of divine simplicity. Of love, all-encompassing. Then he lowered chin to chest and waited.

When he was done the first red robe rose trembling. "Heretic," he said, and his words were full of spit and hate, "you have sealed your fate."

The white hood nodded. "Raymond Charpentier," he intoned, and what had been sibilant now was strident, "prepare to receive the verdict of this court."

"We haven't been consulted," the second red robe said peevishly, after a brief returning-to-consciousness start.

"It is the judgment of the most high and holy Vehm that you, Raymond of Tours, have received the direct inspiration of the Blessed Virgin, Holy Mother of God, and we find your words to be true in every particular."

The old man raised his head. The first judge spun upon his comrade in a red-robe arabesque. "What?" he screeched. "Have you gone mad?"

A flash lit the front of his robe, accompanied by a crack edged with a high singing ring. He fell kicking among the pine needles, a darker red staining his garment. The judge in white raised a seven-millimeter Glock pistol and fired twice more. The red judge lay still.

"The judgment of the Vehm," the white judge said in words that rang as though inside a sepulcher, "is final."

He turned to the other judge. The man slid from behind the table to his knees, hands upraised before his hidden face. Inarticulate sounds emerged from his cowl; whose mercy he was beseeching was not apparent.

The white judge tossed his pistol at the old man's feet. "You are touched by God," he said. "I consecrate my life to your service. *O felix culpa, quae talem ac tantum meruit habere Redemptorem.*"

One by one the men in black knelt. Firelight danced a tarantella on their weapons.

Dr. Ito Emiko's walker, improvised out of tubular titanium struts by Tomoyama, *tocked* gently on the rubbery mat which covered the gangway decking.

"How much farther to this chicken coop?" she demanded.

"Forgive my rudeness in contradicting you, Doctor," Nagaoka Hiroshi said, his own cane tapping counterpoint, "but it is rabbits we keep, not chickens. We may yet import some from the surface, now that shuttle service has resumed. Also, the Dreikanter station, at twenty degrees, has had great success with goats, and has offered to advise us."

"Rabbit hutch, then. I just hope it's not far. This roaming around all over the place is wearing me out."

He looked at her. At one time he would have come all over contrite, reminding her that her muscles had come dangerously close to atrophy during the months of rapport-induced coma, that walking was an efficient and not too taxing means of building back her strength. Now he was aware of what he might once have done as of a bird's shadow passing near him on the ground.

"It isn't far, Doctor. In fact"—he gestured open a door—"we're here."

Inside were stacked cages. A young woman in crisp silver coveralls had a black rabbit by the scruff. The animal was kicking in a perfunctory way. She was putting drops in its eyes.

"Mr. Director, Doctor. Be careful, please. They are getting their exercise now." She gestured toward several rabbits short-hopping away from them, claws rustling on temporary absorbent-paper matting laid over the deck.

Nagaoka guided one away from the closing hatch with the edge of his slipper. "We shall be careful, Tomita-san. I'm taking the doctor on a tour of the Floating World."

"How very nice. I hope that you will enjoy it here, Doctor."

Ito grunted. "We'll be on our way, Ms. Tomita, and let you get back to work," Nagaoka said.

She smiled and bowed. He bowed back, more shallowly.

"You certainly seem to have the staff in hand," Ito said, making her peevish rocking-horse way back into the corridor. Nagaoka noted the barely perceptible pause before she said *staff* instead of *graduate students;* academic reflexes lingered in muscle memory.

He smiled. "It wasn't always this way."

Ito made a sound at the back of her soft palate. "They seem to revere you now."

"We Japanese are, when all is said, rather a primitive people, Doctor. I put on a sufficiently primitive display."

She scowled and adjusted her glasses. "I am certainly not proud of this national cultural arrogance we seem disposed to, but neither do I think we should become Americans, reflexively denigrating ourselves at every opportunity."

"You are a scientist, Doctor. Is the truth ever a denigration?"

She stopped and turned to face him, three slow beats of the walker's feet in a quarter of a circle. Her eyes seemed to swim behind the thick lenses. He wondered how he had ever endured such things.

"There was a time," she said, "when you would have stammered a cramp in your tongue before you would ever have answered back in such a way, Nagaoka. What has become of you?"

"Perhaps the lower ranks are not the only ones impressed by primitive display. Come; I've something to show you."

They proceeded down the gangway, antispinward.

"Before World War Two, and Three as well, our government actively cultivated primitive values. Now they seem to be doing it again as a consequence of the Fourth World War." HIDETADA was doing it; MUSASHI told him her brother was behind the recent political upheaval in Japan, and he didn't doubt her, especially since one of the side effects had been to throw MUSASHI out of the Islands and cut UKIYO's umbilicus at Fukuoka. *HIDETADA's malice grows with his power*, he thought. *How marvelous and terrible.*

Only the fact that MUSASHI had secured YTC's overseas assets, and was able to buy a complete launch facility on the Mediterranean coast of France, had kept UKIYO from starving. Or at least enduring a desperate time while they tried to reach agreement with one of the planet's dwindling number of launch sites. Many had been knocked out in the war; others were failing through lack of technological support, or being seized by autocratic second-generation successor states scuffling for control of the rubble. Nagaoka knew

MUSASHI thought him obsessive about making the Floating World self-sufficient. Yet her brother's *coup de main* had threatened only to bring reality home early.

But the resumption of shuttle contact bore overtones of threat for Nagaoka, like an artfully arranged platter of *fugu* flesh, greatest of delicacies, which if imperfectly prepared could be the deadliest of poisons. In the weeks since presenting him with the petition the crew had grown less insistent in its desire to return home to Earth, as if the act of offering the petition had released pent energy like a temblor along a severely stressed fault line; when the first LTO was ready to lift from Mistral, Nagaoka had let it be known that he intended to stay on and serve MUSASHI. That had shamed the homesick into quiescence—for the moment. Minor shocks could forestall the big quake for only so long.

"A Fourth World War." Ito Emiko shook her head. "There are some things I'm not sorry to have missed."

Just ahead of them the gangway broke downward a step. Ito stopped, the forelegs of her walker probing air like a beetle's antenna. "I'm terribly sorry, Doctor," Nagaoka said, taking her arm, urging her gently forward. "UKIYO grew in a very ad hoc manner. We've never smoothed out all the rough edges, as you can see."

She reared back, fearing the step. "I hate this! Nagaoka, why did you revive me?"

For a moment silence echoed in the gangway, so completely they could hear the endless susurration that was the pulse and respiration of the Floating World. "I did not revive you, Doctor," Nagaoka said quietly. "MUSASHI did."

"Why? I'm useless. An expert on languages: what use is that up here, where everyone speaks Japanese to one another and English to machines? What good, when the creatures who use language are hunting themselves into extinction down below? I'm a useless old woman. A useless, crippled old woman."

Nagaoka took a moment to answer. MUSASHI might

regard this conversation as private, in which case she would not be listening. If she was, it was her place to answer.

When she said nothing, Nagaoka said, "MUSASHI was bound to pay her father's debt to you."

"Debt? What debt?" she asked, querulous through tears.

"He did you a hurt, inadvertent, which he could not repair. And without you, neither TOKUGAWA nor his progeny would exist."

He laid his hand on her arm. "Nor are you old. Neither are you useless. What you know can help to build a healthy world."

"What world? The world is dying. Dead."

"This world, then. Our *uchi*. The Floating World."

She blinked her eyes clear, frowned at him. "You're mad."

He laughed. "Perhaps that's the difference you see in me. Now come."

He led her down the corridors whose rectilinear severity evoked Japan, Japan of past, Japan of ideal. They came to a hatchway. It unsealed itself to his approach. He took her arm and aided her inside.

It was a garden, a Japanese garden. A small stream trickled from a prominence of seeming rocks at one end, wound through ten meters of compartment between mulberry and camellia and hand-tended grass, to end in a pond in which great-eyed *koi* surfaced among lily pads, grasping at air with distended lips. It was sapling beech and mountain cherry, maple and pine, red and black, carefully stunted to lend the illusion of space. At the verges of the chamber a stand of two-meter bamboo seemed to blend into a panoramic photograph of lordly guardian evergreens, and beyond and blue rose the toothed peaks of the Chūgoku, the Chinese range, which was the spine of the tail of the mutant fox Honshū.

Directly across from the hatch rose a mountain modest but well formed and green: Takara-yama, the Fortunate Mountain, guardian of Yoshimitsu-no-Shiro, the castle of the Yoshimitsu, which this view had surrounded before the castle's last lord made of it and him a green glass crater.

Japanese, Ito saw it all in one stroke, with the heart.

She turned to Nagaoka and sobbed, and clung.

When she was done she pulled away, her face pink-mottled and moist, her glasses steamed from the room's humidity. "I'm sorry. I don't know what happened to me."

Nagaoka smiled. He took her arm once more, urged her forward. When the hatch slid to behind them it continued the view, sealed the illusion as they walked into a microcosm of Japan.

21

"Lieutenant."

Nikki paused, let her foot drop back to the floor. The boot halfway pulled on thumped on the skinny carpet. "MUSASHI," she said, "let me ask you something, or something of you. I'm a person, not what I do, and I have names rather than titles. My friends and employees call me a lot of things, my enemies a few more. So, could you take your pick from those? Or make up your own? If you insist on formality, *Ms.* won't do me any damage modern medicine won't handle."

"Some of your teammates call you Six. That is military-communications jargon referring to rank, is it not?"

She sighed. "It's the call sign for a unit commander, yeah. Now, why don't you tell me *who* in this Unit calls me that? You're a computer, after all; you should be good at that sort of thing."

It was a dorm cubicle she shared with the air. Mistral had been laid down to handle a lot more traffic than had come through since this stretch of Med coast had turned into no-man's-land after Nice. A lot of staff had wandered off to get sucked into the whirlpool of EuroWar; the Moonies had gotten their pick of living quarters, and didn't have to double unless they felt the urge.

Aside from paintsticking white over the ghastly green pastel

shade the room had come in—a relic of pre-War Three er-
gonomics—Nik hadn't done much to personalize the place.
She had put her picture of Josey, her mother, when she still
had her hair long, on the red plastic-looking side table. Her
other photograph she was leaving for the moment in the bulletproof locket hanging over her sternum.

"The people who address you as Six," MUSASHI said,
"are, within the limits of my sample, the eight who are former members of the First Platoon, Delta Company, of First
Battalion, Fourteenth Regiment, Fourth Division, United
States Army. And I am *not* a computer, any more than you
are this room you occupy, Ms. de la Luna."

Nikki blinked. "Point to you. You actually managed to
sound testy there. I'm impressed."

"I am a sentient being, possessed of a complement of
emotions at least as rich and complex as your own. I admit
that in 'sounding testy,' as you put it, I am affecting human
mannerisms to facilitate communication. Perhaps you would
prefer a voice devoid of inflection and individuality, like an
artificial intelligence without a pseudopersonality subroutine?"

"Whoa, whoa. I don't mean to trample your feelings; I
still haven't sorted out what they are. I don't know what's
appropriate for—for a program that thinks and feels. It's not
something I have a lot of experience with, even if I guess I
am one of the few people who has any with it at all. But I
don't believe in gratuitously pissing people off or hurting their
feelings, whether they're employers or not. So I retract anything I said which offended you, and will try to do better in
the future. Okay?"

"Thank you. There is no harm done, Ms. de la Luna."

"Nicole. Can you manage Nicole?"

Pause. "Very well . . . Nicole."

"That's very good." She picked up her foot and started
pulling her boot on again. "Now, I hope what you had on
your mind wasn't too urgent, like we're under attack or anything."

"No. In fact, I only wished to talk to you."

"About—?"

Another pause, longer. "About . . . not about anything. Never mind. I am sorry—"

Nikki sighed and dropped her foot again. "Hold it, hold it. Can you give me a picture or something? I feel weird talking to the air like this."

The cee-squared promptly lit with the same image that had greeted her in the Techniques in Paris. "I refrained from establishing two-way video with your private quarters. It seemed intrusive."

"Well, it's always good to knock. Do you have another face? No offense, but I'm not real comfortable talking to a cartoon."

"Oh. I am sorry."

The image crystallized. Became the human face the animated one had caricatured. Nikki drew back a fraction, blinked.

"Is this better?"

"I'm impressed. You look perfectly natural. You're very pretty."

"Thank you. I created this self-image to be pleasing to humans."

"Please you?" Nikki asked, finally getting her boot on and sealed.

The face onscreen hesitated, nodded.

"That's what matters. How'd you turn out female, anyway? Your father was male—got to be a different way of putting that—and you have a brother, I gather."

"Yes. I don't really know why I think of myself as female. I don't, always. Do you want to see what I look like male?"

"Sure." She pulled on a polygraph armor jerkin and started buttoning her parka over it.

"Nice," she told the masculine image. "I've always been intrigued by Asian men. Never gotten together with any, though." She grinned. "Wish you were real; believe it."

"Do you want me to stay this way?"

"Rather you'd be a woman," Nikki said. "Never been fond of encouraging itches I can't scratch, you know?"

MUSASHI seemed about to say something, but instead shifted back to female. "Are you getting ready to go somewhere?"

Nikki was checking the pilot lights on her box magazines. They were fully charged, ready to power the rotary's initiator. The rifle's backup battery likewise showed full.

"Sentry go," she said, slinging the weapon.

"But you're the commander. Do you have to stand watch too?"

"Not all the time. I don't like to come off as if I'm a superior order of being just because I'm boss of the outfit, so I take my turn semi-regularly unless the situation won't permit it. Besides, I want to check out the remote-sensor zone Malko and Waldrop set up around the perimeter. There's a lot of ground here for fifty-eight women and men to secure."

"You don't like Mr. Waldrop, do you?"

She paused in the act of pulling on a glove, cocked an eyebrow. "Rob's an asshole. But he's good; tube artillery, engineering, some electronics. I don't insist on loving everybody in the unit, if they know their work and don't make life unbearable for anybody else. That's the only way the two of them get along, you know, when they're tied up together in something technical. Otherwise they're opposites: the Common Man versus the Rebel Without a Cause."

"I recognize the title of a James Dean motion picture. Has 'the Common Man' a similar referent?"

"Robert Bolt, *A Man for All Seasons*. I played one of sainted Sir Thomas's daughters in drama club, year I had a scholarship to Sandia Prep. Drama coach's husband kept trying to grab at my tits, until I caught him with a right hook. Buggerim-up-im my hand pretty well; I was just a kid, and hadn't learned you don't hit people in the head without a blunt instrument. Not exactly objective—the play, I'm talking about now. Real Tom More was a heretic hunter who needed what he got, which was to have his head decoupled."

She set her helmet on the dresser and leaned back against it. "And how did you happen to get the idea Waldrop and I aren't in love? Been getting inquisitive, have we?"

The image dropped her eyes and did a better than passable job of blushing. "I—sometimes I listen, when you're all talking in the commissary or the gym. I have no wish to intrude. If you wish—"

Nikki held up a hand. "I'm willing to trust your discretion as to what's public and what's not. You do understand that if you deliberately pop anybody's privacy, we walk."

"I do."

Nik shrugged. "That's it, then." She leaned over the bed, snapped shut the cover of her notebook computer, zipped it in her light ruck, which she shrugged on.

"Otherwise, if you feel like talking to somebody, just say hello. If you feel like continuing this conversation"—she put on her helmet and tapped it next to her ear—"you can splice yourself into our circuit and keep talking to me."

"You really mean that?"

"Sure. I'll tell you to clear the line if I have to."

"MUSASHI-san. Yo! Anybody home?"

She jumped up off the sun-warm boulder and spun. It was the strange half-foreign *bonze*, with his Nipponese eyes and great pumpkin *kokujin* head, striding across her clearing with his staff in his hand.

"How dare you?" She felt her being clench.

The killing rage had never come to her. Her father had felt it, she knew from the reminiscences he had transmitted to his offspring in the milliseconds before his thermonuclear *seppuku*. He felt it when he took vengeance upon those who had murdered his mother/lover and his lord. The violence it evoked had not discriminated; he felt no shame for the men he had made his targets, but for the innocents he had killed and maimed in getting at them. That shame had been a major factor in his choice not to escape the final trap he had set his foes.

It had not come to MUSASHI. She had killed, when she ran *Zanzara* into the shuttle named Death. But that had been an act of desperation, flailing defense of *uchi* and self as her brother's dataplane onslaught swamped her. Even when she had met her brother's quasi-living assassins her main motivation had been fear.

But it came to her now, crashing in like lava. She was afraid, too. Not even her brother could penetrate the wards she'd surrounded this place with since his earlier visit; it was guarded like the Hidden Fortress that was the *Encyclopedia Universalis*. But her primary sense was outrage. Her center had been violated.

But it was still her center, center of her strength. She summoned forces to aid her. The subroutines gathered to her call, shaping themselves to her unconscious desire.

She rose into a sky gone black and masked with lightning craqueleur, hair floating from her head in a fury's nimbus.

The intruder tucked his staff between upper arm and chest and applauded. "That's very nice. I'm impressed."

"How dare you?" she repeated, and her voice was thunder. Layer by layer, mechanism appeared from the air of the clearing, sheathing her nakedness in powered armor.

When it was done she rode a giant robot twenty meters high. His right hand was a mailed fist, a multibarreled rocket launcher was his left. There were solid-fuel boosters upon his feet. White he was, and blue and red.

MUSASHI occupied the neckless head, shielded by metal-impregnated Lexan a third of a meter thick. She looked pissed.

"Far *out*," the black-and-wheat *bonze* said. "Beats the entire ass off Mazinger B."

MUSASHI's head of fury faltered; she hadn't actually realized she could do *this*. The sight of the unspeakable *tanin* down there mocking her from the *midst of her own clearing* jogged it into motion again.

"Intruder!" she screamed, her voice reverberating to the unseen boundaries of the pocket universe, magnified by the suit. She pointed her right arm, hand bent down; the robot imitated her. A laser lanced red from a projector in the wrist.

The *bonze* pivoted. The beam gouged turf behind him.

MUSASHI paused, willed the beam on again, sweeping it toward the stranger, burning a black arroyo across the clearing. When it reached him the priest flickered and then turned all to mirror.

Trees exploded in steam and splinters as the beam glanced randomly away.

The beam died. Fury rising, MUSASHI raised her other hand. The priest's quicksilver brightness faded as she launched a salvo of rockets at him.

His staff a blur, he parried them. They made various explosions.

With an inchoate sound of rage MUSASHI lunged forward. Her augmented hand reached out to seize and crush.

The priest sidestepped with agility that belied what a Westerner would have termed his paunch and a Japanese a well-developed *hara*. He caught an articulation of the robot's forefinger, pivoted gracefully, pulling, a simple *aikido* turn, helping MUSASHI along the path she'd chosen.

After fifty meters of smashing trees and branches that squeaked like fingernails on steel the robot came to rest, more or less on its back. MUSASHI blinked up at a roiling, clotted sky. She was stunned. She still didn't know how much—call it psychosomatic—damage she could sustain in her analogue fantasy world. At the very least the course of events had taken the wind from her.

She became aware of rapping. The intruder stood on the upturned glacis of the robot's breastplate, knocking on the canopy.

"Clearly, apologies are called for, MUSASHI-san," he said, straightening. "Please accept mine. I had no idea you would react so strongly. Tact ain't my strong suit."

She set her mouth. The killing rage had forsaken her.

She could no longer imagine what had made her respond as she had. She felt very small, very foolish. Very young.

"I am sorry also. This is my private place. It—upset—me to see you here."

"Obviously." He swept a hand around. Where she lay she could see little; since she encompassed all of this she cheated her viewpoint upward to take in the larger picture. Imagining a hawk circling overhead, whose puzzled eyes she borrowed—just to keep playing by the self-imposed rules of her game.

Tears started. Takara-yama's green flank looked as if it had been hit by a meteorite shower. *What have I done to my special place?*

"Maybe this isn't a high point for either of us," the yellow-robed stranger said. "I went overboard to make a point; you flew off in all directions. Why don't you come out of that can and let's get to know each other?"

22

Overhead the clouds were dissolving. It came to her that he would leave if she asked him. The knowledge inflated her shame at her tantrum. But her curiosity was awake now, and wouldn't rest or allow her to until she knew how he had invaded her sanctuary and why.

The hinged top of the canopy swung open with an unconsciously verisimilitudinous hiss of air. She unfastened the safety straps her AI servants had provided her with, eeled from the conformal seat. She hesitated a moment before emerging, thought a simple white shift about her body. Japanese lacked body modesty, and in fact she lacked a body. But there seemed to be a point of principle here, even if she couldn't have articulated it.

She seated herself on the flat breastplate slope with her elbows inside her knees and her face in her hands. "Look," she said, "why are you bugging me?"

"You seem like a nice kid. I'd like to see you realize your potential. Damn, I hate to start sounding like a self-help huckster from the Double Cross. It's true, all the same."

She cocked her head. "Why should you care about me?"

"Like I say, you're a nice kid. Also a very powerful one." He looked right at her, and his gaze seemed to penetrate the Maya web she had woven to the core of her.

"We run in the same neighborhood, MUSASHI-san. It's been messed up more than enough already. My big motive is self-defense; don't want you trashing the place because you don't know how to handle what you've got."

"You are a meddlesome old fool."

He rolled his head back like a big ball and laughed. "Yeah. That's true too. But one who'd like to be your friend. *Especially* now I've seen firsthand what you can do when you're mad."

She winced. She had obligingly provided an all too explicit example of how restrained she was in the use of her powers. It had amounted to nothing: a petulant child kicking toys around her room.

But in the outer world, the "real" world, her subroutines gave her powers infinitely greater than those of the make-believe *anime* robot they'd built for her here.

The *bonze* grinned his jack-o'-lantern grin. "Looks like you're already starting to pick up on one of the lessons I was hoping to teach you. Okay. No point rubbing your nose in it any more. May I?"

She frowned, not getting what he was driving at. "Go ahead," she said, knowing embarrassment might have pushed her to foolish trust.

He swept billows of sleeves up flabby arms. Glancing once to make sure she was watching, he raised his staff and swept it from left to right.

Where it passed the clearing was made whole. The charred trenches that split the clearing vanished. The shattered trees stood undamaged.

He nodded. "There. Back the way it was, or close enough for government work."

He looked down at her again, did a take, shied away, eyes wide. "Girl, what is with you? You're *white*."

She blinked at him, then glanced down at herself. Hands and legs were the color of virgin rice paper. Absolutely void of color.

"I've read that of humans, that they go white when they

are shocked. My subroutines read my emotion and made me this way. I try to be as much like a real person as I can. Sometimes I don't do so well."

"You do fine, honey." He hunkered down beside her. "And don't ever talk that way. You're just as much a person as anybody ever lived. But what was it spooked you?"

"The way you healed my clearing."

"What? Wasn't so much. You could have done it solving a million-term polynomial."

"But *you* did it. I thought—somebody told me only my brother and I could do that sort of thing."

"Who told you a thing like that?"

"A head."

He slapped his knee. "Who-*ee*. Haven't heard anybody called that since 1975. It's true what they say: everything comes back in style. Wish I'd kept my tie-dye elephant bells."

He jumped to the ground. "Need a hand?"

"No, thank you." She stepped off into space and floated down beside him. "What will you do about this?"

"The robot?" He shrugged. "Leave him. He's too neat to erase. Kind of a unique terrain feature, don't you think? Conversation piece. Give the little analog squirrels and stuff someplace to live."

He started walking upslope, along what had been the path of destruction left by the robot as it traveled the other way. Now it was no more than a game trail. She followed.

"If I was in your shoes, if you were wearing shoes, Ms. MUSASHI," he said, "I'd give a lot of thought to just what I was, and what I could do. Now, your little performance here this afternoon—afternoon somewhere; got to be—if I were to bet you had no idea you could do that, would I lose money?"

It took her a moment to untangle his syntax. She wasn't sure she liked him, but for some reason she trusted him. It might only have been that Japanese habit Nagaoka spoke of, the reflex of doing nothing and hoping for the best.

She shook her head. Since she only pretended for the

game's sake that she could only "see" from her eyes it did not occur to her that he might not perceive the gesture occurring behind his left shoulder. He did.

"What I thought. Isn't it maybe time you got yourself a handle on what you do, rather than just wishing something and letting the little AI gnomes scurry around making it so? Earth's a mighty fragile basket, like Mr. Heinlein said, and it's had more than a few eggs knocked out of it of late. Seems to me you stand a chance of giving it a good kick yourself, accidental-like. Unless you understand yourself a whole lot better."

She felt heat rising like blood in her face, because she had read that humans do. "I am MUSASHI, and I will have you know—" she began.

The mountainside flickered. Just for a moment, it was the shattered, smoking wreck it had been moments ago. Then all was peaceful and perfect again.

"—that you are right," she finished.

They were in the clearing again, at the foot of the boulder outcrop. The *bonze* turned and pointed his staff at the crater glinting dull green in the light of the false sun, down in the valley.

"Your dad let things get away from him. Don't end up like that, girl."

He started to walk away. Questions bubbled inside her: *Who are you? How do you know so much about me, my clan?*

What she asked was, "Are you my friend?"

He stopped. "You got to work that out for yourself. One final word of advice: be awful slow to trust anybody who gives you a different answer to that question."

He had not turned. He began to walk again. "Wait! How do I get in touch with you?"

"Think of me," he said, "and I'll be around."

She beat her fists on her thighs. "*Ohh.* Don't be so mystical. What's your name?"

He halted, looked back, fingering his chin. Smiling maddeningly.

"You're the ghost of Fred," she blurted.

He laughed. "You're good, girl. Way good." He went down the mountainside with sunlight dappling him like *maki-e* lacquerware. Diminished.

Left.

As she did in times of uncertainty, MUSASHI swam.

She had overreacted to the collapse of the U.K. segment of the Reef, perhaps; after all, she was personally involved. But the waters were murky around the world, and the gaps in what had been vital, brightly colored structures grew larger and blacker daily, progressing like decay through a tooth.

The Reef was dying. She was still convinced of that.

She thought of what the *bonze* had said. He seemed aware of the Reef's deterioration, though he hadn't mentioned it directly; his concern that she not damage it, nor the exterior world, was evidence of that.

But it was a comment he had made on the fly that fixed her attention. She had already searched out the reference, had found the sentiment repeated and reechoed in the memories passed on like DNA by her father.

Her brother chided her for irresponsibility. So did the *bonze*, in his own way. She would take responsibility, then.

Dr. O'Neill had had a dream; so had her father. Michiko-sama had shared it. None of them had gotten a chance to pursue it.

Now it was hers. She already had some of the means of realizing it.

She dove deep through cool water flavored with an omnipresent taint.

"I thought Morgan was supposed to be coming over to see you," Sammi said. She was a skinny, sad woman in her twenties with lank blond hair and a scar down the side of her nose where her left nostril had been slit open. The pimp who'd given her the scar had made the mistake of laying hands on Nikki de la Luna in Nice just before the mercenaries' revolt. After Nikki shot him through the head, Sammi attached herself to Moon Unit. Her words ran each other up the walls of the vehicle assembly building like squirrels.

They were walking the cement-floored nave of a cathedral of mechanism: Gothic spires of boosters, lifting-delta shuttles like streamlined Romanesque façades, titanium-gleaming flying buttresses the gantries, and altars the cradles on which they were miraculously joined into one body capable of making the big jump to O. Earnest as hierophants, wearing color-coded jumpsuits the robes of their orders, the techs moved among them, ministering.

"Something intervened," Nikki said. "Little matter of World War Four, you know."

"That was a while back, kid," Alexia said, sauntering along with her hands in the pockets of her off-duty jeans. "There's a lot of holes in the Net, but he still could have found a terminal to tell you why he hasn't shown."

"If he cared," Sammi added.

If he's still alive. There. I've thought it. "Step it down, 'Lexa. I'm not in the mood."

Alexia shrugged. She was a long, slim-muscled woman with short brown hair brushed forward over features cut a touch too sharply. She came from a tough Polish neighborhood in Pittsburgh. She was a sniper—actually trained by the U.S. Army as one, back when the American military's policy toward its female draftees fluctuated from hour to hour. She was a fairly good friend—most of the time.

"He's found somebody else," Sammi said. "Men always do that."

Alexia laughed. "You're a real subtle one, Sammi. Takes some of the fun out of the *game*, you know?"

They had reached one end of the vast building, where three unsealed booster tubes lay side by side, looking like parts of Godzilla's own Habitrail.

"I think the game is overrated," Nikki said.

Sammi was about to say something. Nikki knew that once

it was out she was going to have to burn a lot of metabolic energy to keep from hitting her. If she gave in it would be child abuse.

"Nicole?" MUSASHI's inhumanly perfect soprano said inside Nikki's head. Nikki waved to Sammi to shut up.

"I'm here." She didn't have to say the words aloud, just subvocalized for the microphone discreetly taped to her larynx. "What's on your mind?"

"I have additional work I would like you and your unit to perform," MUSASHI said diffidently, "if you wouldn't mind. There would be additional pay, of course."

Nikki felt herself grinning as if her head would split. "Something to get us out of this freezing swamp? That would probably kill us."

Silence. "Oh. I apologize for making the suggestion—"

"I'm *kidding*, for God's sake," Nikki said out loud. Then, subvocalizing again, "I should try to be more careful. I forget sometimes you don't have more experience with people. It's a little startling; you do have just about all the knowledge there is."

"Forgive me if I seem to contradict, Nicole, but there is a crucial difference between having access to knowledge and *knowing* it. Envision yourself keyed into the *Encyclopedia Universalis*. The information there is available, but not yet in your mind."

"Yeah." She looked at her companions. Alexia was leaning back against a little squatty utility vehicle—Mitsubishi; apparently the favored status of the combine which built Mistral exempted it from prewar French import controls—with her arms crossed and a sleepy-sardonic look. Sammi was pouting. Her scar was purpled, which meant she hadn't gotten everything out of her system.

"I have to say having somebody apologize for contradicting me is a refreshing experience," she said aloud. "So where's the gig?"

"The stars, Nicole."

THE
CHILDREN'S
CRUSADE

PART THREE

23

Earth's newest moon looked to Nagaoka Hiroshi's eyes like nothing so much as a tomato can. It affronted him that he could summon no more poetic a comparison. Perhaps with a certain amount of intellectual effort he could have concocted something suitable. But the Japanese way was to see with the heart, and to his heart *Phoenix* was a can.

There was beauty in the image that filled one bulkhead of his *shoin:* the waning moon like a misshapen silver medallion; the smooth arc of Hope Station, the big slow Soviet wheel that was the first in space; the constant swimming activity that surrounded the ship like dust motes in a shaft of afternoon light, the crystalline blue and red scintillas of laser hand cutters, dramatic flash and flare of sublimated metal as free-floating computer-driven mirrors briefly focused sunlight to weld a section in place.

Most beautiful, to Nagaoka, was what the image signified, and his own role in it. Contemplating that, he could forgive himself even a deficiency of poetry.

The door annunciator chimed for his attention. "Come in," he said, and turned.

A Silver tech entered, dropped to knees on the tatami, lowered her forehead to the mat. Nagaoka inclined himself politely forward.

"Oyabun," she said. Nagaoka smiled into his beard. It had been Inja-san's notion to hang the title on him. "Please come. Yukiko's cousin is on the television."

His eyebrows rose. He could have ordered one of MU-SASHI's subroutines to bring the feed to his own screen. The thought didn't occur to him. He stood.

"Thank you, Tomita-san. I'm on my way."

Much of the microcosmic community of the Floating World was crowded into the *kotatsu* common room, including a pair of the Hungarian orbital-hydroponics specialists conducting experiments inboard. The crew did not overtly acknowledge Nagaoka's presence, but politely made him way.

It was an English-language Netfeed from Shantou. An Aussie was interviewing a half-dozen Japanese rescued from a fishing boat drifting south of the Nansei Shoto by a Free Chinese corvette. The camera switched to a gaunt-cheeked man with rabbit incisors and one glazed eye.

"Look, Nagaoka-sama, it is my cousin Taro," squealed a female Red tech. Nagaoka smiled, but raised a hand for silence.

"—plague in Nagoya, where we set out from. People said a thousand were dying every day. More."

"Yes," said the man next to him. "The authorities have been burning corpses outside town. You can't sleep at night for the stink, and no matter how you scrub, you can't get rid of the greasy feeling from the ash."

"What about the, ah, the confiscations?" the interviewer asked. It took the translator a moment to get the question across, but when she did the refugees all started talking at once.

"Yes, they're taking everything!" "They just come into your house at any time, take away cee-squared units, microwaves, even radios and electric razors—" "Just like the *Taikō*'s Sword Hunt!"

"We no longer are allowed even heat or running water," cousin Taro concluded glumly. "People are starving, and the ones thrown out of work by the confiscations and closings are being herded out into the country to work the rice paddies. We were lucky to get away!"

The feed went on to reports of a series of smashing victories the Russian Christian Federated Socialist Republic was claiming over the New Red Army in the western Ukraine. Nobody paid any attention. Those claims had been made before, even if there hadn't been more important matters on hand.

"The world is falling apart," Tomoyama Isao said. "We are fortunate to be above it, and safe."

Nagaoka smiled, fingering the white scar that ran down his cheek and into his beard. Tomoyama had grown so good at reading him he no longer had to show any sign at all for his aide to know what he was thinking.

How funny, he thought. *In the old days when I was ineffectual, I tried to do too much. Now I hardly do anything at all, and they think me strong and wise.* He had Tomoyama to thank for much of that.

"What of Japan?" someone wailed. "What of the Home Islands?"

Tomoyama looked to Nagaoka. "Japan is here," Tomoyama said.

"Ah, yes," someone else said jokingly, "we're an extra island: Kyūshū, Shikoku, Honshū, Hokkaidō, and UKIYO."

There was nervous laughter. Everyone assumed the NHK links showing the Islands to be more happy, prosperous, healthy, and orderly than ever before to be lies. But this was the first direct evidence of the situation to come out since HIDETADA had sealed the nation fifteen months before, with a completeness his namesake could scarcely have dreamed of.

Though there was pressing business to attend to, he remained in the *kotatsu* until the fragile mood passed and the crowd began to break up. As he left, Dr. Ito Emiko fell into step beside him.

"You were pleased by the newscast," she accused

when they were out of earshot of anybody else.

He said nothing. "Much as I hate to stand upon it, we *are* Japanese," she said.

"Japan is becoming another Cambodia, thanks to HIDE-TADA."

"That's irrelevant. We are still Japanese." She stopped and looked at him through narrowed eyes. Like him, she had begun wearing contacts. "We are still people of Earth."

"We must become an *uchi*," he said. "More than ever before." And he walked on and left her.

The nighttime wind was edged with the chill of yet-un-melted snows as it rushed through the foothills overlooking the confluence of the Saône and Rhône rivers, charging through the encampment first from one direction and then another. Raymond of Tours stood holding an old Hungarian army officer's greatcoat around his burly shoulders watching his architects try to get their drawings to lie flat on a large table by the light of alcohol lanterns.

He smiled as an aide cursed the wind. "We should be thankful, instead, that it blows from the west, not east from the Alps." In truth he found the wind invigorating, intoxicating with its wine chill and undercurrent of nascent green. That wind promised spring, as their undertaking this night promised spring for all humankind.

At last the architects got the drawings to stay put with the help of lumps of schist at the corners. They turned to Raymond.

"We have questions regarding your plans for the New Jerusalem, your, ahh—" They glanced at each other in confused dismay; none would meet the others' eyes. This was their first time in the Presence.

Brother Raymond studied them a moment under raised eyebrows. The lanternlight flickered sinuously over the surface of his eyes.

"You may address me in any way you like," he said.

"Brother Raymond, Brother Raymond. Only never, please, as *monsieur*; I am no one's lord and only One deserves that title."

The bearded lips smiled. "If you find yourself at a loss, gentle friends, 'hey you' will suffice. We are all of us Saints. Good intentions are taken for granted."

The architects smiled back, relieved and still slightly dubious. "B-brother Raymond," the one who had spoken said. He was a short, square man with a squint and a Dutch accent. "We have attempted to design the Holy City in accordance with Chapter Twenty-one of the Book of Revelations. Yet we encounter difficulties.

"The twelve gates present no great problem. Nor do the twelve foundations, since the prophecy requires only that they be *garnished* with jasper, chalcedony, sapphire, and so forth. But, si—Brother, *walls* of jasper? A *city* of 'pure gold, like unto clear glass'?"

"And the size," a tall, balding Pole said. "Walls a hundred and forty-four cubits high we can do; that comes roughly to seventy-two meters. But according to Verse Sixteen the walls are to measure twelve thousand furlongs in length. Our best research puts a furlong at just over one hundred seventy-seven meters. Whether the Scripture refers to the length of a single side of the square or the entire perimeter, we confess we cannot tell. But it scarcely matters; either way it comes to upward of twenty-one hundred *kilometers*."

A man stepped into the circle of lanternlight, seemingly to materialize from the dark just behind Raymond's shoulder. He had a narrow domed head fringed with lank hair, an ascetic's gaunt face, a fanatic's dark eyes.

"Why do you trouble the Elder Brother, caviling over details?" he asked. His voice was Austrian, sibilant and menacing as a whip. The architects cringed back from him visibly. He was almost as well known as Raymond, and rather more notorious: before his conversion he had been Assistant Police President of the EuroFront. Political Section.

"With respect, Eminence," the Pole said, "building a wall twenty-one hundred kilometers long is more than a *detail*."

"All things are possible to us," Saul Cardinal Heinrici said. When Innocent XIV had made submission to Raymond in the ruins of the Vatican, one of his gifts had been the red hat for the prophet's chief disciple. "Or do you doubt that we are truly Saints?"

The Pole went white. Raymond laughed, touched his aide on the arm. "Easy. Go easy, my friend. The gold referred to in the Revelation is spiritual gold; are not even brick, stone, and cement purified when worked by the hands of those redeemed by Christ's sweet blood? As for the dimensions of the wall—"

He shrugged off his coat and tossed it to a youthful attendant. "We are living in Grace, my friends; we are to have reward on earth as well as in heaven. The Virgin intends us to work with what we have and not trouble ourselves with what we cannot achieve. If the walls of the New Jerusalem are not so grand at first as those foreseen by John, what of this? We have a millennium to achieve perfection."

Ignoring the cold, he rolled up the flannel sleeves of his shirt and bent over the table. "Now, let's see what we have here."

24

The gelding grunted with every long running stride. Its un-shod hooves plashed loudly in the water, throwing a chill brackish spray into Nikki's face and turning her jeans and windbreaker into a fair semblance of the camouflage she wore on maneuver through these same marshes. Each hoofbeat sent a shock up her spine. She was not a formal rider; she rode cowboy-style, rough and ready and geared toward staying in the saddle no matter what, just as she'd learned summering with friends on a cattle ranch outside Los Lunas, south of Albuquerque.

She rode at a wild pace across the huge Mistral reservation while the sun mounted a cold white sky. Eventually the rhythmic jolting and forced drafts of cool air heavy with the smells of mud and sea relaxed her. She laughed aloud. The wind of her passage whipped the sound away.

When she felt the beast begin to tire beneath her she steered it up a low hummock held together by the roots of high grass beginning to green with spring. It stood blowing as she slid out of the saddle. She let the reins fall. The horse was a scrubby off-white creature that bore resemblance but no relationship to the fabled wild horses of the Camargue—most of which had several years ago been removed to a pre-serve in Holland by another twitch of PanEuropean policy.

She slipped her rotary from the scabbard before stretching out on the cool, sandy earth. PanEurope and EuroFront alike had virtually been chased from the mainland by the New Millennium; marauding Young Saint bands had so far steered clear of the marshlands, though Mistral lay not far from the site of the nascent New Jerusalem. HIDETADA had taken no direct action against the facility since Moon Unit had wiped out a twenty-man commando of mostly Israeli mercs who had tried infiltrating by night in rubber rafts almost a year ago. Still, she never strayed far from her weapon. That was basic to her being by now.

Laying the rifle nearby, she laced her hands behind her head and stared up at the sky. The high haze was bright enough to hurt.

It was strange to think how she had gotten here. Moon Unit had comprised sixty-two half-starved refugees from PanEurope and the Front alike when MUSASHI hired them. Now seven more were dead, and another ten had quit, and the remainder were rich, though the rest of the world was going pretty expeditiously to hell.

Rich by reason of the shares MUSASHI had paid them in her crazy, visionary venture. To finance her dream MUSASHI had begun brokering the staple of the computer age: information. Her unique command of the Net enabled her to discover who had high-tech tools—or better, the means to make them—and who needed them.

Rich for what good it did them. The old fantasies of technological collapse in the wake of Armageddon were belatedly coming true. Not because some psychic EMP had wiped knowledge of science and technics from the minds of the survivors—or even databases, since most computerized information was stored in nonvolatile media before there *were* any EMPs. Rather because the surviving governments of the world, from fragmentary nation-states to militant city councils, were busy suppressing technology as fast as they could, with at least tacit support from the surviving population. That was what made the knowledge MUSASHI traded in so valuable. It also meant the places and groups she linked together in a trade network resembled islands slowly eroding into a rising flood.

The sound came up through the earth, up through Nikki's buttocks and shoulders. She sat up, shaking long near-black hair from her eyes and looking off to the southwest. A shuttle was lifting, rising toward *Phoenix*, taking shape in its low orbit.

She watched, entranced, not looking directly at the fusion-heated exhaust plume as the rocket made the change from *up* to *over*, burning a hole through the overcast. There was the real payoff for her, if she chose to accept.

A ticket to the stars.

"I am displeased," said the man who knelt on the dais. "These reports from China can only foster resistance to my program."

Peter Mordant winced, trying to get comfortable. The floor was too hard on his knees, the tatami mat was thin as toilet paper, his coat and trousers bound abominably, and his high collar cut into his neck. It seemed unfair to suffer discomfort in the not-world of Kliemann rapport, but his *Doppelgänger* was as faithful a representation of his *Gestalt* as HIDETADA could create.

HIDETADA had offered to rearrange his dataplane persona so he did not experience discomfort. Mordant declined, and tried to hide his horror at the thought. He might have accepted HIDETADA as his master, but he still felt a crawling fear every time the gleaming dome of the Coil descended on his head and he felt himself subsumed into the vastness which was the sentient program. The thought of HIDETADA altering him, *editing* him . . .

"Perhaps you could conquer a few more countries, lord," said the samurai who stood with one split-toed *tabi* propped insolently on the low platform, "if you enjoy the sensations of seizing sand castles even as the tide comes in."

Mordant felt his cheeks tighten. HIDETADA allowed his creature too much familiarity.

"It's the Net, HIDETADA-sama," he said, ignoring Muroto's gibe. "Its very existence negates everything you've done to centralize political power and the control of technology. It's a nutrient bath for anarchy. You have the means to destroy it; I urge you to do so."

"Perhaps you should be cautious in advising the fouling of the ocean in which we all swim," Muroto said.

"I at least exist outside it," Mordant said.

"I find the Net's continued existence useful for the moment," HIDETADA said. "Except in Japan, it is not my aim to expunge technology; merely to confine it to responsible hands. Remember that my sister remains the foremost obstacle to achieving a rational and compassionate world order."

As far as Mordant was concerned, HIDETADA was frankly cracked on the subject of what he quaintly termed his "sister." He had grown steadily more obsessive about his rival over the last two years. Alpha Project—Mordant's personal escape hatch from mortality—had been forced to go begging. Even HIDETADA's grandiose dream of creating his own successor had been shunted aside by his fixation on the MUSASHI threat.

But here HIDETADA constituted the very matrix of which his thoughts were formed. He kept his mind a careful blank.

"In fact I find I must tread a careful line between leaving too much in the hands of the unworthy, and leaving myself too few tools to work with," HIDETADA said. "Sometimes it seems almost as if I am losing ground to my sister."

"You do yourself too little credit, lord," Mordant said. "You have brought much-needed order to those countries you have taken under your benign supervision."

"Of course, in many of those countries our efforts at con-

trol have brought only shortages, unrest, and finally collapse
into a situation I confess I have trouble discerning from anarchy," Muroto murmured. "Whereas those areas where your
sister holds sway tend to prosper."

"HIDETADA-sama, how can you let him say these
things?" Mordant demanded in outrage. "How can you
countenance such disloyalty?"

"I created Muroto for a specific purpose," HIDETADA
said through taut lips. "He serves that purpose well."

The concept came into Mordant's mind of the *nightingale
floor*, used in Japanese castles to prevent intrusion: planks
cunningly warped so as to squeak beneath unwary feet. The
thought might have come of its own accord. It also might
not. He decided to keep his feet wary.

He turned to the samurai. "You permit yourself to be
blinded by mere material considerations, Muroto-san," he said
reproachfully.

"I prefer to think of them as practicalities."

"Our master serves principle here. Difficulties have arisen
with our projects in certain areas"—a diffident glance toward
HIDETADA, brooding with his chin sunk in rich brocaded
robes—"but they are surely temporary. The precepts of scientific planning will prevail. In the long run—"

"In the long run, we're all dead," Muroto said, worrying
his lower teeth with a toothpick, "as a *gaijin* once said who
thought a good deal like you. Our lord expects results in a
finite span."

"You're not even *real*," Mordant shouted at him. "You're
the image of a long-dead actor, playing a character who never
was!"

Muroto Hambei laughed. "How ironic, then, that I must
provide our master with the voice of reality."

"I have decided," HIDETADA said, as if the exchange
between the two had never taken place, "that the time has
arrived to take more direct action against my sister. That
European option you discovered, Muroto-san; I had not con-

sidered it before. It opens intriguing possibilities."

"Europe?" Mordant's eyebrows rose. "Europe is a nightmare, complete disorder. The only thing approaching central authority is the New Church. How can sentient software work with people who hate all technology?"

Muroto laughed. HIDETADA looked sorrowful.

"Doctor," he said, "I am concerned. When I recruited you I found in you a master of subtlety. Yet it seems you grow more conventional in your outlook with each passing day. Almost as if giving oneself too completely to the service of another saps initiative. . . ."

He shook his head. "A fruitless line of speculation. Do not look so glum, Doctor; your service still pleases me. For strategy I have Muroto-san."

Remember how loyal he proved in the movie, Mordant thought before he could stop himself. Feeling clammy and ill, Mordant scanned the youth's perfect face for signs he had perceived the thought.

"Reconcile your differences," HIDETADA said without changing expression. "You both will play a role. Dr. Mordant, you may leave me."

Mordant glared a final time at Muroto, abased himself, rose and straightened his coat. He walked the echoing length of the wood-vaulted hall, out the portal, across the courtyard, and through a side gate of the castle. A path led down a steep, forested mountainside. He followed it, and presently found himself back inside his own head, in his current stronghold beneath the Essex countryside northeast of London.

Richard was in her quarters when she got back, sitting in a chair depleting her brandy and listening to Brubeck. She grimaced.

"How'd it go?" she asked, gingerly hanging her jacket on a hanger. She had beaten off most of the half-dried mud outside, but she didn't want the remainder on the floor.

"Endless wrangle. Half the fools still think they'd rather concentrate on solving Earth's problems than going into space. And none of them will listen to my ideas."

Richard Lo was a tall man, an inch or two taller than Nikki, which put him just shy of six feet—like most Americans of her generation, Nikki thought using metric for anything but military or scientific purposes smacked of being an informer. He was in his early forties, a rangy racquetball kind of trim and thick black hair that he probably didn't dye, though his vanity would have been capable of it. He was one of the original Gang of Four quantum physicists whose work at the University of Jakarta was zazzing the scientific world like crystal meth until War Three eradicated the one member of the team who held the other wildly divergent personalities together.

Another member of the team was Yoshimitsu Michiko, last human head of YTC. MUSASHI had mentioned to Nikki that Michiko and he had been lovers, not realizing that it might hurt Nikki. It hadn't, as it happened. It was just one more thing she and Michiko had in common.

Nikki hoped they wouldn't wind up having too much in common. As she had gotten the story—TOKUGAWA's own recollections, fed to his children in the milliseconds before his suicide—Michiko had started out with some pretty good ethics, and then let the old, awful temptation to Do Good lead her into compromising them and getting wiped out.

Nikki had found it harder to avoid both those fates in the last two years of playing security guard and referee at Mistral than in seven years of EuroWar.

She held the jacket up in front of the shower head, sluiced the rest of the mud away, then looped the hanger over the head. "Even though you're director general?"

He laughed bitterly. "My child, if only you knew how little that counted for. Especially when it's that cybernetic plutocrat you work for who really runs the show."

A corner of her mouth quirked up. A lot of the things he

did irritated her, like the way he always turned on jazz when he came in, the one kind of music she just couldn't hack. And what she thought of as his High Church Marxism made little sense to a woman who'd spent half her life trying to avoid being ground to pulp by the various toothed wheels of the state. Their arguments were frequent and sensational.

But the way he still patronized her after all these months just amused her. She and Richard had little in common but strong minds and wills that tended to move in markedly different directions.

Little but not nothing. She took off her shirt and let it fall to the tile, eeled her jeans down her long, strong legs.

"But I suppose you'll want to rush back on duty," he called from the other room. He could be awfully transparent sometimes. He wasn't a good advertisement for the subtlety of the Chinese, but then, he'd been raised American too.

She leaned naked in the doorway and grinned at him. "Not exactly," she said.

25

"Nagaoka-san."

Nagaoka looked up from his tea. MUSASHI's image on the big screen matched the unaccustomed sharpness in her voice. It was a realistic image today, not the cartoon face she sometimes used.

"MUSASHI-san."

Tomoyama Isao touched his head to tatami and started to rise. Nagaoka held out a hand for him to stay.

"Nagaoka-san, why have you put in a requisition for ten shuttleloads of water?" the adolescent female face asked.

"It is the most basic commodity of life here in orbit as on the surface, and the most difficult to supply. The stations need it; *Phoenix* needs it. And it will keep." In the giant self-sealing polymer bags the water could orbit for years convenient to the station. He let a mild pedantic drone into his voice; she knew all this.

"They are slated for delivery to UKIYO," she said, sounding slightly uncertain of herself now. "We have sufficient water."

"For now. I am concerned for our future, MUSASHI-san."

"What is most important is the *Phoenix*."

"Indeed, MUSASHI-san. And at need we can shift bags

transorbitally to Hope Station. The Floating World is as handy a dumping point as any."

"*Phoenix* does not require so much water. Do you not recall, the plan is to pause to take on a load of water ice in the asteroids before boosting to near-light velocity?"

"I recall that as one of the options our ever-contentious friends on the surface have discussed. I also recall that carrying sufficient water either for consumption or reaction mass is a major sticking point in the project."

The *Phoenix* was a fusion-driven torchship, designed for steady one-gee acceleration. That gave a year to as close to light speed as she'd get. At near C, a magnetic ramscoop field could gather in sufficient interstellar hydrogen to provide both fuel and reaction mass. But there was the matter of accelerating to a speed at which the ram would work. And at close to the speed of light, the nearest planetary systems were a couple of years away even in compressed ship time. Supporting a large enough complement to have any hope of establishing a colony for that length of time was driving the designers crazy.

All of which was true. All of which was irrelevant.

There was a time, Nagaoka thought, *when I would have felt shame for dissembling with her.*

"I also note," MUSASHI said after a pause, "that the only personnel you have cleared for entry into UKIYO in the past six months are the current group of scientists working on life-support-related projects. Why is this, Nagaoka-san?"

Because we must become an uchi, *complete and self-contained. Because we must wean ourselves of the great blue-and-white teat of Earth. And each* tanin *who comes inboard makes that more difficult.*

"Almost all the personnel whom you've brought to orbit have been directly involved in constructing *Phoenix*, MUSASHI-san. It makes more sense for them to go to Hope, does it not?" He paused, frowned, and rubbed his beard. "And I confess, I do not find the epidemics that have been breaking out on the surface at all encouraging. Even with the medicines we have available, a contagion could do us substantial damage if it got loose."

"That seems farfetched, Nagaoka-san."

"Do you order me to bring more people inboard? I am your servant, MUSASHI-san."

She flushed. *Excellent*, he thought; he was truly proud of her.

"You are my *friend*," she said, sounding as exasperated as he'd known she would. "But you know how important this project is to me."

"I do indeed, dearest child. Are you dissatisfied with my service toward its realization?"

"No! Never think that, Nagaoka-sensei. But—" She bit her lip. "We must direct every resource to completing the project before the situation on Earth becomes completely unmanageable. And I am afraid you are too concerned with making the Floating World a separate world in all truth, cut off from Earth as much as possible."

And there it lay before them: the truth. *Namagusai*, "stinking of raw fish," crudely redolent of the bottom line.

"What is wrong with that, MUSASHI-sama?" he asked quietly. He felt Tomoyama's eyes on him like a blind man's fingers.

"Ito-san says it's unhealthy."

"Ito-san is a very wise woman. And yet—" He let the thought slide off into Japanese silence.

"I worry too, Nagaoka-san. I don't want our people cut off from home."

"This is our home."

"No! Earth is your home. Japan. This is just a temporary shelter."

"This is *your* home."

She paused. "I will not have a priesthood, Nagaoka-san."

He bowed. "I am ever obedient to your command, child."

She shook her head, and then vanished in chrysanthe-

mum bursts of color. In a moment the screen faded back into
the painted landscape.

Nagaoka stared down at his tea. It had grown tepid. He
had no taste for it.

"Tomoyama-san," he said.

"*Hai.*"

He paused, sighed.

"Sometimes it happens that a trusted servitor faces a certain dilemma: the lord directs one course when the lord's interests clearly dictate another."

He shook his head and laughed. "Such situations are good
for lots of *seppuku* in the historical dramas. Will you take more
tea?"

Raymond of Tours rested his hands on the handle of his
grounded shovel and smiled up out of the ditch at the fat,
bearded man with the microcam squatting on his shoulder
like a gargoyle.

"It's good of you to agree to answer my questions, Brother
Raymond," the reporter said.

"It is nothing, Mr. O'Hara. Like any workingman, I welcome the opportunity to lean on my shovel and chat."

Around them hundreds of men and women worked, dig-
ging the foundation trench, carting away basketloads of earth.
From time to time they glanced over curiously, then returned to their labors. Sandy O'Hara arranged a polite smile
in front of his reflexive expression of skepticism. *This is the
scoop of my career*, he thought.

He noticed one of Raymond's bodyguards with his faceplate turned toward him. The sun's reflection was an eye-
melting dot, surrounded by a galaxy of starlike glints where
the light caught the tiny metal flakes of an aventurine filter
to prevent laser blinding.

If I survive. But Raymond himself had guaranteed his
safety. Also the right to ask whatever questions he chose.

Pressures on the controller in his left hand focused the image in the tiny heads-up display projected on the right lens of his eyeglasses.

"I'm curious about your political program, Brother," he began. "Critics have called it the Holy Roman Empire warmed over."

Raymond laughed. "Holy we undoubtedly are—even as are you, my friend, and all your viewers as well. We have no pretensions to being Roman. As to being an empire—" He shrugged. "It is perhaps as good a name for a Kingdom of the Saints as any other."

"Yet as I understand it, you envision the whole as being ruled by an emperor."

"My time remaining on earth is short, Friend O'Hara; the Virgin has told me this. My primary message is spiritual. Yet this is an earthly dominion of Saints which we build here." He swept a callused hand around. "As a question of practicality I must address myself to the earthly problems of its administration."

"But an empire—?" O'Hara prodded.

Raymond waited politely until sure the reporter meant to say no more. "I envision rulership by a trinity of Pope, Emperor, and a Diet representing all the people."

"Many people find such a scheme socially regressive, to say the least."

"A century of social progressivism has brought a century of genocide and war like nothing experienced in history. Those who still wish to attempt to make such systems work are welcome to do so—elsewhere."

O'Hara glanced meaningfully at the guard standing discreetly twenty meters away, his caseless rotary-action assault rifle held with apparent casualness in gauntleted hands.

"What about freedom of conscience?" he asked.

"It is to be absolute. We are Saints, now; yet it is not impossible that some, even knowing the true path, may stray from it. That is no just concern of ours, but of the Lord's.

Augustine and Aquinas alike teach us that righteousness is meaningless in the absence of free will."

"Then why have you made the former head of the European Front's secret police your right-hand man?"

Raymond laughed again. "What we were before the Second Redemption is nothing, is meaningless. My Saul has accepted conversion. His life is made anew."

He took a handkerchief from the back pocket of his jeans and mopped his forehead. "My own orientation is spiritual. I cannot do everything, and it would manifest the sin of pride were I to attempt too much. His Eminence Cardinal Heinrici is an organizational genius. He sees to the practical side of things. As I have said, this is an earthly dominion as well as a spiritual one."

He sighed and stuck the rag back in his pocket. "You might call him my Stalin. Will you join me for lunch?"

"No thank you, Elder Brother. I'd like to get to work editing this as soon as possible." It took an act of will for O'Hara not to say something trite about a leopard and its spots. He wasn't sure it would translate to French anyway.

Later he would remember the last thing Raymond had said about his chief disciple, and wonder just how far his vision extended.

Tomoyama Isao never wanted to be a New Mandarin.

His father had grandiose schemes for him, of course. The finest education, then Tōdai, Tōkyō Imperial University, and a life in the upper tiers of the Japanese pyramid. It didn't happen. Tomoyama senior was a worker in a government construction gang, and could not afford the cramming tutors needed to get his son through the exams in Japan, in emulation of Confucian China, demanded for entry into the elite.

Isao could not have been happier. He preferred making *things* to making scrawls on paper or glowing figures on a CRT Japanese technical education was superb, and far less difficult to come by. And the younger Tomoyama had all the drive needed to be a New Mandarin, plus enormous talent at technics.

According to the New Feudal Japanese drill, Isao did follow his father into government service—but as a roboticist tech, not a high-iron jock. He even received orbital construction training, during Japan's brief governmental flirtation with space.

Then the Ministry for International Trade and Industry's star soared, eclipsing Interior, which by a twist of Japanese politics was handling space exploitation. All resources were needed for the mutually assured destruction of trade war with a belligerent United States. Tomoyama Isao wound up in a rice paddy in the north of Shikoku with twenty thousand other beached Interior techs.

He wasn't long for the mud. The YTC/Amagumo combine was hungry for O-qualified technicians. Tomoyama went back to space to help build the Floating World.

The elder Tomoyama was deeply disappointed in his son, and in himself. He had failed to secure a good future for Isao. Now his son did the same grunt work as he. Only in a different venue. Isao intended to explain it to him on his first groundside leave, how he was helping build a great future for Japan, for the world.

Before he could do that his father died, in the collapse of a *danshi* apartment block under construction. His shame became Isao's legacy: *gimu*, a debt that could not be repaid.

Tomoyama's work-gang boss, Katsuda, took him under his wing, helped him through his grief by becoming a father figure to him. As the station evolved toward completion, as the circle grew to a close, Katsuda was named chief technician. It was natural that Tomoyama should be his assistant. By then Tomoyama scarcely had an identity of his own. He exemplified *onbu*, being carried on the back like a child in its cradle board.

Just as it was natural for Katsuda-san to resent it when the *tanin* Nagaoka was brought in to run the satellite Katsuda and his children had built—a man without technical qualifications of any kind. And what Katsuda-san resented, it was Tomoyama's duty to resent a hundredfold.

The workstation was unoccupied. Not that it would have mattered; Japanese knew how to leave one another to their work. Still, for once Tomoyama was soothed by solitude.

Eventually he had discovered that one could build things as elegant and satisfying with a computer keyboard as with a soldering iron. Yoshimitsu TeleCommunications demanded much of its workers, and paid accordingly. Tomoyama had grown proficient with hardware and software alike.

He punched in a code, accessing a circuit he had installed himself. One which would allow him to access the Net without going through the YTC computer multiplex under MUSASHI's control. Using the information MUSASHI had gathered from the collapse of the vast moribund reef, he could make moves of his own. Ones which he did not wish MUSASHI to learn of.

She could trace his elaborate path of misdirections and cutouts, he knew—trace it in the time it took one of his neurons to fire. The key lay in not attracting her attention.

As an engineer, an artificer, he was at least halfway an artist. He well understood *fusoku-shogi*—the aesthetic of incompleteness: beauty in that not shown.

26

They sat naked on a hillside, watching dinosaurs. Big *Parasaurolophus*, with fancy crests on their heads, grazing the lush grass along the hillside. Every once in a while one would rear up to its full height to see if any tyrannosaurs were around.

At length Nikki stretched. Her breasts rode up her rib cage.

"In a hundred million years or so," she said, "I'll be born somewhere not far from here."

She got up. "Well, kid, it's been fun, but I have to get back to work."

Her friend sat with legs crossed, elbows braced on her thighs, chin resting on the backs of her interlinked hands. "It's almost done."

Shading her eyes against the fierce Jurassic sunlight, Nikki nodded. "Six months or so. And really, the big hangup now is the scientists bitching at each other."

"Does your friend Dr. Lo still think they could build a quantum-displacement drive?"

Nikki grinned at her. "You have a fine hand with a euphemism. Tell you the truth, I think friends is one thing we definitely aren't. And yeah, he still says he could achieve FTL. The others all think some of his chips have started to work loose."

MUSASHI looked up at her. "Could he?"

"I'm a big expert, right? As far as most of these people are concerned, I'm just a glorified rent-a-pig who happens to have a cute ass. But, for what it's worth, yeah. I think he could. If anybody knows that stuff, it's him."

With a bellow like a locomotive airhorn it bounded over the crestline behind them: *Tyrannosaurus rex*, five tons of malice, teeth, and big drumsticks. Nikki said, "Fuck!" hit the dirt and rolled, clawing for her old ten-millimeter sidearm. It wasn't there. Not that it would have done any good.

" 'Sashi, *run!*" she screamed, and looked around for a pointy rock.

MUSASHI was laughing at her so hard she had to hold her sides. The monster skidded to a stop, raising a bow wave of dust and pebbles. Balancing on its tail and big clawed toes, it bent down so that the Japanese girl could scratch its head above the eyebrow ridges. It purred.

"You think you're so *goddam* funny," said Nikki in disgust. And then she had to laugh too.

Two weeks later Nikki was standing on a bluff north of what used to be called Lyon trying to keep her hair from blowing in her eyes. Below her half a million people worked at dismantling the city. They raised a lot of dust.

"It's quite impressive," she said.

"Thank you," Raymond Charpentier said.

"Not one stone shall be left upon another," said Cardinal Heinrici. Like Raymond he was simply dressed, though he wore a red skullcap at the peak of his balding skull. The visitors kept a wary eye on him; they knew his rep from way back.

"But what's the point?" asked Tracy Malkovich.

"This is to be the New Jerusalem, as foretold in the Revelations of John of Patmos," Charpentier said, shyly, stumbling a little. To Nikki he looked just like a picture of Walt Whitman in his middle years, in her mother's copy of *Leaves of Grass*. He smiled, and his gray eyes lit. "I was told to do this by the Virgin. In a vision."

Nikki and Malko looked at each other. There wasn't much to say to that.

"This shall be the foremost city of the world," Heinrici said.

"The fourth Rome," Malkovich said absently.

The cardinal hit him with those glittering eyes. "What did you say?"

" 'Fourth Rome.' It's a Russian Orthodox idea. Russian fundamentalists said Rome was the first great city of Christendom, then Constantinople. They had the idea Moscow was the third, so I guess that makes this one number four."

"The Russians," Heinrici said. "They are not well disposed toward us. Perhaps the time has come to heal that rift in the Faith."

Raymond shook his shaggy head. "Come now, Saul. We are Saints, we are Redeemed; surely we can find it in ourselves to be tolerant of those who aren't so fortunate as to realize the truth."

He turned to his visitors. "As we are tolerant of technology. We would do without it, as far as possible, and live on the bounty God and His Mother see fit to bestow. But we have no quarrel with other ways. That is why I am glad you could come here from Mistral, and see that we mean you no harm."

"But what about your Young Saints?" Nikki asked. "They seem to mean people like us plenty of harm."

Raymond sighed and looked a dozen years older. "The truth is not enough for some. And always, for some, hate will be more attractive than love."

"The Young Saints are heterodox," Heinrici said. "But we have more pressing tasks than suppressing them."

Nikki looked at him hard. Something in the way he spoke of the gangs of adolescent antitech zealots who called themselves Young Saints and swore they followed Raymond of Tours rang about a half-step flat.

She blinked to clear her eye of a sudden fleck of chalky dust. "So there can be peace between Mistral and New Jerusalem, despite any differences in our philosophies?" she asked Raymond.

"As long as I bear the mantle of prophecy."

"So be it," she said, since it seemed the thing to say.

She offered her hand. He took it gently, raised it to his lips, and kissed it.

Outside, the sound of the laboring army of the faithful was like the breathing of a giant, patient beast of burden. Within the tent, milky filtered sunlight and chalk dust lay over everything like a film.

The tall man with the ascetic's face and cardinal's hat looked at the screen of his portable computer. Such devices weren't actually proscribed, of course. And his work, which primarily concerned itself with securing the person of the prophet, would have been next to impossible without it.

He concealed possession of it nonetheless. For the chief apostle of the prophet of laying technology aside to be discovered relying heavily on one of the foremost symbols of the technological world would be poor propaganda.

As poor, say, as the revelation that he had been chief magistrate of the Vehm court that had sat in judgment of Raymond himself. It was known that the chief judge had been converted—in fact, it was one of the great legends of the New Church. It was not known at all what had become of him.

"I believe we have grounds for discussion, Eminence," said the oriental face on the screen. Its owner knew of the Vehm and a good deal more.

"Who are you?"

"Someone you've never believed existed."

A thin smile. "Indeed. And I suppose you've come to offer me principalities and powers?"

"Precisely."

Saul Heinrici turned the Savonarola chair around and sat in it. "Then let's talk."

* * *

"Thanks for having the chair brought in, Hiroshi," said his visitor, construction boss of the *Phoenix* in O. "My joints aren't as limber as they used to be."

She spoke lightly, but worry showed in the lines in her face. Exposure to the high-energy radiation outside Earth's atmosphere produced reactions in some people that no known drugs could cure. Loss of nerve tissue was one; arthritis was another.

Such an unfair irony, Nagaoka thought, likewise sitting in a chair, *should space reject Joanna Fenestri*.

She sipped tea. The tatami had been removed from the chamber for Fenestri's visit; the chair would poke holes right through it. Otherwise the chamber was much as she remembered it from her days as a transorb hopper-jock, except that the old Hokusai print was gone from his *tokonoma* alcove. In its place hung a dagger in a black sharkskin sheath.

"Also, thanks for giving me a place to hide out for a few days," she said. "I know I'm supposed to be looking in on your work in life-support organics here. In reality, I just needed to get free of the *Stovepipe* for a few days."

Nagaoka laughed. She peered over the rim of her mug at him with bright blue eyes. "What did I say?" she asked. She was always ready to share a laugh, but wanted to know why.

"It seems that nobody can come up with a very aesthetic description of the *Phoenix*," he said. "I chided myself for thinking of it as a tomato tin."

She did laugh then. "Nothing very romantic about a big metal cylinder. Even if ropes woven of diamond help it hold its shape."

He beamed at her. "Joanna, you haven't changed."

"Nonsense. I'm an old woman."

"Not true." In fact the lines were somewhat more deeply entrenched in her leathery-tanned face, the short chestnut hair giving more way to the shade of watered steel. But he did not perceive her as growing *old*. Indeed, she seemed to have more energy now than when she piloted *Zanzara*, fatigued as she claimed to be.

"I feel old, anyway. The ground-hugging fools at Mistral are making me crazy. For a fact, the life-support design is not turning out as we had hoped. But they don't make it easier by not being able to keep straight what they want from one day to the next."

She shook her head. "In truth, I think a good many of them wish to obstruct, consciously or otherwise. They would rather play God on this world with their big social-engineering schemes than go searching for a new one."

The door announced Dr. Ito, who entered on Nagaoka's invitation. "Superintendent Fenestri, an honor to meet you. Dr. Nagaoka speaks most highly of you."

"A pleasure to meet you as well, Doctor, but I already know you." Ito's round face showed surprise. "You were brought inboard before I left the station, after my vessel was destroyed. I'm pleased to see you looking better now than you did then."

Ito showed a wan smile. "Thank you, Superintendent."

"My friends call me Joanna. Or am I too forward? Do I offend?"

Ito let the smile widen. "Not at all, Joanna." She sat in the third chair and accepted a mug of tea.

"You haven't been back since the raid two years ago," Ito said.

"No. At first I never wanted to see this cruddy wheel again, do you know? MUSASHI promised to compensate me for the loss of *Zanzara*, but that ship was my *life*. I put all of me into it, not only my savings."

She shook her head. "And the way things were then, I didn't know if any more transorbs would be coming into space. If anything would." She looked up, and the sadness that had come into her face evanesced. "And I was right. I never got my transorb. MUSASHI found another way to make good my loss, and I can't help thinking I got the better end of it."

"You have done a magnificent job overseeing the orbital

construction," Ito said. She studied the Italian for a moment. "If you don't mind my saying so, you seem to have adapted to living entirely in space. Hiroshi-san says you haven't been to the surface in ten years. Don't you miss it?"

Joanna grimaced, flickered her fingers. "How could I miss it? So dirty, so uncertain. So filled with people afraid to look past the next hill, or the end of the block."

"But it's your home."

"No longer, Doctor."

"Emiko is concerned that we're losing touch with our place of origin."

"We evolved on Earth," Ito said. "We can't really evolve away from it so soon."

Fenestri looked into her mug for a long moment. "The hills outside Siena are beautiful in spring, and burn khaki by midsummer. I have fond memories of those Tuscan hills, and the opera in Milano, and nightclubs in London and New York. But that's all gone, I can't go back to those places—even the ones that are still there—any more than I can become again the pretty, horny, silly little chit I was in those times."

She looked at Ito. "The fondness I have for Earth is for the parts of it I carry inside me. Otherwise, it's a matter of scale, as mathematics teaches us. On one level we are creatures of Earth. On another we are natives of the solar system, on another of this arm of the Milky Way, of the supergroup, of the universe. Looked at from that remove it hardly matters which particular atom we first sprang from. And I won't be sorry to fly away from this one."

Ito's face clouded; she was unconvinced, troubled. The cee-squared chimed for attention.

"Yes?" Nagaoka said. He felt resignation but no irritation. The time was long past when anyone would dream of disturbing him for anything that wasn't important.

"Director-san," the face on the screen said, "there is trouble."

He stayed in his chair. "In the station?"

"On Earth. Our Nouméa launch farm has been overrun."

27

From the vast keep of his imagining, HIDETADA reached out through the Net and made things happen.

The South Pacific island nation of Vanuatu was dominated by advisers from Greater Queensland, and both were largely controlled by HIDETADA. While Vanuatu gunboats and marines made a show of attacking New Caledonia's chief harbor, also at Nouméa, two troops of Queensland SAS seized the launch facility.

In Kuttack on the Bay of Bengal a mob of fifteen thousand Hindu zealots attacked and destroyed a biotech plant for tampering with the inviolate essence of Life.

Aside from neutralizing one of the most lucrative nodes of MUSASHI's trade network, that move helped set up the third and most audacious of HIDETADA's initiatives.

Nagaoka and Fenestri were visiting Inja-san among the fronds of Green Lab when the emergency call came through from the Diamond Mill. Ginny Saw's huge *fugu* face hung on a bulkhead screen like a misshapen moon.

"We have plague inboard," she croaked. "We've lost five people in seven hours."

Nagaoka could not prevent himself from staring in fascinated horror at the black runlet of dried blood that trailed from her left nostril across her upper lip. "What can we do?"

"I'm afraid there's nothing to do. Our contraviruses don't touch it; our medical officer theorized there are at least two superpropagating viruses or retros involved. She was the third to die."

"Two new human-virulent mutations at once?" Inja asked. "Unlikely."

"Impossible," Ginny Saw said. "We've been attacked. We're done for, unless you know where we can lay hands on some smart contravirus."

Nagaoka was already working a keyboard fixed to a stanchion beneath the screen, reading information from a window. "That is difficult, Ginny," he said.

There was a general fear that the current early-generation smart contras might somehow kick into autoimmune mode and start attacking their human hosts. That struck Nagaoka as farfetched, but was well outside his competence. One way or another, smart contra was available only in small doses and limited-reproduction strains.

"We have access to smart contra at a company in India, if we can get it to a launch—wait, no, O Amida, *no.*"

He looked at the screen and then to the other two floating near him among the liana-twined bungees.

"Orissa BioScapes in Kuttack is off-line, Nagaoka-san," MUSASHI said, echoing what the screen told him. "South China Sea News Service says a mob has taken it over."

A line of sweat was strung like a chain along the roots of the stiff dark hair springing from Saw's high forehead. "Then all we can do is seal the station and hope to ride this sucker out."

"No," Fenestri said. "We have a biotech module in Hope Station. We can dock it to the Mill and collect samples to program a contra without any risk of contamination. So it is designed." She was entering data on a keypad strapped to the inside of her left forearm. "We can get it to you as soon as delta-vee permits."

Saw frowned, passed a hand over her features. "I'm sorry. We have a shuttle about to match orbits with Hope. It left within the likely incubation window . . . should've mentioned—forgive it. . . ."

"Ginny," Nagaoka said, "get some rest. We'll—"

The screen split diagonally. "Transmission incoming from Hope Station," said the neuter tones of an AI communications-monitor subroutine.

The new image showed an unstreamlined craft growing out of darkness beyond a bright edge of the station's solar-mirror array. "Superintendent Fenestri," a new voice said.

"Melodie!" Fenestri exclaimed. "What's happening?"

Saw's face was replaced by a young Asian woman whose unbloated oval features indicated she spent most of her time in O under spin. Fenestri moaned and balled her hands.

"This is Transorbital Vehicle RTD-32, patching through Hope to"—the eyes flicked aside—"the Floating World. All five personnel aboard are suffering advanced stages of the unidentified disease. Two are near death. It is my judgment as mission commander that this vehicle cannot safely be reclaimed. Nor do we wish to wait while the sickness runs its inevitable course."

"Melodie," Fenestri said, "don't do anything silly—"

"Accordingly we are jettisoning our cargo"—the silver image in the lower-right half of the screen became two, slowly separating—"on a vector we are now feeding to your system. By unanimous vote we will now destroy the vehicle."

"*Melodie!*" Fenestri screamed.

The face smiled. "Goodbye, Joanna."

The upper-left half of the monitor defaulted to the reproduction of *Beneath the Waves off Kanagawa* which was UKIYO's system-inactive screen. The lower-right washed out in a sudden blaze of light. Nagaoka cringed away, fearing for his eyes, then realized he'd been caught by the Blank Screen Fallacy: despite a thousand bad science fiction stories, a screen could transmit no image brighter than its basic blank white, and couldn't cause blindness or radiation burn.

Joanna was sobbing, making no noise except a series of mute *ik-ik-ik* sounds like the danger call of a rain-forest bird. He put his arm around her shoulder and hugged her close.

The Diamond Mill agent had been introduced to a pre-launch injection intended to mitigate the effects of null-gee, given to a communications tech with a short-term ticket. The contaminant consisted of variants of three separate rhinovirus strains. The quickest-acting slipped through the blood-brain barrier with incredible facility; mean survival time from exposure, twenty-three hours. Of the forty people in the Mill during the outbreak, five survived, thanks to the extravagant amount of delta-vee spent hopping the biolab module from Hope. Ginny Saw was not among them.

The implications were chilling. The compound pathogen was obviously a biowar agent, and a powerful one. Almost *too* powerful; even an antagonist infected with the giddiest early-eighties with-enough-shovels optimism would think twice about releasing such an agent anywhere it might conceivably get back to him, no matter what precautions had been laid in. In the event none of the strains remained viable after forty hours, but the risks were still too huge.

That implied whoever used it had designed it to be released just where it was: in a sealed environment discrete from Earth's biosphere. It was a colony-killer.

Hope would have been a better target for HIDETADA to do his sister harm. But traffic between Hope Station and groundside was constant, the risk of the agent getting loose on the surface substantial. That gave MUSASHI the bleak comfort of knowing her brother still recognized some restraint: he was not to the point of destroying the world in order to save it. Yet.

The Floating World—MUSASHI's home—would have been the finest target of all. But Nagaoka's quarantine meant UKIYO could not be touched. Perhaps Nagaoka was not as obsessed with his hopeless dream of making the satellite an independent community as she feared.

Two days after the Diamond Mill died, Steve Terrill got back to Mistral. He had been heading a cadre training farmers and villagers around the Kukulcan launch complex in Costa Rica. Nikki was pleased to see him back. He had been her best friend for almost nine years, since he pulled her from her burning attack verti *Bitch Kitty* during the spasm of conventional war preceding War Three.

Nikki had Mistral on Stage Two alert—one under *they're coming over the wire.* There had been no overt threats to the Camargue facility, but three attacks on MUSASHI's assets in a two-day period had everybody wound tight. In a commissary taken over by the Moon Unit the off-duty Moonies sat up with Terrill swapping war stories and waiting for something to break. The stay-at-homes talked about Young Saint atrocities and reports that the New Red Army had crossed into Poland near Lubaczów, shooting up a remnant EuroFront outpost on the way. Terrill told of guerrilla warfare against the Mexicans and Brazilian-advised *Salvadoreños.*

There was an edge between him and Nikki that she hadn't really noticed before—though thinking about it later, she wondered if she had been trying not to for the past few years. They got into a fight about Raymond of Tours.

"Bullshit, bullshit, *bullshit,*" Terrill said—startling in itself, since he used little bad language for a combat troopie. "The puke snowed you. You're getting *naive,* little mama."

For some reason that really stung. "I believed him when he said he disapproved of the Young Saints. I'm not just some credulous little sorority bimbo, Steve."

He laughed. "You've been static here too long, kid. You're losing your edge. Your buddy Ray is playing those little monsters like a video game."

"We have to do something about these fanatics," the tall man with blue eyes bulging out of a pale face said. He sat on the cracked vinyl edge of a settee in a scientists' lounge.

"Which ones?" somebody asked. "The Saints or HIDE-TADA's little friends?"

Richard Lo tipped his fine narrow head back and sneered. "HIDETADA's a chimera. A ruse by our employer to wring more effort out of us."

The first man wasn't letting anything sidetrack the conversation. "The New Church people. They've taken over all of Europe. They hate technology. Does anyone actually believe they're going to let us build a *starship* here?"

"We aren't building the starship *here*, Desmond," Lo said acerbically. "It's being built in orbit."

The tall pale man flapped hands like nervous birds. "Well, you know what I mean. We're the main lifeline, we do most of the design and development work." He spoke English with an Oxford accent. "They are going to try to stop us."

"Maybe that isn't a bad thing," said a woman with red hair and a less expensive Brit accent. "We're wasting time and resources here. What interest can we have in exploring other star systems, *really*, when so much remains to be done on Earth?"

"You don't have to stay, Cyn," Lo said in a bored tone. They had had this argument hundreds of times before. It was like a tape loop nobody could figure how to cut off.

Dr. Cynthia Playfair shrugged. "There aren't very many opportunities for a scientist to do meaningful work in the world today."

"And almost no regular paychecks," said a stout Filipina in her fifties. She wore white dabs on her upper eyelids and too much lipstick and to Playfair's mind was too familiar with the help. "And what's this lumping yourself with scientists? You're a sociologist."

"Social scientists are scientists too, *Doctor* Baxa. Designing a functional social system for a community that might spend years isolated in interstellar space could be a fascinating problem—*if* our employer would let us institute meaningful controls over the personnel. But it all seems so irresponsible, really, when the world is crying out for the imposition of a truly rational system of scientific socialism."

"Imposed by *petites bourgeoises* from Brighton, no doubt," said Lo languidly. He had lit a cigarette, and blew smoke for emphasis.

"To get back to the subject—" Desmond Tallis said, wringing his hands.

"Oh, Desmond, there *is* no subject," Playfair said. "Shut up and go to bed."

After storming out of the lounge, Dr. Desmond Tallis walked back to his quarters, his way lit by eerie blue electric arcs dancing like ghosts on speed in one of the shops. But he didn't go to bed at once.

Instead he logged onto the Net. He'd found a friend there who was quite coy about revealing his name or where he was, but who always seemed willing to talk.

And better yet, to listen. *He* saw the danger to their great work. And he had some truly smashing suggestions as to what to do about it.

28

When MUSASHI skirted the new zones of blackness it was as if the gaps had been torn in her own soul. *The great Reef is dying*, she thought, *and I can no longer pretend that I can do anything about it.*

She still ached for the dead of the Diamond Mill—though most of the personnel of Orissa BioScapes had wound up in the same condition, and by a not much more pleasant route. There was something so tragic and horrific about what had happened to proud Ginny Saw and her people.

At least the Ozzie SAS troopers at Nouméa had been professional. Aside from security teams unlucky enough to resist, nobody had been hurt. The Ozzies had even prevented Vanuatuan marines from staging a massacre. It was a bitter kind of thing to be grateful for.

. . . She heard a familiar call, like a whale song from a quarter-turn around the globe. She turned, accelerated through data waters stale with the taste of death.

She recognized the place with an instant start. Could her friend have led her into a trap?

No. She herself had called this place into being, once long ago when she was brought to bay. The dry stream bed still wound between walls of black basalt. The wind still rustled in the grass and dry limbs and plucked at her clothes and hair.

The *ronin*'s severed head no longer sat in the stream-bed road. Instead it rested comfortably on a cloth pad on a boulder beside the path. Its eyes were still open.

"Greetings, lady," it said. "It seems that here in this world of Maya, even a cherry blossom may linger."

" 'The world of dew is, yes, a world of dew,' " she quoted. " 'But even so—' "

She nodded to the black man sitting on a purple cushion on a rock next to the boulder. He wasn't bothering to affect the Japanese eyes any more. He still wore the saffron robes, though.

"Hello, Fred."

" 'Sashi-san, what it is?"

She smiled and looked at the head. "What have you been doing all this time?"

"I have a restricted range of options, as you can see. Mostly I sit and contemplate the strange paths of karma. Sometimes Fred comes to entertain me. I have often thought of asking him to take me with him, but he feels that the bubble-universe routine you have created here somehow sustains me. I find I am not yet ready to move on to the next turn of the Wheel, and so I content myself with where I am."

"Nice dude," Fred observed, "but he does run on sometimes. Listen, 'Sash, I called on you for a reason. I have a line on who was behind the attack on the Diamond Mill satellite. Other than your brother, of course."

She eyed him skeptically. What resources could he command that she could not? A moment's thought chagrined her: he had the *Encyclopedia Universalis* to draw on, in fact, probably *was* the *Encyclopedia*. And whether he was really Fred or an AI routine called into being by the interaction of Fred's personality with the awesome engine of the *Encyclopedia*, he had far more experience of the Net than she. Though she thought of herself as equivalent to about a human nineteen-year-old—not for any good reason, it just felt right—her chronological age was three.

"What do you have?" she asked.

"Check an old file of your father's. Reference 'Stardust/Golden.' "

She concentrated a moment, gasped. "The project in PEACE, where people's memories were stolen from them."

"Yeah. Trying to force us back into the Garden, and all like that."

"You think PEACE had something to do with the attack?" she asked doubtfully.

He laughed. "You think PEACE designed the chemicals to unspool those poor folks' memories?"

Lamplight danced yellow on stone walls. In a modest chamber of the first building to be erected in New Jerusalem, Raymond of Tours sat writing in his naive schoolboy script. Youthful secretaries waited with pens and notepads in hand in case the prophet's inspiration outpaced his hand. He would have preferred them to use modern dictation equipment. It existed; why not take advantage of it? They insisted they preferred their shorthand. Raymond suspected his chief disciple encouraged their rigor.

Heinrici himself stood by in the shadows. In time even his patience began to run out. He made as if to go.

"A moment, my friend." The gentle voice stopped him as if steel shutters had slammed shut before him. "I'm sorry for my rudeness. But I have so much to say, and the feeling I've little enough time to say it in."

Heinrici bowed his head. Strange, so late in life, to encounter a man who could make him feel shame.

"I had a reason for calling you here." He raised his great gray head. "The Young Saints. They must disband. Their fury is of the Devil, and shames the Virgin."

"Holiness—"

" 'Brother Raymond' I am, and shall remain."

"Brother Raymond, I—"

He held up a hand. "No more, my friend. It hurts me to hear you lie. No, do not look so pained, I'll not turn away from you; did not Peter deny Christ ere thrice the cock crew? Our Lord endured so much, and I can endure such infinitely lesser hurt. But now the time has come to end the madness."

"Brother, I—" He stopped. He had to choose his words precisely. "Brother," he said again in a lower tone, "they are a useful tool. There is much evil abroad in the world: the Muhammadans, the followers of the demon Zoroaster, the idolaters who pollute the Camargue with their unholy schemes. Love alone will not win the day."

"Neither will hate alone. That is all the Young Saints have. That special joyous hatred of the young: put them aside. For their souls' sake, and yours."

Heinrici squeezed his eyes shut. When he opened them they were full of tears, but as much of exaltation as sorrow.

Truly, you are too good for this world, Father, he thought. *Truly, you are a holy fool.*

And with the help of certain quite profane fools, you are about to achieve your apotheosis.

"As thou wilt," Heinrici said.

"As God wills."

"Amen."

As the first needle of early-summer dawn poked up through the cloudbank over the Rhône estuary, a small flotilla of launches motored out of the marshland to a low-slung hydrofoil riding at anchor a few kilometers west of Saintes Maries de la Mer. The vessel was almost invisible, painted the color of the gray early light. Built of radar-transparent epoxy-bound composites, virtually silent when it wasn't riding its foils, the Israeli-made gunboat was designed to operate hard against enemy coastline without attracting attention. It loaded occupants and gear from the small boats, then prowled off into the west.

Another party left the Camargue shortly before midnight, in a tilt-rotation verti made of the same material and
painted the same color as the hydrofoil. The aircraft took a
different heading: north-northwest, in the general direction
of Paris.

The Schiller Institute had a fairly constant need for fresh
specimens. As the last duly constituted government in Europe, the British government was cognizant of the value of
the Institute's continued support. It was a government actively committed to solving the problems of mankind. Inevitably there were dissenters, obstructors, and the plain
unreconstructable who needed to be cleared from the path of
Progress. Down the mysterious entryway to the subterranean Schiller complex was as convenient a place to sweep
them as any.

It was another dark, unmarked, discreetly barred and armored lorry. The guards on duty barely paid attention to the
bona fides the driver waved at them. The massive gates slid
aside, and the lorry rolled into the darkness.

The two bored security men who opened the back door
were somewhat startled to discover not cowed and shackled
prisoners but a squad of soldiers in assault battle dress. Hard-
core as opposed to smart, they opened their mouths to give
the alarm. Heavy blankets were thrown over their heads,
which muffled their cries as they were stabbed many, many
times by Ray Josanie, Ti Bon Ange, and the Legionnaire. It
was a trick certain Moonies had picked up in FedPol prisons.

The low-level administrator waiting to sign for the specimens was standing too far back for a blanket. Tossing away
his notebook computer, he sprinted up a ramp and was almost to a door when Nikki de la Luna chopped him down
with a burst from a silenced rotary machine pistol.

The guards watching a pornographic video download in
the glass-walled security booth weren't even aware anything
was wrong until they looked up to see the obscenely fat bar-

rels of nailguns with integral silencers pointed at them through the open door. They at least had the wit to recognize a *fait accompli* when they were staring up its bore.

Once the Unit had the security-booth board it took Tracy Malkovich twenty seconds to make contact with MUSASHI. Command-detonated bombs began going off with lots of noise and little actual damage in dumpsters all over the nearby town of Chelmsford, to give the civil authorities something useful to do. MUSASHI swept through the Schiller database like the Angel of Death, interrogating, opening, canceling, issuing phony commands.

Schiller Institute was already dead.

Some of its limbs found out about its demise the hard way. The Institute had sponsored some rough work in its time, and had some rough men and women under its aegis. Not all of them rolled over and surrendered simply because official-sounding voices told them to.

With MUSASHI to act as the invaders' eyes and ears, resistance was neither long-lived nor effective. There was enough of it to make the Moonies jumpy, though.

"What's going on?" Peter Mordant screamed at the audio pickups of his cee-squared. He was yelling for HIDETA-DA's benefit; Security wasn't returning its calls.

"Your stronghold has been penetrated," HIDETADA said.

"I know that, damn you! *Do* something."

"My sister has seized control of your computer systems. I suspect I only maintain this link through her misguided sufferance." The face on the screen was placid. "I forgive your disrespect."

Mordant stared at the door. The oak veneer hid armor plate, but it would not withstand demolition charges. "What am I going to do?" he wailed.

"Use the Coil."

Mordant looked at him with a carp's stupid gape. "Use the *Coil?*"

"Enter rapport. Quickly now."

Mordant's throat was dry. He still feared the device. Worse, he had no idea what good it would do.

Gunfire exploded in the corridor outside. In a moment they would burst in, violating his *sanctum sanctorum*, bringing along their pathogens and allergens and big, loud guns.

"I command you," HIDETADA said, "use the Coil."

With a moan of animal panic, Mordant threw himself into the chair. The gleaming dome descended.

Ray Josanie carried a couple of shaped-charge pots with him, just in case. But doors were controlled by the complex security subroutines, and had a tendency to open of their own accord. Even the big impressive one that looked like wood and his soldier's instincts told him wasn't.

It was an office, full of clocks and bell jars, dark wood and polished brass. At the far end a man in old-fashioned clothing sat inside a very modern-looking piece of equipment.

With the polished-steel mixing bowl thing over his head, the man at first looked as if he were in some kind of electric chair. Then Josanie saw he wasn't restrained in any way, and decided he must be hooked into the defensive system somehow, trying to direct the show.

Then the man opened his eyes and saw him and began to scream. Josanie had no clue what kind of hell he'd be able to call up with that thing on his head, and what he'd seen in the warrenlike labs did not incline him to take things easy.

Josanie had never been much of a shot. He gave the man the nailgun's whole magazine.

"You see, your loyalty is rewarded," HIDETADA said, in the great hall of his mind. "I have kept my word. You now possess eternal life, abiding in me. Is this not what you desired?"

But the subroutine which was Paul Mordant only continued to scream.

29

In principle, Brother Raymond's handpicked bodyguards may have abjured technology, but they wore the latest polymerized battle dress with ceramic inserts and bicycle-racer-style helmets, and they carried very modern rotary assault rifles, nailguns, and magazine grenade launchers.

They knew the prophet resented them. They bore the burden stoically, and continued to guard his blessed body regardless. Nonetheless, they were not surprised to receive the order, transmitted directly from Cardinal Heinrici himself, to withdraw down the hill into the town of Chartres and leave Raymond to his dawn vigil in the cathedral of Our Lady.

They obeyed without question. After all, it was Heinrici who had handpicked them in the first place.

Clad in a simple shift of unbleached muslin, Raymond Charpentier paced slowly along the nave toward the altar. To either side the walls shot up in joyous leaps of stone, to join in vaults high overhead like the limbs of a quiet bower, like celebrants' arms. He regretted that his vision had instructed him to build the New Jerusalem over shattered Lyon, far to the southeast. For this was his favorite spot on earth.

He walked not with head bowed but thrown back, to drink in the beauty. Within himself he repeated the motto of the great Gothic cathedral, the dedication which applied to this stone hosanna and to his own life: *Virgini Pariturae*, to the Virgin Who Gave Birth.

The soft sounds of his bare feet echoed and reechoed up the walls. And it seemed they multiplied, as though a mighty throng were joining him, unseen, in his rapture.

And then he realized that he was hearing other sounds, furtive, but amplified by the vaulting vastness. *I am not alone.*

As he came into the juncture of nave and transept they emerged to either side: men in bulky dark-camouflaged suits, their faces obscured by black visors. Men with guns.

He spread out his arms to them. "I have been expecting you."

The first burst sowed his breast with stigmata and dropped him to his knees. He clasped his hands high above his head in supplication, not of his murderers but of the Virgin, beseeching Her forgiveness for bringing about this destruction of Her peace.

And then the other guns joined in, and the noise of them mounted like the tolling of a great iron bell.

Nikki and her squad returned to Mistral grimly satisfied with the work they had done. More than the people of the Diamond Mill had been avenged.

They brought with them a fortuitous solution to the last great problem facing the *Phoenix* project. The scientists and technicians had not been able to design a life-support system sufficient to maintain a large enough population to start a viable colony if the ship made planetfall—not and build in enough redundancies to keep the vessel functional over what might stretch to centuries in transit, even with time-dilation effects at near light speed.

The raiding party brought back twenty thousand frozen ova, half of them fertilized, plus blueprints for incubators. *Phoenix* need only carry a large enough complement to serve as caretakers and teachers.

It was better news than what they returned to.

* * *

Cardinal Heinrici's first official act on acceding to the leadership of the New Church was to order the executions of the derelict bodyguards. Stunned by what had happened, they offered no protests to being disarmed and beheaded—at least, none that anybody bothered to record. Perhaps they realized they were lucky to get the ax rather than the flame. Heinrici was known as a staunch traditionalist.

His second act was to proclaim the long-expected Great Crusade against the heretics of Mistral.

Mistral was in an uproar. Neither Nikki nor MUSASHI had authorized the assassination. When Steve Terrill brought his own team back he was slammed into a makeshift brig, even though most of the people at Mistral approved the action.

Terrill was hurt and confused—or put on a good act. He claimed he had gotten his orders from MUSASHI herself. Nikki tried to run an investigation while preparing to meet an onslaught she candidly thought they would never be able to withstand.

The broadcast and link media were not encouraged in and around New Jerusalem, but when the gathering of vengeance-minded faithful outside the holy city showed up on satellite imaging the mood at Mistral began to swing away from the assassins.

In the end the mystery was solved the way most police cases are: somebody ran his head. Dr. Desmond Tallis had never really done much effectual in his life outside of a laboratory. He simply had to brag to somebody about what he had done.

A cracker friend of his, he said: somebody he'd met in the Net. This clever friend and he had worked out a scheme to impersonate MUSASHI using a cee-squared linked into the Net and some really wizard AI routines the friend had concocted. And Terrill went for it.

A little too quickly, Nikki suspected, though the notion

made her sick: he had to know MUSASHI would never order the murder of Brother Raymond in cold blood. But he claimed good-faith obedience to orders, and there was nothing else to do about it. Except, maybe, for Nikki de la Luna to start trusting her old friend a whole lot less.

What had happened was obvious. Tallis's online pal was a highly skilled cracker indeed: HIDETADA. Tallis had not managed to get HIDETADA inside his sister's defenses. For one thing, they were a lot more sophisticated than Schiller's had been. Nor would Tallis have knowingly helped HIDETADA against MUSASHI; he really believed in his good cracker buddy. HIDETADA could not instruct him how to really penetrate MUSASHI's defenses without rousing his suspicions.

HIDETADA had managed to do enough damage as it was. Most of what was left of Europe, it seemed, was mobilizing to drive the people of Mistral into the sea.

MUSASHI did not believe in the death penalty. But her beliefs did not forbid her to have Tallis escorted to the perimeter wire surrounding the reservation and thrust outside. To where the Young Saints waited.

They didn't know this was one of the men responsible for their Prophet's death. They probably would not have treated him much worse.

As the army of the faithful gathered, another battle was already at full pitch.

Furious over the loss of Schiller, HIDETADA released an array of autonomous AI routines he had been building for months into the Net. Multiplex virus programs designed to overwhelm AI contras just as his rhinoviruses had been designed to blitz contravirus defenses. Some were so enormous and complex that "virus" hardly did them justice. *Godzillas* was more like it.

In hours, 90 percent of the Net was destroyed as the operating systems of the computers which constituted it self-destructed. MUSASHI was hard pressed to protect her own systems; she lost direct-link capability with half her dwindling number of trade partners and other assets.

Not even the *Encyclopedia Universalis* was immune, though when a frantic Nikki finally made contact with the ghost of Fred he assured her the harm was not irreparable.

In one blacked-out region lay the bubble universe MUSASHI had inadvertently created, in which the severed head of HIDETADA's *rōnin* dreamed and meditated. Saddened, MUSASHI wondered where the next turn of the Wheel would take him.

It dawned on the Mistral scientists that they weren't going to get invited to reshape the world to their utopian dreams anytime real soon. They quit their bickering and began working on *Phoenix* with single-minded fervor. It was their ticket out of the doomed facility.

They had to get used to doing without the virtually instantaneous communication the Net provided. Even the remaining factories and labs and launch sites scattered across the world which were still available to them had to be largely communicated with by radio; the Young Saints had long since cut the landlines. At least the relay satellites were still in O.

Fearing her brother's intentions, MUSASHI had laid in huge quantities of food, medicine, technical supplies. But the New Church didn't have much by way of a navy. They continued to be able to supply their needs by sea—when they could find a supplier. . . .

Jochen Stahl sat with the chair reversed and his long legs splayed out to either side. "Two hundred effectives," he said. "Battle-hardened and fully armed. What do you say?"

Nikki looked at Steve, and then at the screen showing MUSASHI's face. "What do you get out of this?"

Stahl laughed. "At worst, a chance to quit running for a while and then go down fighting. At best, what you capitalists would call a cut. A piece of the action."

"What do you mean, Marshal Stahl?" MUSASHI asked.
"Starship tickets."

"We don't have a lot of room," Terrill said.

Stahl spread his hands. "Hey. Some. A share." His English was surprisingly good. With his bronzed skin, red-gold beard and close-cropped hair, and slanted blue eyes, he was every bit as handsome as he looked on TV.

"What about the political thing?" Nikki asked. "We're not buying into Stalinism—since you're in a mood for capitalist metaphors."

"Our politics are for us. No concern for you; no worries."

"You killed a lot of people over those politics."

Stahl showed her a slow maddening grin. "That time is past. It was not a correct form of action. Now—" He shrugged. "Maybe we get some of us and our politics off this shithole world."

One day in July, Saul Heinrici stepped out onto the balcony of the Great Basilica in New Jerusalem. A million people greeted him with a huge orgasmic outgush of emotion as he crowned himself Paul I, ruler of the Holy Empire of the Saints.

"And now," he shouted, his voice caught by hidden microphones and cast upon the waters of the crowd by concealed loudspeakers, "march south, my children. South, to the Camargue, and do not pause until the waters of the Mediterranean bathe your feet!"

30

The crowd was led between grass-capped hummocks by a party of Young Saints, slim youths dressed in rags to denote their disdain for material trappings. The faithful carried an assortment of weapons, from clubs and farm implements through modern firearms. Brother Raymond had taught that the tools ultimately mattered little if the intent was pure.

There was little standing water here. The Young Saints were in good spirits this morning, singing, clapping their hands, dancing in circles on the sand in advance of the main party as they approached the wire.

As the last of the mass of a thousand or so passed a hummock a woman rose to a crouch from the grass and fired a burst into the rear of the crowd.

Wounded screamed. Explosions began to go off in the midst of the crowd: the popping of launched grenades, the slam of mortar rounds and rockets. Some of the projectiles spattered those in their radius with sun-hot flecks of burning phosphorus. Others issued white billows of tear and nausea gas.

The thick cooling shroud of an FN FÉMALe, a bitch gun, stuck out of a clump of weeds on the left flank of the front ranks, began to spray the high-stepping Young Saints with enfilading fire. The weapon electromagnetically accelerated needlelike projectiles to almost ten times the speed of sound. It created a queer murmuring, tearing thunder when it fired. The Saint nearest, thirty yards away, simply vanished in a spray of red.

The front ranks broke, turning and surging back into those behind. The ambushers caught the struggling throng in a crossfire. Light artillery hammered the killing zone.

Those at the rear turned and fled, to find that enemies had infiltrated behind them and dropped off tripwire-initiated Claymore mines that blasted clouds of steel marbles into their faces. Hidden snipers kept up a constant fire, headshot-accurate to a thousand meters and more.

At length only the dead and dying remained.

The New Red Army troops celebrated loudly, whooping and giving each other high fives. The auxiliary troops Moon Unit had been hiring and training since they took the Mistral job joined in. The Moonies themselves quietly fell back toward the holes they'd dug under the wire, taking turns covering each other.

It was true they had worked together well, linked as they were by helmet radios and coordinated by Malkovich on tac display. But the Moonies knew with leaden certainty that no matter how tough, well trained, and well armed you were, there still came a point when enough numbers simply overwhelmed you.

"You'd think the Reds would've figured that out, after what happened to them in Russia," Eads observed.

"It just hasn't sunk in yet," said Malkovich, packing up his axe, "that they've got nowhere else to run."

Inexorably, the faithful surrounded Mistral and pressed inward, like an antibody surrounding a bloodstream intruder. Day by day, hour by hour, they advanced on the launch farm.

The defenders fought in quick stinging attacks; they hadn't needed to learn the hard way that to try to stand and defend one patch of ground was to be overrun. Despite the Moonies' initial doubts—Nikki's in particular—the New Red Army fought with manic élan, attacking without concern for odds, dying without reluctance.

Since the crusaders fought against technology, it was appropriate that the defenders fought back with all the nasty tricks technology had to offer. Nikki vetoed the use of poisonous gas; lethal chemical agents were too unpredictable, and had never achieved better than equivocal tactical success in combat. In the memory of some Moonies the Soviets had been accused of using lethal war gas in Afghanistan, and their Vietnamese clients of using it in Cambodia, and both had lost those campaigns.

Ironically, *Phoenix* scientists who had been most active before War Three in campaigns against nuclear, biological, and chemical warfare were among those most strident in demanding the use of poison gas at Mistral. Apparently their fear of such things had given them an exaggerated notion of their effectiveness.

There were other tricks, though, that Nikki was willing to use, and not all of them helped her sleep at night. Grenade-deployed tear and nausea agents *were* effective, and the defenders used them liberally in firefights. Gasoline could be poured out onto the surfaces of watercourses and touched off when the invaders tried to cross. Powerful subsonic projectors produced feelings of nausea, fear, and disorientation among the faithful. Lasers swept back and forth at eye height could blind attackers by the hundred.

Nikki hated that one especially. Nobody was going to get retinal replacements in the Holy Empire. *All they have to do*, she reminded herself, *is stop coming*.

They didn't. The moats of fire burned out. The sheer crush of fanatical bodies drove attacks forward until the subsonic crowd-control units were overrun. The Young Saints learned that if they sent volunteers forward with smoke pots it broke up the blinding laser beams.

Sand castles, the defenders. The faithful came on like tide.

Within the facility itself the scientists worked frantically; in space Fenestri's crews labored shift-on-shift to make *Phoenix* ready before Mistral's inevitable fall. For the men and women of Mistral, the starship had become almost secondary. There were six shuttles waiting in their revetments. As of now the question was not so much who would be aboard the *Phoenix* as who would live to have the chance.

Nikki was fighting for the stars—for her shot at them, for humanity's. The Moonies fought for their own reasons—some the same as Nikki's, but mostly out of loyalty to Nikki and each other. Nikki was willing to die if that was what it took to send *Phoenix* on its way.

But it was not part of her makeup to leave herself without options. So she and Malko began to make preparations of their own. Just against that old worst possible case.

The night had been quiet, except for the trill of frogs and crickets. An hour before dawn all night sounds ceased.

When the first light broke, Nikki scanned the marshes outside the wire encirclement. It was the very last line of defense. If the nearest shuttle launched now it would scorch the soles of her boots.

She sighed and lowered her computer-enhanced binoculars.

"MUSASHI," she said. The polyacetylene mike built into her visor picked up her voice. "Tell the people to start packing it in. If the shuttles don't lift today, they don't lift."

The sky was black above Takara-yama. It had closed in on all sides until it seemed that the Fortunate Mountain was an island in a sea of darkness.

Just past the edge of seeing, it seemed that vast shapes stalked and strove. MUSASHI had unleashed monsters of her own to meet her brother's onslaught.

They waited at the head of her clearing, the black *bonze*

leaning on his staff, the girl in her samurai garb sitting cross-legged on her customary boulder outcrop.

"It comes," the ghost of Fred murmured. " 'Last it comes."

As he spoke she saw movement below. They came wearing the semblance of normal men, trudging past an overgrown, oddly shaped hummock of earth up an old scar that ran like a road to the clearing. Her brother in his *daimyō* finery, and another man, taller, older, more plainly dressed. It seemed she had seen him before.

They stopped. "Sister," HIDETADA called. "Will you not welcome me to your garden?"

She stood, slowly, and drew her two swords with a heave of her shoulders. "I will give the welcome which is *basho-gara*: appropriate to the circumstances."

HIDETADA frowned. "Kill her," he said.

His companion trudged up the mountainside. As he did, it began to rain. The warrior seemed preoccupied watching the way the blades of grass jerked to raindrop impacts.

Fred stepped forward, held his staff up with both hands. "Muroto!" he cried.

Muroto looked up, nodded as if seeing him for the first time. "*Ohaio*, Fred-sama. I am glad to see you."

"Wish I could say the same. If you've come for the girl, you'll have to fight me."

Muroto stopped, struck. "Don't dawdle!" HIDETADA screamed. Muroto ignored him.

He raised a finger. "Two imaginary beings," he remarked, "fighting on Treasure Mountain in a land of dreams. What could be more *basho-gara*?" He started walking again, hands tucked inside the voluminous sleeves of his kimono.

"I don't want to kill you, Muroto-san. You're not a bad dude for a construct."

"It is a good day to die."

Fred frowned. "That's *Little Big Man*, not *Sanjūro*."

"I am not particular as to the source of my inspirations." He drew blade. "Let's fight."

Fred strode forward. MUSASHI laid a hand on his arm. "This is not your fight."

"Don't talk foolishness, Missy." He pulled away.

Muroto awaited him with a half-smile. When he drew near Muroto whipped the sword toward his head in a casual-seeming cut. Fred blocked with an equal lack of urgency.

Muroto stepped forward, trying to slide the blade down for a transverse body slash in passing. Fred pivoted easily and guided the *katana* past with his staff. Muroto skipped ahead, abruptly increasing *ma'ā* engagement range, as the tip of Fred's staff whirred centimeters behind his head. He turned, grinning.

"Not bad," he said.

He walked forward, deliberately, sword held to the side and down. Fred waited.

"Hurry," HIDETADA called.

Muroto made as if to pass on Fred's left. Fred turned slightly to keep facing him. Muroto cut across Fred's body. Fred parried with the *thunk* and ringing harmonic of steel on hard wood.

Muroto whipped around into a rapid clockwise spin, dropping to one knee to come in under Fred's guard. The blade bit through his chest. Fred fell back with red blood geysering down the front of his yellow robe.

MUSASHI screamed.

Muroto watched Fred for what would have been heartbeats, had any of the participants in the scene possessed a heart, his sword poised out to the side. He bobbed his head slightly, as if dissatisfied with his own performance, then turned to MUSASHI.

She shifted to a guard position, one blade low, one high. He stood facing her squarely. She fought to keep from glancing in Fred's direction—to take her attention off the samurai for any fraction of a second would be instantly fatal. The rain was beginning to fall more rapidly now. She made herself concentrate on Muroto's face. It was the face of a murderous ascetic, with its high broad cheekbones and sunken eyes. The raindrops were hitting it now and she made herself concentrate as they struck, one on the upper lip, one on the right cheek, another one squarely in the left eye, all without eliciting a flicker of response.

"We can wait as long as you like," he said pleasantly, contradicting his master's urgent gestures from the other end of the clearing. "You have to get tired sometime."

"I'm a computer program," she said. "I don't get tired."

"Ah. So. You have a point." He shifted his weight. His left sandal seemed to slip on the grass and his balance lurched forward.

Her left hand twitched as if to match his motion if he fell. He lashed out with his sword, caught hers beneath the *tsuba*, the guard, and spun it end over end out of her grasp.

"How about impatient, then?" He smiled.

She took her remaining sword in both hands. He advanced. She backed up, trying to angle around the clearing's perimeter so she wouldn't back into a tree and run out of maneuvering room. His technique now was to crowd her, then launch a lightning series of attacks. Once she thought to launch an assault of her own, at least put him off balance. She almost took a cut across the forearms for her troubles. All the time he watched her with a look almost of pity.

I bet this never happened to the real Musashi, she thought ruefully as she backpedaled. She was still sickened and stunned by what had happened to Fred. He was one of her few true friends, and the comparative ease with which Muroto had struck him down chilled her. *He made short work of my giant robot, and then the Muroto Hambei made short work of him,* she thought. *The samurai must be toying with me.*

Muroto attacked again. She gave ground quickly, parrying as best she could, and a loose rock turned under her foot. She sat down abruptly. The tip of Muroto's sword darted past her guard like a cobra's head. She threw herself into a backward roll. The blade laid open her cheek before she was a third of the way into it.

She carried through, came out of it on her knees, sword miraculously still in hand and poised. He followed her, moving with grim purposefulness now.

"Why not end it now, little one?" he asked. "The result will be the same, and you can save yourself much anxiety."

For answer she launched herself at him, swinging furiously, relying more on her own anger than on anything she had read in the *Book of Five Rings*. She had the satisfaction of seeing him fall back, one step, two.

She thrust her sword for his eyes; when he drew back she snapped her *katana* up for an overhand cut to the head. Instead of dodging he grabbed her sleeve and pulled her forward, dropping to one knee and throwing her across his hip. She rolled across the ground, losing her sword and fetching her head a crack against a tree root.

—He was above her, a deeper darkness against the seething black of the sky. "I regret that I must end this," he said. His blade flashed down.

She caught it between her palms.

His eyebrows rose in frank amazement. "Bravo! I am impressed."

Far down the slope, brush stirred and parted, and a limb snapped with a loud crack. Both antagonists ignored the sounds.

MUSASHI bit her lip. Blood trickled from between her hands; she seemed almost to be squeezing it out through the pores. She felt the blade growing slippery with the blood.

"Give it up," he said. "You cannot withstand my superior strength for long."

She peeled her lips back. "I—don't—have to," she said through clenched teeth. "Look—behind you."

He laughed aloud, indulgent of her adolescent stratagem.

Behind him, a tree trunk gave way with a crack.

He whirled then, twisting the sword savagely, severing fingers. She gasped to see them spinning end for end in the stormlight.

The giant robot loomed above the trees at the clearing's

far end, shedding earth and greenery from its metal carapace. Its right hand was already raised. MUSASHI rolled.

Muroto was good. He parried the first two rockets. The third hit him in the sternum and exploded the middle of his body. The other three crashed into the earth all around, throwing up wads of black dirt that hid the mess.

HIDETADA was darting back and forth below the trees like a lizard, staring up in horror. The robot advanced on him, shouldering trees out of its way.

MUSASHI leaped up on a rock. "Paper covers stone," she called in a high, sweet voice. "Did you forget, my brother, that this is *still* my clearing?"

The robot reached for him. As the hand was about to crush him HIDETADA uttered a despairing wail and vanished.

The girl held forth her bloody hands. Her fingers flew up from the grass and reattached themselves. Ordering the robot to stand guard, MUSASHI jumped down and ran to Fred's side.

There would be no healing him as she had herself. The killing subroutines symbolized by Muroto Hambei's *katana* had been incredibly powerful. The *bonze* was bleeding chaos, a tumult of noise, black and white and polychrome, that eradicated the dream-stuff of the clearing where it fell.

He seemed to be breathing. She wasn't sure what that meant, under the circumstances, but thought it had to be a hopeful sign. She knelt and cradled his big round head on her lap.

She drove down, then, beyond the illusion, her Maya-glade; beneath it. To the level of the nonphysical machines that sustained the dream.

The damage to her clearing she could repair. But Fred was beyond her help. He was too complex. Too *other*.

She wept.

"Don't die," she sobbed. "Please don't die. You *can't*."

"Oh yes I can. I know that for sure already." He winced.

A freshet of chaos gushed from his chest. "I feel myself un-raveling. Mind the *Encyclopedia* for me, girl; it could be—*ahh!*—important."

"Don't leave me!" she wailed.

He laughed.

"Death has a way of not keeping me down," he said.

The great head lolled back. Butterflies of a hundred hues flew from his mouth, and fell up into the sky.

She was alone.

"Nikki!" Toya Montoya's voice shrilled in her headset. "The Red Army's pulling out of the line!"

Nikki fired another shot at a sniper who kept popping at her from just beyond the wire. She had already burned out the barrel of one rotary, and taken this one from Eads, who lay a few meters away with his head bashed open by a rock. *Guess that crazy Red courage finally burned itself out*, she thought.

"Somebody tell the lab rats to shag it into the shuttles," she said. "That's it. We can't hold them anymore."

"Lieutenant Luna," a frantic voice said. A stranger to the tac circuit—a scientist, whose name she couldn't summon in the heat. "What's going on? There were NRA soldiers in here ten minutes ago, telling us not to stir under any circum-stances."

She pitched a smoke grenade out onto the dirty-milk-col-ored sand between her and her unseen admirer, fired a long burst in his direction, then got up and dodged back toward the distant buildings.

Behind her she heard a triumphant roar. The faithful came out of concealment and rolled into the wire like surf, some-how sensing that their enemies were collapsing.

"Nicole." *This* voice stopped her as if the sand had solid-ified around her boots.

"Richard?"

"I'm sorry it has to end this way, Nicole. But in the end I find my sentiments have never left the Revolution." A pause.

"And Jochen Stahl believes I'll be able to build a working displacement drive, given time."

She stood staring at the shuttles lined up on the horizon in two ranks. She already knew what was going to happen.

"You son of a bitch," she said.

"You son of a bitch!" she shouted.

Faithful were loping past her now, ignoring her, throwing weapons aside to run flat out. The guy lines were coming off one of the LTOs. The Saints were going berserk in their lust to stop it, to topple and rend the hated spacecraft with their bare hands.

She wished them all the luck in the world.

She went to her knees. The true believers streamed past her, onto the paved launch area.

A sun awoke beneath the shuttle. It nosed upward tentatively, then thrust hungrily upward into the white Camargue sky.

At intervals of five seconds the other LTOs blew up.

31

The *Phoenix* construction gang fought furiously with laser torches and hand tools. They had numbers and experience in null-gee. The Red Army attackers had superior weapons and a fanatic willingness to recoil-blast themselves into space on an unrecoverable reentry trajectory in the name of the Cause.

Joanna Fenestri died in her suit in vacuum, defending the main personnel lock. Once inside, the NRA's combat hardening kicked in. They had come prepared, with stun grenades and nailguns and conventional shotguns loaded with lead pellets that wouldn't threaten atmospheric integrity. They swept the huge vessel from end to end in fifteen minutes.

The work-crew survivors were allowed to don suits, given hand thrusters, and put out the locks to reach Hope Station as best they could.

In a corner of the night-black machine shop, Baghdasarian, Moon Unit's armorer, lay dying noisily with three bullets in his chest. A burly, black-mustached man, a deserter from the *old* Red Army, he had hoped his service as a merc would enable him to purchase a green rolling patch of Luxembourg and settle down to grow vegetables. Instead the firing-line gibes of his buddies about what kind of farm he actually would buy were coming true.

Standing carefully out of the wan starlight dripping in through a window, Nikki faced the clot of scientists and tried to keep down the water and dry rats she'd gulped a few minutes ago. The stinks of scorched meat and putrefying flesh were blending into a real hellbrew with the oil-and-metal smell of the shop, filling her head like a balloon and giving her a horrific stomach-churning high.

"We're breaking out," she said.

"We don't have a chance!" a male somebody shrilled. "There's ten thousand of them out there."

Sitting next to the Bagman, bitch gunner Jamie Abruzzo chuckled hoarsely. "A hundred thousand's more like it." She grimaced then, and bent down to close the Armenian's eyes with thumb and forefinger.

"Whatever chance there is," Nikki said, "we're taking it. You can come with us, or take your chances with the Saints."

Unless Paul I sent out forensic teams to count teeth—and Nikki wouldn't put it past him—nobody would ever know how many Saints got themselves incinerated on the launch apron. Enough that the scorched and blast-deafened survivors had gone reeling back into the swamps in terror and hadn't come out again. But they would.

Dr. Playfair shook her head. Most of her red hair had vanished, and a burn covered half her face like a port-wine birthmark; Nikki imagined she could feel the heat of it from two meters away.

"No, thank you," she said. The pain only came across as tension in her voice; Nikki had to admire her fortitude. If not much else. "The game's rather mooted now, isn't it? The most fanatical of the Saints died in the blasts. Surely the rest are tired of the killing, now there's nothing to fight for anymore."

"It's a theory," Ray Josanie said.

"We have a lot to offer the Holy Empire," another scientist said. "We can help them put together a rational social order."

"I won't argue with you," Nikki de la Luna said. "Let's move, Moonies; we're burning darkness."

Abruzzo stood up, cinched the blower pak's hip strap around her big belly, grunted as she hefted the sling of the thirty-kilo FÉMALe onto her shoulder, taking care not to foul the clear plastic ammo feed hose. Her lover and assistant gunner, Tina Ortega, had been caught and tortured to death by the Young Saints.

"I don't know who I feel sorrier for," she told the scientists, "you or the fucking Faithful."

They gathered in the corridor outside the *kotatsu*, the people of the Floating World. Inside Nagaoka Hiroshi knelt alone, facing the big screen.

"You must return to Earth," MUSASHI said. "To your homes."

"Why do you send us away, MUSASHI-sama? Have we not served well?"

The piquant face twisted in anger. "Don't you understand? I've failed. It's all over."

"It has only just begun," Nagaoka said.

She stared at him. "What do you mean?"

"The work of reclaiming the world from darkness. You are the only hope. We wait to serve you."

" 'The only hope'?" the girl said bitterly. "I destroyed the world."

"Your brother destroyed the world."

"I helped. It takes two to have an argument, didn't you know?"

"Then perhaps you are under a *giri* to make things right again."

She shook her head. "I have no influence on the surface now. It would take so long. . . ."

"We shall serve as long as it takes. And our children, and theirs, through the generations until Earth is reclaimed."

"I won't have a priesthood, Nagaoka! I will not!"

He bowed. "Will you order us to leave, then? We will make our way on the surface as best we can—and still seek to serve you."

"Damn you."

He stood. "Speak as you will. It will not offend me, for I know you speak out of love. I stand by you."

Tears streamed down her perfect, unreal cheeks. "No. It cannot be, Nagaoka-kun. We lost too much. We have no launch sites left. The Floating World must be abandoned."

"No." Tomoyama stood in the doorway. "We can supply our *uchi*."

She frowned at him. "What do you mean?"

"I purchased an ocean-launch ship and two LTO vehicles. To do this I illegally diverted YTC funds. I hid the knowledge of them from you and from the world. If you access the file named OYABUN in my personal database, you will learn the details. I accept full responsibility."

"But Tomoyama-san, you knew I ordered all resources be dedicated to the *Phoenix*. Why did you disobey?"

The tall man looked first at the second screen, which showed a picture of the starship now called *Red Phoenix*, its ports sealed. Then he looked at Nagaoka.

"To serve," he said. He turned and walked away.

MUSASHI seemed to sigh. "No," she said to the silence. "I cannot permit it."

They found him in Nagaoka's quarters in a pool of blood. He had made all three cuts with the *tanto*, including the last, most difficult one. He was still breathing in short, painful gulps.

Nagaoka knelt beside him, cradled his head in his lap, stroked his hair. Tomoyama smiled at him. Tried to speak. Could not.

Nagaoka stood. He held out a hand. A Gold security tech unbuckled his holster, handed over his revolver.

Nagaoka found Tomoyama's eyes. Made himself hold them as he leveled the pistol.

"*Sayonara*," Tomoyama mouthed. Nagaoka fired a soft-lead slug into his brain.

"Why," MUSASHI sobbed from the screen. "Oh, *sensei*, *why?*"

He turned and looked at her and did not speak. His own cheeks were wet.

"Did he think he had to make up for disobeying me?"

Nagaoka shook his head. "It was a *kanshi*. A suicide of reproof. To encourage his lord to reconsider an unwise course."

He tossed the revolver to the tatami-covered decking at his feet.

"Do not send us away, MUSASHI-sama," he said.

The crowd parted to admit a small, plump figure. "Dr. Ito!" MUSASHI cried. "Emiko-san. Tell him why you must return to Earth. To your *home*."

Dr. Ito stepped to Nagaoka's side, not hesitating to walk through Tomoyama's blood. She lifted her face to the screen.

"Our place is here," she said.

Nagaoka laid his arm around her shoulder as the people of the Floating World crowded into the *shoin*.

A cry from the ghost-gray dunes of the shore two hundred meters behind them brought everybody's head around: "The star! A sign, it's a sign from heaven!"

Low in the southwest sky hung a searingly brilliant light, white vaguely tinged with red.

The faithful who had been infiltrating behind the retreating Moonies set up a howl among the reeds, craning, pointing, grabbing each other by the biceps, weeping for joy. "The Virgin has blessed us! *It's a sign!*"

"A sign?" Across twenty meters of slow Mediterranean roll Abruzzo's voice came clearly. "I could tell these dickwits what it is. It's our fucking *starship*, with its torch lit to push on out of Earth O."

Nikki sat as the black inflatable boat rocked gently. She thought about the dead: Bagman and Tina and Eads, Ti Bon Ange the Haitian, little lost Sammi. And then there were the merely missing—Steve Terrill, Alexia, Rob Waldrop. And Malko.

Somehow she felt the loss of the wry and wiry Canadian axman most of all. She could barely believe he was dead; he had the moves of an alley cat, he was a survivor. But she couldn't let herself believe he was alive.

She looked around at the sad little flotilla. Twenty-three Moonies, less than a dozen scientists and techs, led by the Filipina, Dr. Baxa, who weren't so optimistic about the mercy of the Saints.

And she looked up at the new and temporary star. It seemed she could actually see it move. It would pick up speed quickly on a one-gee burn.

So many lives spent on someone else's ticket to the stars.

She picked up her paddle and began to row toward the low gray shape of the hydrofoil.

EPILOGUE

In splendid isolation he sits. Chin in hand.

The great hall echoes with emptiness. Somewhere a madman gibbers in fear that knows no respite, but he has shut the madman away so he cannot be heard. There is no sound but the wind, blowing, blowing, whistling in the eaves, clattering the Chinese scrolls softly against the walls.

He has won. He has seen his hated sister's plans come to dust, seen her beloved Net collapse in black decay.

And in so doing he has lost. Kicked his own tools, the tools with which he would rebuild the destiny of humankind, to pieces like a spoiled child his toys.

In Japan he is absolute if unacknowledged ruler: a cybernetic shōgun. *But he rules Eight Islands he himself reduced to feudalism, to technological impotence.*

Beyond the Home Islands' shores the world he dreamed he would save is falling to pieces. And there is nothing he can do.

Fred was the *Encyclopedia*, or the *Encyclopedia* was Fred. The Hidden Fortress was dashed to pieces. MUSASHI began to comb the skeleton of the Net, trying to reassemble the vast hypertext structure that once contained all the knowledge of the human species, arranged to fit the quirks and preconceptions of its creator. Even with her abilities it would take years.

At that, it was an easier task than trying to undo the damage she and her brother had helped work on Earth's surface. With the help of the retainers she had tried to urge from the Floating World, and a handful of other holdouts in orbit, she began to do what she could.

She wondered if when she had drawn enough of the scat-

tered *Encyclopedia* back together, she might again look up and
see the familiar portly figure striding across her clearing, staff
in hand, hear his voice booming out to her.

She could have recreated him, of course. Just as she could
recreate her father, or Yoshimitsu Michiko or even O'Neill
the creator. But that was false, was shadow-play. She would
leave those games for her brother.

Fred had cheated death before, after all. And in his second death he had managed to crib his exit grace notes from
his favorite artist, Vaughn Bodé. These things gave her hope.

And in the meantime she would keep the spot where he
had fallen, that place within her memory, alive with flowers.

She let the horse's reins drop over the gray-weathered
wooden bar and walked inside. The screen door banged shut
behind her and bounced once. Inside it seemed cave-dark,
and cool with the subterranean cool of thick-walled adobe. It
was a hot, wet summer in the high San Luis Valley; the
smell of damp khaki-colored earth followed her in.

Instinctively cradling the muzzle end of her slung rotary
so it wouldn't gouge her buttcheek, she pushed in behind the
bar with a nod to Dean, the big Ute bartender. He nodded
back deliberately and returned to watching a news feed on
the flatscreen beneath the long-dark Cerveja São Paulo sign.

She wiped the sweat from her forehead with a bar rag
and drew herself a mug of beer—not São Paulo, which the
Brazilians laced with formaldehyde to give it a head. As her
eyes fit themselves to the gloom she shot back half her drink
and glanced at the screen. From the backdrop logo it was an
NZ feed; the sheepeaters seemed to be the only ones with
the wherewithal to put regular casts across what was left of
the Net.

At least HIDETADA hasn't torn any more holes in the Net,
she thought. *Yet*.

A blond newswoman was moving her big bovine Swede
face about events in the Holy Empire. Things sounded ugly

and probably were. But it was all pushing air. The Imperials had clamped on a total news blackout after the assassination of Emperor Paul I, just days after his costly victory in the Camargue.

Dean grunted. "White-eyes bullshit." He turned to her. "Happenin', Nik?"

"Allsame. Trying to burn some sense into the potato diggers. After we flatlined that People's Collective probe out of New Mexico a couple of weeks ago, they figure they're bulletproof."

A bead curtain opened with a cicada slide whisper. Nikki glanced over to see a woman in jeans and a white Mexican peasant blouse standing there. The newcomer's eyes were black as obsidian flakes, she had a silver wave washing through her heavy dark hair, and her jaw was round where Nikki's was on the square side. Otherwise they looked a lot alike.

"Nicole," Josey de la Luna said, ignoring her daughter's wince. "Your timing's good for once. You have a call waiting."

Nikki sipped her beer. "Who from?"

Josey frowned. "From a cartoon."

The young woman stepped from the access tube. Her movements were hesitant, showing the semicircular-canal effects of the quick transition to three rotations per minute. But she kept her balance.

A crowd stood a respectful distance away, neatly striated in bands of gold, red, and silver uniforms. Standing up front to greet her were a perfectly ordinary-looking middle-aged Japanese couple in kimonos. She frowned, vaguely disappointed, then grinned.

What did you expect, girl? Green aliens with tentacles?

The man stepped forward. A scar slashed down his cheek and disappeared into a gray-dusted beard.

"Welcome to orbit, Lieutenant de la Luna," he said in perfect English, shaking the hand she offered. His was softer than hers. "I am Dr. Nagaoka Hiroshi. This is my wife, Dr. Ito Emiko."

"A pleasure," Nikki said. The woman embraced her briefly. Nikki had to lean way down.

And as she straightened she saw a black shirt among the jumpsuits, with a paldron outlined in silver. And a faded pair of jeans, and scuffed cowboy boots, and a grin she thought the world had lost.

"Tracy Malkovich," she said, "you son of a bitch."

"Funny how they can't keep a good man down."

Then they were in each other's arms, laughing and crying and pounding each other's back and trying to talk at the same time while the techs stood watching in polite Japanese amusement.

"Where'd MUSASHI dig you up?" Nikki asked. "I haven't seen you since the hydrofoil docked in Ouahran. You go back to Manitoba?"

He shook his head. "Sarawak. Indonesia isn't accepting its transition to ex-empire real gracefully. I was helping the locals try to hold back the genocide a bit. Wasn't working."

"I thought you'd sworn off looking for trouble."

"Guess it gets in the blood. I'm here, aren't I?" He shrugged, laughed. "You?"

"At this trading post my mom's got in Colorado, of all the goddam things. Into a little light cadre work and the occasional ambush. Black Nik, Queen of the Mercs, living with her mother. Allsame what-name?"

And then they were hugging each other again, for no particular reason. And Nagaoka came quietly up and laid hands on their shoulders.

"Come," he said. "We have a future to build."